Sita Romero

words we cannot say

Words We Cannot Say
Red Adept Publishing, LLC
104 Bugenfield Court
Garner, NC 27529
https://RedAdeptPublishing.com/
Copyright © 2022 by Sita Romero. All rights reserved.
Cover Art by Streetlight Graphics[1]

---

1.   http://StreetlightGraphics.com

For all the silenced mothers. I hear you.

Chapter 1

Nurses in Labor and Delivery blamed the full moon for the crazy patients—whether they truly believed the superstition or not. Penelope didn't subscribe to that nonsense, but she was still relieved to be assigned to triage that night so she could assess and admit patients instead of caring for them. She wasn't wary of the patients—she was worried about the raw emotion that might burst from her at any moment.

Jasper's words echoed in her mind: "I can't do this anymore. It's over."

A birdlike woman all of five feet tall buzzed through the locked double doors onto the labor-and-delivery unit, looking timid and leading with a round belly. Beside her, a man loaded down like a pack animal carried three bags and cradled a large blue birth ball beneath one arm. At about six and a half feet tall, he towered over the pregnant woman. He might be a linebacker, although most of the Atlanta Falcons' wives delivered at Northside, the fancy baby factory.

Penelope swallowed, forcing the disquiet in her stomach back down, and led them to the triage room, where she helped the patient gown up and started a baseline of monitoring on the baby. His heart rate looked great. Next, the cervical check. She waited for a mild contraction to end before inserting a gloved hand. The patient's partner—her husband, it turned out—had put the bags down and now stood beside the bed, shifting from foot to foot. Penelope was amused that a tough guy could be brought to his knees while watching his wife labor.

Midcheck, a wave of nausea rolled over Penelope. The contents of her stomach pressed upward, threatening to leave. She refused to believe she was physically sick over the breakup. Swallowing, she forced the feeling back down. *Shit. Not now.* She couldn't afford the

1

mental drain of thinking about Jasper, but his words—"I have to focus on my wife. It's over"—played on a loop in her mind.

"Is everything okay?" asked the dad-to-be.

"Mm-hmm." Penelope pulled her gloved hand out and slid her
free hand beneath the wrist of the blue latex to remove it. "Be right
back."

Penelope darted down the hall, whipping her blond hair into a
messy ponytail and barely making it to the nurses' bathroom before
losing her lunch. It lurched up her throat and out, burning. An un-
stoppable force. Afterward, she took a deep breath and exhaled, feeling instantly better. Leaving the room like that was not ideal, but she
couldn't risk barfing all over her patient. Penelope rinsed her mouth
out and washed her face, the water cool on her makeup-free skin.

"So sorry about that," she said as she entered the room. Her patient, Alicia, was midcontraction again. "Oh good—looks like we
have some labor going on."

Penelope checked the monitor, tracing the baby's heartbeat as it
dropped during the contraction. She waited. Normal. It would come
back up.

"Great job. Nice breathing," Penelope said when the contraction
ended. "You're in active labor, so I'll call your doctor, but you'll
probably be admitted." She kept her eyes trained on the monitor.
The postcontraction recovery was taking a long time. *The heart rate
should be returning to normal now.*

Alicia smiled up at her husband. "Sounds like we're going to have
a baby." He nodded, a proud look eclipsing his previously worried
one. She turned to Penelope. "I felt something while you were gone.
I think my water broke."

"Okay, I'll check that out for you." Penelope repositioned the
monitor. *Am I tracing the mom's heart rate instead of the baby's?* "I just
need you to put this on your index finger." She handed the pulse ox

to the mom. If she could differentiate the mother's heart rate from the baby's, she could be sure.

Penelope removed the drape from the mother's lap, pulled back Alicia's gown, and tilted the adjustable bed with the push of a button. "Yes, it looks like your water broke. I'm just going to check you again to determine the position of the baby."

She watched the monitor, gloved up, and reached in for another check. In front of the baby's head, a spongy cord descended out of the cervix. *Son of a bitch.*

Penelope reached farther. "Nice deep breaths, Alicia—that's it."

She pushed through the slightly open cervix with two fingers, feeling for the baby's head. Curling her fingers, Penelope tried to nudge the cord back and tuck it where it belonged.

It wouldn't go.

She settled on supporting the baby's head with her hand outstretched as if balancing a baseball on two fingers. The cord was like a kinked hose, the baby's head an immoveable rock, cutting off his oxygen supply.

With her free hand, Penelope pressed the call button. "I'm going to need hands in triage two. Code thirteen." She looked up from between Alicia's knees, meeting her eyes, which were wide with fear. "Alicia, look at me. The umbilical cord has come down. It's being compressed by the baby's head. I'm going to keep my hand here to support his head and keep it off the cord. In just a minute, this room is going to get *very* busy. We're going to help you have your baby now. I want you to stay calm. I'll explain everything after. Things are going to happen very fast. Do you understand?"

One minute. The mental countdown started. *How many minutes will it take to get the baby out? Ten? Twenty?* Ten would be a record. Twenty would likely not end well. She wondered how she could keep her hand steady for that long. In that moment, the only thing keeping Alicia's baby from dying was the tenuous balance of his crown on Penelope's fingertips. The heart rate had recovered. *For now.*

"Is—is my baby okay?" Alicia asked.

Penelope wanted to tell her everything would be okay. But she couldn't make any promises. "I'm keeping my hand here to give your baby more oxygen. We're going to get him out. That's the most important thing right now. I'm going to stay right here with you."

Hannah and Kathy crashed into the room.

"I need oxygen, Hannah. Kathy, we need a line in, and I'm one-handed now."

Hannah pulled the mask from the wall, opened the line to the oxygen, and placed the mask over Alicia's nose and mouth. More oxygen for Mom meant more for baby.

"Hannah, call the OR and tell them we're coming." Now that Penelope had called the code, they didn't have time for anything but action. It was a checklist. "Then call the OB and anesthesia. We need everyone ready to go."

Three minutes.

Kathy put the line in.

"Before you run the fluids, I need labs," Penelope said.

"On it." Kathy didn't look up from Alicia's veins as she moved to collecting the blood.

Penelope turned to the father. "I'm sorry, tell me your name again?"

"Dan," he croaked.

"Dan, you're going to go to the other side of the operating room, outside the nursery. The baby will go straight to the nursery once he's out, and you can be there with his nurse." She hoped that was true.

He kissed his wife on the forehead, mumbling to her before following Penelope's orders. He stumbled out of the room, dazed.

The triage door opened again, and Dr. Ramirez entered. "Ready?" His typical impatience as a doctor annoyed her, but in this case, it made all the difference.

"As soon as the lines are in," Penelope said.

Kathy connected the tubes and hung the fluid bag on the pole attached to the stretcher. The rest of them looked as helpless as Penelope felt. "Done," Kathy said.

Six minutes.

The hospital bed gave a loud click as Ramirez removed the lock and turned it into a rolling transport. Alicia's eyes were trained on the ceiling.

"Alicia, I'm going to stay right here, okay?" Penelope said.

She nodded.

Penelope pulled her feet up, trying to make herself small as she tucked into the bed with Alicia. She had no choice but to ride the bed to the OR with her hand forcing the baby's head back until he was safe. The hallway stretched before them. Penelope's hand braced the baby's head. The squishy umbilical cord hung loose, hanging out of the cervix.

Her fingers stretched and cramped. She forced them to attention. As uncomfortable as she was, this poor mama had to ride to the OR with a nurse's hand inside her. Penelope swallowed, still tasting acid in her mouth. Fluorescent lights shone down on them as they pushed down the hallway and through the double doors to the operating room.

Eight minutes. Eight minutes to the OR was record time.

Ramirez prepared to move the patient to the operating table. "Doing great. Penelope, stay right where you are. Ready for transfer? One, two, three." The team shifted Alicia from the hospital bed to the table with Penelope still attached.

The anesthesiologist offered a few clipped words to explain what was coming next. There was no time. A mask descended on Alicia's face, putting her under general anesthesia. There was no way to administer anything else quickly enough. *Horrifying.* She'd go to sleep pregnant, with a nurse's hand inside her, and wake up a mother.

The surgical team draped them both as if Penelope was an appendage of the woman, like a bizarre Siamese twin, dangling between her legs. Her hand wobbled, and she fought to steady it. Sweat beaded on her forehead.

"Making the first incision now," Ramirez said.

Ten minutes.

She couldn't see anything but a sea of sterile green surgical draping. Penelope felt an instrument land on the drape somewhere above her. This was not her usual position in the OR—crouched beneath the drape, immobilized, frantically holding back a baby who was crushing his own life support. She imagined Ramirez's precise surgical incision first breaking the outer layer of skin then severing the abdominal muscle beneath.

There was movement inside the mother, and the doctor's fingertips swiped Penelope's. The baby lurched, and the pressure fighting against her outstretched fingers receded. She stayed still, frozen, waiting until the doctor made the official call.

"Time of birth?" Ramirez called.

"One fifty-two," Kathy said.

Penelope pulled her cramped hand from the mother's body and extracted herself from beneath the drape. She stripped off the glove and flexed her fingers, which were jammed from staying in one position. Thirteen minutes had passed from the time she discovered the compressed umbilical cord until the baby was free from his mother's womb.

A loud cry echoed.

"There we go," Kathy said. "Holler for me, little one."

The baby's cry released Penelope's clenched teeth. She'd been holding tension everywhere, not just in her fingers. Ramirez delivered the placenta.

"Can I go check on the father?" Penelope asked. "I'd like to let him know everyone is fine."

Ramirez nodded, flopping the bloody placenta into the bowl and handing it off to Hannah for inspection.

Penelope rolled her shoulders as she left the OR. She imagined herself crouched like a puppeteer beneath the stage, hand forced into position, back bent as the audience watched. The performance was all that mattered. And her performance that night had saved a baby.

Dan paced the hall outside the nursery.

"He's okay. He's out. Good cry. Doc is still working on Mom right now, but she's doing great too."

Tears of relief flooded down the father's face. Penelope reached up and patted his massive shoulder. "I know—that was intense. But it all worked out. I'm so glad you were in here when the water broke."

He nodded.

"Your baby boy will be out shortly. Stay right here."

"Thank you," he choked out.

She smiled at him. "You're welcome. And congratulations."

She turned down the hall, and the wave of nausea returned. No doubt it had been held at bay because she'd been so focused on keeping the baby alive. *Not again.*

She raced into the nurses' bathroom and let it out. Hopefully, she wasn't actually sick and spreading some gross stomach bug to everyone she came in contact with. She had to get a grip and get over him.

Penelope went back to the nurses' station and sat. She'd been fighting an ominous feeling since the breakup, but that night, it was worse.

Kathy approached her. "Penelope, you were a rock star in there."

"Just doing my job," she said, not looking up.

"You okay, darlin'?" Kathy's slight Southern accent made her particularly endearing. "You look like you might toss your cookies."

"Do I look that bad? And I already *did* toss my cookies. Twice."

"Oh, honey, you going to make it through your shift?"

Hannah rounded the corner and sighed. "What's your problem?" she asked Penelope.

"Be nice, Hannah. She's been throwing up all night. Probably caught that bug that's goin' around."

Hannah raised an eyebrow. "Sick? Or pregnant?"

"Just because you see pregnant women everywhere doesn't mean someone is pregnant anytime they're sick. That's enough," Kathy said.

Hannah stretched the gum in her mouth with her tongue and then smiled at Penelope.

Pregnant? No. I can't be pregnant, can I? Penelope ran the numbers through her mind, counting backward. Her last period had been light and spotty, but she'd had it recently.

No way. They'd been careful. She was on the pill. She wasn't pregnant.

"Of course I'm not pregnant." Penelope could hear the nervousness in her own voice.

For the rest of the night, thoughts of Jasper and her denial of Hannah's stupid idea warred in Penelope's mind. In the morning, just after shift change, she stripped out of her scrubs in the locker room and slipped into the supply cabinet. A few test strips wouldn't be missed. Once she confirmed that Hannah was wrong and stupid, she would sleep like a baby.

At her apartment, she went straight to the kitchen, plucked out a disposable red plastic cup, and headed into the bathroom. The hospital strips were not like the store-bought pregnancy tests. They were missing the housing and designed to be dipped straight into a urine sample.

She placed the cup, warm with urine, on the counter and dipped the thin stick inside. After counting to three, she removed it, laid it flat, and waited for the control line to appear.

I'm not pregnant. Of course I'm not pregnant.

When the requisite time had passed, she looked down at the thin strip. "I'm pregnant."

Chapter 2

"Jesenia Menendez-Simmons," Nia said.

The nurse looked at her and then the computer and back again. It always took a minute when Nia said her full name. People were thrown by her accent, and her name on paper didn't look the way it sounded.

If someone had told Nia six years before that she'd be standing at the counter in the IVF clinic, she wouldn't have believed it. Back then, Nia's life had consisted of standing backstage, removing a sleek Dior beaded slip dress and sliding into a Prada crepe midi then stepping out onto the runway. She hadn't been sure she would ever want to have kids. And now that she was finally ready, she didn't know if she was able to have a child anymore, despite her mother's reassurance that she would one day. It was hard to imagine replacing the trips to Paris and dinners at Michelin three-star restaurants with trips to Disney World and dinners at Chuck E. Cheese. She'd thought she might never want to trade her Fendi bag for a diaper bag.

But those days were gone, replaced by the best thing that had ever happened to her—Edward. She'd had all the success she could stomach in the fashion industry, and with Edward's new medical practice, she would never work again unless she wanted to. Now they were settled into their high-rise apartment in Buckhead, surrounded by the skyline of the uptown district. They had Pixie, their teacup Yorkie. Everything was shaping up to be the life she wanted. Except she couldn't get pregnant this time.

Once she was checked in, Nia settled next to a pretty redhead who looked tired and overwhelmed. "Is this your first cycle?" the woman asked. She reminded Nia of an older, redder version of Penelope. Her hair was pulled back into that characteristic Penelope-style ponytail, and her dress hung off her like she was too interested in other things to trifle with clothing choices.

10

Nia tried to keep her face passive and curious, but the question had startled her. *What ever happened to "Hello, how are you?"* It was as if her spot next to the woman in the fertility clinic had somehow invited her into an intimate space.

"Um... yes. How can you tell?" Nia let out a nervous laugh.

"You look so excited. I mean, we're all excited. I just mean, you look... new." The woman blushed and looked down at her lap.

"You're right. What cycle is this for you?" Nia already suspected she knew the answer. The desperation in the woman's face was a giveaway. But after the awkward exchange, Nia wanted to reciprocate.

"Sixth," the redhead said.

Nia's stomach clenched. *Sixth.* "Oh, wow. So, how are you feeling about this cycle? I have a friend who got pregnant on her sixth." By *friend*, she meant a woman from the trying-to-conceive message board, but she wasn't about to explain that little detail. "Statistically, your chances have gone way up by making it to cycle six." She hoped that her words encouraged the woman.

"I feel good. We're going to implant more this time. I'm willing to risk triplets at this point, to be honest."

Nia swallowed. *Triplets.* She wanted a baby, of course. It was all she wanted lately, but three of them at once... she'd have to hire an au pair to survive. Maybe two of them.

"Well, good luck to you."

Baby dust. That was message-board lingo. Or *sticky dust*, as in *I hope this time the baby sticks.* While she might not have said it out loud, that didn't stop Nia from thinking it.

The nurse called Nia's name before she had to interact again with the six-cycle lady. *Six cycles.* Fortunately, she and Edward could afford to try for six cycles if they needed to. But even though Edward had assured her they would try as many times as they needed, Nia wouldn't do that. After the failed IUIs, they'd decided to pursue adoption as well. They were going to have a baby one way or another, regardless of what Mami might think of it.

Nia clutched her brown-and-tan Louis beneath her arm, keeping a hand on the strap near her shoulder. Edward wouldn't make it because he had someone in labor, leaving her at the fertility clinic alone. *You have to* go, he'd said that morning, taking her hands in his. *We don't want to miss a whole cycle.* His enthusiasm made her feel even worse about her inability to get pregnant.

Dr. Jeff was an old friend of Edward's. By luck, they'd both ended up in Atlanta. Edward did his residency at Grady, and once Nia was in the picture, Atlanta became home. His mother had even followed him there. Nia used to think it was some weird only-child thing, but now that they were about to be parents, she didn't mind.

"How was the cruise?" she asked Jeff casually.

She was more accustomed to seeing him at happy-hour get-togethers, and she felt odd addressing him as her doctor. But Edward trusted Jeff implicitly, and she trusted Edward. Even if small talk was the last thing on her mind and her nerves were getting to her, she was determined to make the best of it.

A smile broke across Jeff's smooth face. He had skin like a baby. What Nia wouldn't give to look like she wasn't aging. If she hadn't known Jeff's age, she would have guessed he was much younger than her and Edward.

"Fiji is amazing. You guys should really go."

She smiled at him, feigning interest as he prattled. She didn't want to go to Fiji—she wanted to have a baby. It was all she and Edward could talk about lately, and she was failing him by still not being pregnant yet. *Besides, what does he think I'm going to do—take a big pregnant belly on a trip across the ocean to see an island and risk getting sick with the norovirus or worse? No, thanks.* And she certainly wasn't planning on taking her newborn to Fiji.

"Sounds beautiful," she said.

She used to care about people's trips to Fiji. She used to want to hear about travel and what made others feel passionate. But lately, it was all she could do to keep from crying. Three years into it, they were still dealing with her stupid hormones and trying to figure out why she wasn't pregnant. Edward had finally pushed her to change fertility doctors. *Trust me, you've got to see Jeff. He's the best.*

She wanted to close her eyes, rub her temples, and lean her head back into a cushion that wrapped all the way around her neck like the oversized pillow she carried when she traveled. Jeff must have seen it on her face because he finally got to the point.

"I'm sure Edward has explained it to you. The embryo transfer is not painful and will feel much like a regular annual exam. Any questions before we start?"

Nia shook her head—no questions. It wasn't Edward who'd explained it to her. She'd read every post on her Trying-to-Conceive—TTC—message board to find out what to expect. She knew more about cycles, possibilities for conception, and abbreviations on the subject than she cared to admit. She knew enough to be embarrassed to admit it in public. She knew about the shots, the egg retrieval, the supplements. Those women spared no detail.

Some of them were so positive. *They got eleven eggs. So many! But then they called to say only six had fertilized. Such a waiting game to see which ones will thrive.* Even if they'd only gotten two eggs, everyone would have cheered.

Others were more negative. Until they were pregnant. *Absolutely intimidating, horribly isolating, and the best thing we ever did.*

The doomsayers didn't bother Nia. At least they were honest.

Then there was the realist. She didn't want anyone going into it blind. *Oh-Em-Gee, ice before you do the injections. They are the worst! But they brought us the twins, so it's all good.* Always "helping" with some advice or other.

Some of the women were annoying, but most of them were great. And hearing all the minutiae of their journey made it less daunting for Nia. She couldn't bear only knowing the medical version of things, no matter how many lay terms doctors—including Edward—included in their descriptions.

"I know what to expect. I'm ready," Nia said, although she found it ironic that she was trying to get pregnant without her husband in the room.

"And the percentage? Because you're under thirty-five, we are looking at forty to fifty percent here, even on a first try." His tone was positive, like he was delivering *good* news. She imagined how different his words would be if she were over thirty-five.

Less than half of women in her position would end up pregnant at the end of this. Nia shoved the thought aside. It was going to work.

Jeff left the room and brought back a horde of nurses or technicians or whatever they were. One flipped open the stirrups and encouraged her to lie back. Another turned on the ultrasound machine, and it made a low hum as it whirred to life. There was a decorative panel inset above the table over the fluorescent light to mimic a bright, sunny day with fluffy clouds, flowers, and a butterfly. Looking at a panel of fake sky on a plastic light cover didn't take Nia out of the office, off the table, or away from the procedure.

Six cycles. She couldn't see putting herself through that. This was going to work. It *had* to work.

It only took a few minutes. Nia watched the screen as a puff of white, blurry embryos made their way into her uterus. She expected to feel something other than emptiness.

When Jeff and the nurses were gone, she dressed slowly, sliding into her favorite jeans and slipping back into her wedges. This was going to be it. She was going to be pregnant. No more wanting. No more waiting. She often found herself slipping dramatically between these positive thoughts and utter despair. Maybe it was stupid, but hope and Edward were keeping her from slipping completely away.

A knock on the door revealed the nurse, who had returned with a small gift bag.

"What's this?" Nia asked, peering into the bag. It was the petri dish her embryo had been made in. Her eyebrows drew in.

"Most families like it," the nurse said, her tone apologetic.

"Okay. Thanks?"

"Good luck." The nurse's eyes were wide and hopeful. It was obviously a carefully crafted and practiced look.

Chapter 3

Lotus hung the phone up, set it down on the kitchen table and made a note on the updated shipping. Her distributor in Indonesia had ended the call with promises that the mistake wouldn't happen again. Lotus would have to research some other options in case she had to move on.

Everyone makes mistakes. She could forgive them this one.

But the floor mats and meditation pillows were some of her hottest sellers. The Lotus Garden supplied several yoga studios around town, and word of mouth had made them the go-to shop as more studios opened. She closed the spiral book and pressed her fingers to her forehead. She'd never wanted to name the store after herself. When they landed the account with the biggest yoga studio in town, Rob had insisted on it until he won. They had to quit agonizing over the name and move forward, get the doors open, and capitalize on the shop-local trend.

None of it—the Victorian home in Inman Park, the funds to open the Lotus Garden—would have been possible without her generous grandfather. Before she opened the shop, his money had been the reason Lotus had skipped town to spend six months hiking the Appalachian Trail right after college. She maintained the house's original 1930s wood floors. The place was hers, all because her grandfather had died and had loved her the most. The home had passed right over her parents, and the deed had landed in her hands following his funeral.

Maybe she was lucky. Or maybe it was his way of thanking her. Or apologizing.

A crescendo of stomping broke her thoughts as Rob and Blaze bounded down the staircase with their energetic golden retriever, Morgana, snaking around them, almost knocking Blaze off his feet. Rob swept Blaze up and shouldered the small boy as Morgana trotted across the kitchen and greeted Lotus. She ran her fingers through the ever-shedding wheat-colored coat and ignored it when Morgana licked her leg.

Rob loves this dog.

She frequently reminded herself of the needs of others as a way to look past the little annoyances that tried to swallow her whole. Like the muddy paw prints she wiped from the wood floors and the wildly swinging tail that put Blaze off balance and knocked the toddler over more times than she could count. Or like the trips to the vet and the nighttime barking.

Rob leaned over, kissed her forehead, and dropped Blaze into her lap. "Good morning." His long hair swung down and brushed her shoulders. He whipped it back and stood.

Lotus smiled up at him, pushing Blaze's russet bangs out of his face. "How did you sleep?"

"Want mommy milk," Blaze said.

Rob opened the back door and let Morgana out. Lotus exhaled and turned her attention to her toddler. It was going to be one of *those* days.

Lotus glanced around the kitchen for the sippy cup she'd prepared. "Here it is." She offered the cup to the child. "I put it in your cup today."

Blaze's eyebrows drew in and rose at the same time, a cloud of fear coming over his perfect features. "Not a cuppy. Mommy milkie." He groped at her shirt and grabbed it in his fists.

Lotus pried his fingers open and stood, setting her son on the countertop. "Mommy milk is all gone." *Calm. Firm. Kind but firm.* The wailing would come next. She had been trying to allow child-led weaning. The research supported continuing to nurse Blaze as long as he liked. But lately she didn't want to anymore. *Isn't that a good enough reason to stop?*

Tears welled up in his eyes. Dread filled her stomach.

"Mommy milkie. Mommy milkie." The sullen demand continued.

Lotus wanted to wind the clock back an hour and have her early morning to herself. She wanted her warm coconut green tea and her meditation practice. She longed for her quiet and solitude as Rob lay next to their sleeping child upstairs to keep him in bed just a little longer. The morning had been shattered by his persistent cries, and Lotus couldn't escape the repeated demand.

"I can get him some breakfast," Rob offered, shrugging. "You want to help Daddy make breakfast, buddy?"

"Want mommy milkie. Want mommy milkie."

Lotus sighed. They all knew how the tantrum would end. *How am I ever going to wean him?*

She pulled him off the counter and plopped back down so he could climb into her lap. His repetitions quieted into gulping as he nursed, cradled in her lap, twirling the bottom edge of her cotton shirt in his tiny fingers. His insistence, coupled with mommy guilt and the inevitable outcome, had pushed her to cave. He lay curled into her body, soft and warm. He smelled of lavender honey soap. She exhaled in defeat.

Rob shrugged again. In the quiet of Blaze's distraction, he refilled her teacup and joined her at the table.

"Thank you," Lotus said quietly.

He never let anything frazzle him, and she admired that. It was the little things Rob did that made her love him. Refilling the teacup. Never saying "I told you so," and always sitting in comfortable silence with her—even from their first encounter on the Appalachian Trail all those years ago.

This time, Rob broke the comfortable silence. "I wanted to check in with you about Jagannath coming to stay."

Lotus tried to smooth the irritation rising in her chest, threatening to register on her face. Ignoring their dilemma wasn't going to make it go away. "Do you think now is the best time?" She gestured to herself and to the squirming boy as he yanked her shirt, switched sides, and clamped down happily to continue nursing.

"He just needs some support right now. Some community. Can't we give him that? The divorce has been really hard on him. What can we offer the soul of another being if not our own hospitality?"

She used to love the way Rob spoke of another's "soul," but something about this felt greasy and indigestible. Jagannath was a loafer. She'd known the type growing up. It was one thing to live together communally, everyone offering their own piece to share with the greater whole. She missed that communal life sometimes. The adults all cared for each other's children, who ran and played and built things and baked all together. Sometimes, she missed her "aunties" as much as her own parents. But Jagannath was different. He just freeloaded. He would stay until he wasn't welcome. And then he'd stay some more. And the fact that it had to be *Jagannath*, of all people, made her uncomfortable. He and Rob had a history.

"How long will it be?" Lotus put on her best mask of thoughtfulness and concern.

Rob took her free hand and held it in both of his. "I want you to know I hear you. I can hear your concern. He needs help, but he's going to work. It'll be different than you expect. I know it."

Lotus nodded and turned her attention to Blaze. "Okay."

There was no sense in arguing. They'd already been through a too-similar conversation. Twice. Rob wouldn't let it go because Jagannath needed them. So they would help. Maybe Jagannath would work in the shop, and they'd finally get the inventory categorized the way she wanted. Maybe another childlike playmate would be just the distraction needed to wean Blaze. Maybe Rob would handle it better this time.

Maybe.

She checked the time and considered calling Penelope. If she'd just come off a night shift, she'd be sleeping for the day. Lotus settled on sending her a text. *We had the roommate conversation again. It's happening. Call me when you wake up.*

Her phone immediately lit up with a response—odd for so early in the morning after a night shift. *I had the worst night ever. Going to sleep, but we definitely need to chat soon. Maybe coffee Wednesday?*

Lotus confirmed the coffee date. Wednesday was the Mom's Morning Out program and guaranteed her toddler-free peace for three and a half hours. Coffee with her cousin was a perfect kid-free treat.

Chapter 4

Hoping the fertility treatment had worked, Nia turned away from the vanity, leaving her pregnancy test abandoned, swimming in the complexity of the marble-patterned countertop. She couldn't look. She couldn't bear to see that tiny single line one more time—the control line that would tell her, *Yes, you took the test correctly. No, you are not pregnant. Negative.*

Her whole life was a negative.

That wasn't true. But in moments of desperation, she felt it deep under her skin and around her. The nuns at St. Catherine's haunted her memory. Sin.

But what about forgiveness? Is God really punishing me because I'm not a good Catholic?

She left the bathroom without checking the result of the test. The closet lit automatically when she walked in. Walls of clothes and shoes towered on each side of her, flanked by purses and accessories. In the center of her walk-in closet, she plopped into the chair and dug her toes into the thick plush rug. With elbows on knees, her face in her hands, she cried.

How much can one person take? When will I decide I've had enough?

She'd already told Edward this was it. Nia didn't want to be the desperate redheaded six-time IVF woman she'd met at Jeff's office. After one IVF, she could move on. She knew that a single line would mar the test, mocking her. It was so easy for some women.

It was easy for you too, a tiny voice whispered.

Edward went to work every day, delivering baby after baby. Babies conceived on the first try. Babies conceived without anyone trying. In residency, he'd seen it all—teen mothers, babies no one wanted, babies on drugs. And here Nia was—young and healthy. She should be capable of making a baby, of making them into a family.

You were *capable*, the sinister voice whispered.

She rubbed her eyes, trying to press the tears back. They flowed unhampered until she was worn out. She was being melodramatic. Just because she hadn't gotten pregnant yet didn't mean she never would. It was early in her cycle. Maybe it was too early.

Edward had cautioned her about taking the tests at home, warning her about the wait between conception and a positive test. "I promise, you want the blood test. Jeff knows what he's doing. He's the best in town—that's why we're going there. Let Dr. J do his job. Please, baby."

The hormones were making her a lunatic. Cycle after cycle of waiting, wanting, hoping, dreading the outcome, and then boom. Negative.

She heard the front door open and shut. The beep of the alarm signaled that Edward had come home. She didn't want him to find her sobbing in the closet, a blubbering mess, melted into a shell of who she used to be. He'd seen it enough already.

Conceiving a baby wasn't supposed to bring her to her knees. It *had* been easy when she was younger. At seventeen, when she'd let Jimmy lift the chiffon of her Jessica McClintock dress in the back of the limo, she hadn't thought it would happen to her. But those stupid Jack Daniels wine coolers. It hadn't taken much for her to forget the condom. That baby would have been fifteen now.

And it had happened so easily at twenty-three with her sleazeball manager. She pushed the thought away, refusing to travel down that dark road.

The women of the TTC message board had been the ones to clue her in on the early-testing trick. The fertility hormones made her test positive—a false positive. But once the hormones started draining out, the positive looked more and more faint. Each day after the implantation, she'd checked with that little stick, watching the false positive fade. And then nothing. Negative.

If this latest one was positive—if that second little pink line showed up—she would know. She would know that no matter how faint it was, she was pregnant. She would know before she took the blood test. Jackie had gotten one at eight DPO—days past ovulation. Nia measured her life in *days past ovulation.*

Edward knew about her message-board friends, but she hadn't told Penelope. Pen had been there through their whole journey. They'd met through Edward when he was still in residency, three years before. Nia knew it was weird having friends she only knew through the internet. Penelope might not understand.

But the women trying to conceive understood. Some of the ones she chatted with on the late-night message boards had it much worse than she did. Some had lost every baby they'd ever conceived. "Angel babies," they called them. She couldn't think of hers as angel babies. She tried not to think of them at all.

Maybe it was going to be a false negative. She was only ten DPO. Maybe it wasn't time yet. Thirteen point six was the average DPO for a positive pregnancy test.

Nia stood, wiping her face, and walked back to the bathroom. It didn't matter. Even if the test was negative, it was going to be okay.

She approached the vanity slowly, as if the stick on the marble countertop was made of dynamite. She promised everything if she could just see that second line. *I'll go to church. I'll be a really involved mother. Whatever you want, God, I'll do it.*

The redness of her eyes barely marred her features. She still had the beauty that was so envied, with her "tanned" skin—as the unintentional racists would say. "It's not tan," she'd finally told the six-foot-tall stick-thin blonde at the Versace shoot. "That's just the color of my skin."

Nia squeezed her eyes shut. Just the line—that was all she wanted. A faint little pink double line. Opening her eyes, Nia picked up the pregnancy test.

One line.

Not pregnant. Again.

"*Carajo*," she cursed. She dropped the test in the wastebasket just as Edward stepped into their bathroom.

"I heard that." He was still wearing his scrubs.

She could feel herself crumple. He was her rock, and he was there in the moment of pain again. He lifted off his V-neck scrub top and exposed a white tank top hugging his body. His straight black hair touched his eyebrows as he looked down at Nia with a soft expression.

"It's early still." Edward dropped the scrub top and folded her into his arms—her safe space—and she cried anew into his chest. She held him, grateful that he didn't admonish her about the test.

She was making herself crazy, and he didn't point it out. He never told her to stop talking to those desperate women on the TTC message board. He simply held her.

"It's early still," he repeated.

She knew it was killing him to see her like this. *How much longer is he going to stand by and wait for his wife to conceive? What if I never do?*

She pushed the harsh thought away. Edward loved her. He would stand by no matter what.

Even if you never get pregnant? the little voice asked. A sense of complete helplessness threatened to be the only thing she ever felt.

It amazed her, the control that tiny red line held over her life. That line was the difference between nothing and everything.

Chapter 5

"I need your help," Penelope said.

There was no sense in dragging it out. The real reason Penelope sat across from Lotus, drinking a green matcha tea and gazing at her glowing cousin, hung in the air between them. She hadn't expected to get the news that Lotus was pregnant. But Lotus had shown up for the coffee date with a tight tank top, her barely-there belly showing the truth. Penelope pushed forward, even though the belly had thrown her off.

Lotus nodded. "Of course."

Their unspoken agreement had become spoken over the years. Sometimes, there was no avoiding talking about their family. Their childhood, despite the distance, had stretched into adulthood until Lotus had moved to Atlanta. Now that Gram was gone, there was no one in her family she trusted more than Lotus.

Penelope remembered those hastily scrawled letters, the stamps on the front reading *4 your eyes only*, and the bent corners of the beat-up mail. She'd stood at the foot of the driveway some days, waiting to greet their mailman and search through the pile of letters for one from her California cousin. Now Penelope was in the Bean Tree coffee shop, sitting across from the one person she trusted as much as Nia.

Nia. That was who she really wanted to talk to. She'd never kept anything from Nia. Nia had a way of digging in and pointing it out if Penelope was "off." She would see right through her. So Penelope had been avoiding her.

Looking down at the globe of tiny belly on Lotus, a wave of regret washed over Penelope. She swallowed and pushed on. "I'm pregnant." If she hadn't forced it out of her mouth quickly, it was possible she wouldn't have said it at all.

"Oh." Lotus connected the dots between "I need your help" and "I'm pregnant" fast enough to keep her face impassive. "Not happy about it, I take it?"

Penelope shook her head. "I was on birth control. It wasn't supposed to happen like this. I did everything right." Well, not everything. She'd slept with a married man, after all. "I just can't handle it. I'm not all... motherly, like you."

Lotus raised an eyebrow. "I need to know what you need from me in this moment. Do you want advice, or do you want my support?"

"Both."

"This is your body and your choice. But don't walk away because you don't feel 'motherly,' whatever that is supposed to mean. Don't walk away because you don't think you can handle this, because I know you could. Make the choice that's best for you, and I'm here all the way." Lotus took a sip of her drink.

Penelope swallowed hard. She looked down at her hands clasped on the table. "I think I want an abortion. I mean, I know I do. That's what I decided."

"It's going to be okay, Pen. I told you I'd always have your back. I meant it. Even now. Especially now." Lotus reached over, putting her warm hand on Penelope's.

Penelope thought of Gram's funeral and their conversation on the log by the creek. Lotus had been there for her back then too. "I know, but now you're pregnant." She looked into her tea, avoiding Lotus's intense eye contact. "My timing couldn't be worse."

Lotus's head bobbed in understanding. "It doesn't matter. My path is not yours. This pregnancy has nothing to do with yours, and it certainly won't prevent me from being there for you. No matter what."

Penelope could feel her eyebrows draw up in a pained expression. *Gee, thanks for helping me get an abortion. I couldn't ask Nia because of her infertility.* That conversation with Nia would be even more painful than this one.

"I'll need somebody to drive me. To take me home after." She swallowed, thinking of putting on sweatpants and going home with Lotus after the procedure.

Lotus withdrew her hand from Penelope's and took a sip of her soymilk latte. "I'm guessing you haven't told him?"

Penelope shook her head. "And I don't intend to. What business is it of his now? It's my body and my choice." The words came out with a defensive edge, but Penelope couldn't stop them. It *was* her choice.

"I agree," Lotus said.

She was always like that. Supportive. Penelope could have said that she was going to avoid prenatal care and "freebirth" in the woods, and Lotus would have nodded. Penelope found herself considering if the same would be true if she told Lotus she was keeping the baby but scheduling a C-section. Lotus had surprised her with support when Penelope made the choice to disengage from her toxic family. The funeral had been the last straw. Gram's death, the dolls, and the ruby ring had been enough to put an end to the thin relationship she had with her mother. And Lotus had been there for her, aiding in her courage to speak up and let go. At some point, Penelope ought to stop feeling so surprised that people were there for her, but she might never get used to it.

Lotus's phone chimed, and she dug it from the depths of her boho bag and squinted at it. "Fucking Rob," she muttered.

"Uh-oh. What's going on with you two?"

"You know, the biggest difficulty with being in a poly marriage is the damn schedule. I imagine, it's like coordinating a big family when all the kids have a bunch of extracurriculars. He's messed it up again—that's all."

"That doesn't sound good. And the thing with the new roomie? It's a definite?"

Lotus rolled her eyes. The expression made her look like a teenager. "I wish he wasn't coming at all. Too much baggage. But he's moving in this weekend." Over the years, Lotus and Rob had both had live-in partners—that was not the problem. "Partners come and go, but this one is different. This guy broke his heart." She tucked her phone away after sending a quick text. "Like, what made us his best possible scenario? I realize his divorce unexpectedly changed things for him, but I just can't see how we're the best option for him at this point."

Penelope shrugged. She didn't understand having two lovers at once, but it seemed to work for Lotus and her family. Mostly. "A lot of people I know are getting divorced. Maybe we're just at the age for that. It's got to be tough when your entire life intertwines with some-one else's. Who gets to keep the dog and the friends? Still, you know you can say no, right? I mean, you're pregnant. Wasn't that a factor?"

"I know." Lotus let out a forceful *ha* exhalation. It was a weird yoga thing she did that had become so familiar to Penelope that she could watch Lotus do it without stifling a laugh. "I get it. He needed a reset. Okay, okay. But there hasn't been any definitive timeline set. I told Rob I want Jagannath out before the baby comes. That's my deadline. I mean, for the love of Goddess, I'm giving birth at home."

Penelope suppressed a wince. Yes, she knew. Home birth. It wasn't something they talked about often. Lotus hadn't told Pene-lope she'd planned that with Blaze until almost the very end. Pene-lope didn't offer unwavering support, but she respected her choice, even if she wouldn't choose it for herself.

The thought brought her attention to the baby growing inside her. It didn't matter how she would choose to give birth—she didn't want this baby and couldn't handle the idea of becoming a mother. She wouldn't be like Lotus, doting on Blaze and running her whole life around him, making her own baby food and going to La Leche League meetings. It would be a nightmare trying to fit a baby into her life. She found herself grateful that she lived in a world where this decision could be handled with a phone call and an office visit.

Penelope reached across the table, taking Lotus's hand. Unlike Lotus, she wasn't used to displaying affection, and her cousin looked up at her, surprised, like she understood that the gesture was big coming from Penelope. They'd arrived at a level of comfort Penelope had rarely known.

"Thank you," Penelope said. "Thank you for not judging me and always being here for me. I don't think you know how much it means." There was no sense getting all sappy, but she had to thank her. No one—besides Nia and Gram—had ever really shown up for her. "I'll text you the details when I get it scheduled."

They finished their drinks and left the café, and a weight lifted. Penelope still felt a twinge of guilt for keeping the news secret from Nia and asking her pregnant cousin to take her to the clinic. She wanted to confide in her best friend, Nia, but for the moment, Lotus would be there for her. Like she always was. At least Penelope had someone to go with her to the abortion. At least it would be over soon.

Chapter 6

There was something magical about the way a Catholic church smelled. Wax melting off the candles, mixed with incense and oil, brought a sense of familiarity that reminded Nia of childhood. The priest finished the Hail Mary, and Nia kept her eyes shut. Mary, mother of God. That was who she needed to appeal to.

She wasn't a good Catholic, even though she made the effort to bring her mother to mass. The tug of her silent promises to God pulled her there. Not that she truly believed that being devout was going to pay off in the form of a pregnancy.

Ricardo giggled loudly, and she glanced down the pew toward her nephew. Miguel shot him a stern look. Maria snatched her doll out of her brother's hands and squinted at him.

Nia's sister, Ana, hadn't been cursed with infertility. Her mother hadn't been cursed with it either. Nia was the only one.

After mass, everyone went back to her mother's for lunch. Nia plated the empanadas, dodging the chaos in the kitchen.

"*Muévete! Muévete!*" Miguel called to the twins as they circled each other with stick swords. "That's not for inside the house. And certainly not for inside the kitchen." He shooed them.

"*Afuera!*" With one word, Nia banished them.

The children piled out together, spilling into the backyard, giggling. The wooden sticks clanked together in their mock fight.

Nia's mother, Lucia, moved the rice and beans to a serving dish. "Is Edward going to be able to join us?"

"No, Mamá, he's still on call, and now that someone's in labor, he can't leave the hospital." Nia left out the part about him adjusting his call schedule to be home for the adoption home study happening later that evening. Mamá didn't need to know about that.

"Hm," Mamá said. "I know he works so much for his family. Always delivering those babies. When do you think he will deliver one of your babies?"

Subtle, as usual. Lucia was a full foot shorter than Nia, but she was broad and demanding. Nia pictured her mother pulling off her sandal, waving at her like she had when Nia was a willful child, threatening the *chancla* if she didn't hurry up and follow orders to produce more grandchildren.

"The *nietos* will all be grown without them. Don't you want them to have *primos* to grow up with?"

Nia sighed. "Of course we do, Mamá. But you'll have to wait. God knows the perfect timing. Trust."

She hadn't told her mother about the infertility or IVF or any of their baby plans and certainly not about the adoption idea. She wouldn't understand. Nia couldn't handle the thought of anyone else blaming her. She already blamed herself enough.

"Maybe she's already pregnant, Mamá. Look, she's not drinking her wine."

Nia shot Ana a dirty look when her mother turned. She squeezed her eyes shut for a moment, and that single control line mocked her again.

"All right. Gather for the prayer. Lunch is ready. Miguel, bring in the children."

Nia bowed her head, shutting her eyes, shutting out her family. She wished Edward was there to squeeze her hand, to confirm that she was doing the right thing to hide their problems from her family, and to make her feel like someone in the room understood her. Nia's mother said the prayer, but Nia tuned it out. She wanted the Hail Mary. She wanted to think of the mother Mary. She wanted to *be* a mother. But it didn't feel like anyone was listening to her prayers.

That evening, at home, Nia pushed in the upholstered white chair, tucking it beneath the dining room table. Fine china and linens decorated the dark, handcrafted hardwood table. The hand-painted Japanese china had been given to them by Edward's grandmother as a wedding gift. While the rest of the house had a distinctly modern look, the dining room blended the modern with the classic Japanese aesthetic of Edward's heritage. Considering their possessions, Nia reassured herself that they weren't going to fail the adoption home study for being unable to afford kids.

"Stop moving the chairs. Everything is perfect," Edward said from the kitchen.

A flower in the centerpiece drooped to the side, bending at the stem. Brown around the edges and half-limp, it stood out among the fresh white blooms. She plucked it from the arrangement and shifted the remaining flowers.

"I was just tucking the chairs in." She took the flower to the trash can and dropped it in.

Edward stood over the sink, stirring fresh lemonade in the pitcher.

"Should I cut up more lemons? Maybe we need more lemons."

"It will be perfect. She's not judging us on our lemonade."

"I know." She looked up at Edward. "You think she'll ask about my abortions?"

Edward set the wooden spoon on the counter and turned to Nia. He put his hands on her shoulders and met her eyes. "We're going to be wonderful parents. Who knows? We might not even need this." He didn't dare say that she might *be* pregnant. It was too much to hope for. But not saying it out loud didn't mean that it didn't exist for Nia. The home study woman and the IVF—all of it reminded Nia that they were in for a penny, in for a pound. It was all she wanted anymore, and she wasn't going to leave a stone unturned trying to make this a reality for them.

"I know we'll be great parents," she said. "But it's just—I don't want to be judged for..." Nia swallowed. "My past."

"I know. Which is why we didn't go through Catholic Charities. She isn't going to ask, though. Let's just focus on being ourselves and letting her do the assessment."

Nia exhaled heavily. "You're too perfect, you know that?"

Edward kissed her forehead. His soft lips made her shoulders relax a bit. "This is just a step in the process. But once we're through this, we're officially on the waiting list. A couple will choose us—I know it."

"What's not to love?" Nia said weakly.

A buzz from the intercom sounded in the living room. "Ms. Fitzgerald here to see the Simmons family," a voice said over the speaker.

"Come right up," Edward replied, punching the keypad on the intercom to open the door to the building.

Nia dropped the lemon slices into the pitcher and added ice. It was time. She washed the sticky lemon juice from her hands and stopped, staring at the bright-yellow slices floating in the lemonade. Nodding to herself, she took the pitcher to the coffee table and added it to the tray with tumblers in the center.

A sharp rapping on the door announced that the social worker had arrived. Edward opened it to a stern-looking woman with glasses, holding a leather binder and stack of files.

"You must be Mr. and Mrs. Simmons. I'm here for your adoption home study."

They led her into the living room and sat together on the sofa, offering her the wingback chair that flanked the coffee table.

Ms. Fitzgerald cleared her throat with a quiet squeak. "I have your file here. I'd like to go over a few things with you. Then we can talk about your readiness to add a child to your lives."

She smiled. It was likely supposed to be reassuring, but her eyes were tight and suspicious. *Aren't the people who usually do this job pretty personable—or at least a little bit happy?*

Ms. Fitzgerald sat in her perfectly pressed suit and jotted in her notebook while looking over the file and asking questions. It was a lot more tedious than Nia had expected. The nervous energy she'd been holding settled into her stomach. It felt sour, like a chewed-up lump of old food sitting just below her chest. She smiled and answered questions, holding Edward's hand between them on the couch.

"We feel that there are children who deserve a better life than what they may be born into. We hope to be able to give them that life," Edward said.

"And how long were you trying to conceive before you felt that adoption was the right choice for you?"

Is there a right answer? A wrong answer? Does she think this is our last resort? Will that keep us from passing the study? The questions zoomed one after the other in Nia's mind.

"We've always thought adoption was an option," Edward said. "Of course, we thought conceiving our own would be right for our family as well."

Nia nodded. Edward was quicker on his feet.

"And what happens if you conceive during the adoption process?"

"We want a big family," Nia said quickly. "I'm one of three, and Edward always wanted siblings. We've talked about having several kids. Probably three or four."

Ms. Fitzgerald wrote in the notebook perched on her knees.

"We'd still want to go through with the adoption process," Edward said.

Nia smiled again. She couldn't contradict Edward in front of the woman, but she wondered if they really would go forward. *What if that means two babies at the same time?* But the answer had been given. Maybe it was the best one.

Nia nervously offered to refill Ms. Fitzgerald's lemonade. When she said no, Nia refilled her own. She took sips of the cold, tart drink just to distract herself from the main task at hand.

An hour and a half later, they stood at the door, Ms. Fitzgerald's left arm full of the notes she'd taken. A report would go in, stating their fitness to become parents. It was all much more clinical than Nia had anticipated. They were two-dimensional people on a piece of paper who had answered questions, right or wrong, and become a number in the line of people waiting for babies.

As Nia reached forward and shook Ms. Fitzgerald's hand, she was close enough to smell her perfume, and it had a bitter medicinal scent that repulsed her. She smiled through the handshake, feeling the taste of the disturbing perfume in her mouth.

As soon as the woman was out the door, Nia turned to Edward. "Holy shit, her perfume smelled like embalming fluid. I thought I was going to be sick for a second. And wow. Not much of a personality on her, huh? I was thinking she might try to make this more comfortable and relaxed."

Edward laughed and hugged Nia. "It doesn't matter. We were great. We're going to be on the waiting list. We're going to adopt a baby."

Chapter 7

Lotus stood on the porch, arms folded. *Why did I agree to this?* Immediately, she exhaled a sharp "ha," a single fire breath to expel her tension and judgment.

Jagannath arrived with a Lyft driver, laden with a hiking backpack and little else. No car. No suitcase. Just the pack and two brown moving boxes. He didn't hesitate to hug Rob, throwing his arms around Rob's neck and giving him a full embrace. Somewhat more familiar than the bro hug she'd expected.

He gave a strange half bow, dipping his head toward Lotus. He was intentionally bald except for a tuft of hair, which was pulled up into a knot.

Lotus pulled her lip between her teeth, biting back her opinion. "Your room is ready. I just ask that you're quiet during Blaze's nap time and at bedtime."

"Done, and for that matter, what else can I do? I don't want to be here without doing my share. Anything you need, please ask." His eyes were wide with sincerity, crystal blue with an innocence that made Lotus's hair stand on edge.

She wrinkled her nose. "Hmm. Okay, I'll let you know."

Rob took one of the moving boxes into his arms. "What do you have in here, bricks?"

"Just the stuff for my altar. I couldn't leave it, though I didn't take much else."

Rob nodded and headed inside, carrying one of the boxes, and Lotus gestured for Jagannath to follow. She stepped through the doorway, the smell of patchouli and sandalwood from his boxes lingering. Her long skirt kissed the tops of her feet.

Blaze came bounding from the playroom, having leapt off the hammock swing dangling in the doorway. To his credit, Jagannath squatted down and greeted Blaze at eye level. When he held out his hand, Blaze took it and shook it vigorously, pumping it with both arms and giggling.

"Mighty strong shake you have there," Jagannath said. "You must be a really good climber."

"Don't remind me," Lotus said. "We let him explore his own limits. But I'd be lying if I didn't admit that it makes me nervous every time he goes into the big live oak."

"I brought something for you." He stood, fishing a small carved wooden bird from his bag. "A crane for you." He put the open-winged bird in Blaze's hand.

Blaze smiled up at him with an atypical shyness and then zoomed off through the hall, toward the kitchen, holding the bird high and flying it with his hand.

Lotus thanked Jagannath. "Walking feet!" she called to Blaze, turning to go after him.

Jagannath insisted on cooking dinner his first night with them. Lotus came into the kitchen later as he was chopping vegetables like an iron chef. Spice jars of cumin, coriander, and cardamom added to the smell of whatever was bubbling on her stove.

She watched him moving deftly around the kitchen like he knew it. "Rob tells me you went to culinary school." Lotus didn't want to be friends with him, but hostility would only make things harder. He was in her home now. She filled the tea kettle.

"Dropped out of culinary school is more like it," he said.

"But you still like cooking?"

"I didn't leave because of that. I left because of the attitude of most chefs. I couldn't find my place among the angry perfectionists. I love to cook, but I would never want to give up who I am for it."

"I appreciate that you're making dinner for us. Thank you." She liked to cook for her family, but the night off was both surprising and welcome.

"I hope you like Indian food." He glanced over at her, an eyebrow raised.

"I like all kinds of food. Hopefully, Blaze will eat it too. He's a pretty adventurous eater for a toddler."

"There's rice and naan at the very least. Everyone likes that. And I'm sure he'll love the mango lassi."

"You didn't have to go to so much trouble." *Is he trying to outdo me in the kitchen? Is he trying to prove something?* She exhaled a sharp *ha*, expelling the thought, wondering when she'd become so cynical. *Is it just because it's* him?

"It won't always be this intricate. Just tonight or on special occasions."

Does he think his arrival is a special occasion?

The tea kettle whistled a high-pitched whine. She reached around a bubbling dish yellow with turmeric and grabbed the kettle then covered her ball of loose-leaf tea with hot water. "I'll leave you to it."

Lotus went to the living room with her tea and her attitude, wondering how she would ever settle into the new arrangement. She itched to go to work. But she'd promised herself not to. She wanted to feel out this new situation on the first night. *Why did I ever agree to let him live here?*

As if in answer to her thoughts, Morgana bounded through the house, carrying a raggedy, dirty, half-chewed lovey in her mouth. She dropped the mangled toy at Lotus's feet.

Because I love Rob—that's why.

Lotus picked up the soggy toy and threw it then wiped her hand on her skirt. To take her mind off everything, she flipped open her laptop and pulled up the store's POS tracking system. Just a few reports. She'd already broken her promise to herself not to work. It didn't matter. Her goal wasn't to avoid work—it was to avoid leaving the house, and that much she'd accomplished.

At dinner, Blaze ate two bites and then got up from his chair, made a trip around the table, and returned to his spot. After three rounds like this, Rob asked, "Don't you want to sit and eat, Blaze?"

"Do you think that after we let him do his progressive dinner-party routine every night, he's going to sit still tonight to impress someone he doesn't even know?" Lotus asked.

"I thought we were supposed to be introducing the idea repeatedly. Isn't that what you said?" Rob asked.

"It's not like getting him to eat new foods. We have to decide if this behavior is acceptable or not and then intervene appropriately. It's age appropriate. He's not going to be doing laps around the table when he's ten or fifteen." She turned to Jagannath. "The food is delicious. Sorry, we hope his movement isn't too disruptive. He has to move his body a lot. Sometimes, we just have dinner after he's in bed if we can wait that late."

"Doesn't bother me a bit," Jagannath said. "I usually wait until after I eat to do my walking, but hey, his way works for digestion too."

At bedtime, Blaze pressed against Lotus in the twin bed, nursing after she'd read him a story. Rob had gone with Jagannath on an after-dinner walk while she shifted into their nighttime routine. She clenched and unclenched her jaw, forcing herself to take slow, deep breaths. Maybe she should have said no. But now Jagannath was living in her home, eating with her family, and sleeping two doors down from them. *Will Rob want him back?* Jagannath had been the one who got away, Rob's biggest heartbreak. She found it hard to believe he wasn't going to wreak havoc on their lives again.

Chapter 8

After driving by Jasper's house like a psycho, Penelope decided she was not going to be able to handle her shift that night. Despite her decision to have an abortion, she wanted to see him, not to tell him—never that. But driving by his house reminded her why it would never work between them.

She still had spare clothes in her trunk, which had come in handy on gym days or if she decided to meet Jasper somewhere on short notice. When they were first dating, her trunk only held a pair of shoes and a clean pair of panties. But the longer it went on, the more she stuffed into that duffel bag until her trunk had turned into an extra closet.

She ditched her scrubs, slid into a mini skirt and a tank top, and added her makeup using the car mirror. After rimming her eyes with liner and tossing it back into her bag, she pulled out her red lipstick. She'd been wearing it the night she met Jasper.

At first, it had been a fling. She wouldn't have even met him if she hadn't listened to Lotus. Lotus always had an event or a cause. "It'll be fun. You never get out. You work too much," Lotus had said. She'd even made a mask for Penelope to wear. A masquerade—it was so gothic.

Jasper stood at the bar, masked, alone. If only his wife hadn't had the flu that night, she would have been on his arm, and Penelope never would have met him. But there he was, alone, drinking a Moscow mule.

Two glasses of wine later, Penelope approached him. "Surprising amount of feathers for such a masculine look."

He was a head taller than her, blond as a California surfer with thick, broad shoulders beneath a black jacket. His hair was partially hidden by the crown of feathers framing the top of his silver mask and stuck up from behind a harp and rearing stallions.

He smiled, dimples showing beneath the mask. Green eyes shone from the eyeholes of his half-hidden face. "It was either this or one with a phallic-looking beak. I went for the feathers. And yours? Where'd you find that?"

Penelope smiled, knowing the red lipstick accented the enormous red flower beside her left eye. "I've got a hippie friend who makes them. I just got lucky."

His eyes twinkled. It was going to be that kind of night. They bantered, and it amused her to tease him. Not wanting to give him too much, she left him at the bar and danced with Nia and Lotus. She'd dragged Nia to a girls' night out once she realized Lotus was not bringing Rob along. Nia had only agreed because she was between cycles and needed a mental break. Penelope drank more wine. She swirled on the edge of the dance floor, the room twirling with her, and landed in the arms of her feathery bar boy.

"I thought you'd never leave that bar," she said breathlessly.

"I thought you'd come back," he said into her ear. The warmth of his breath gave her chills.

The room pulsed with loud music, and the rhythmic thumping urged her to keep moving. In his arms, her body pulsed with his. *Who is this beautiful man? How did I get the nerve to approach him?* A couple of glasses of wine made her less shy, but they were just talking. Until they weren't.

Then they were just dancing. Until they weren't.

It was supposed to be one night. The masquerade might have been for charity, but there was something provocative about being masked all night, not seeing the other patrons fully. Not revealing herself wholly.

It wasn't until they were in the elevator, with Penelope smearing her red lipstick all over his mouth, that she realized her inhibitions were completely gone. She didn't even ask him his name.

In the morning, she left her number, not really expecting him to call. Not expecting anything from him. It had been a great night, but she didn't think she would start a relationship with a one-night stand. Still, in case he decided he wanted another round, she'd left her number.

When he texted two weeks later, she learned his name.

You want to meet up tonight? With or without the masks? I'd love to see you. Jasper.

When she met Jasper, she'd been just drunk enough to go after what she wanted. But that night, fresh from the results of her pregnancy test, Penelope was so drunk the words jumbled together, and she had a hard time getting them to line up and form a sentence. This time, there was no cute guy at the bar, so she drank alone until everything was fuzzy.

She called Nia. "I need you to not judge me right now and just get down here." Penelope could hear the words slurring even though she tried to separate them.

"Where are you?" Nia asked patiently.

"Juicy Lucy in Sandy Springs. Ooh, that's a lot of esses. Ssss. Like you, Jesenia." She pronounced the name the Spanish way, with the *J* sounding like a *H*, but she slurred the *s* for three seconds then laughed.

"I'm on my way. Don't move."

Nia and Penelope had met at the Labor and Delivery Christmas party. Edward was Penelope's favorite resident at the time. Though she wouldn't normally have talked to the doctors' wives—they were a special breed of women—something had been different about Nia.

Penelope hung up her cell phone and turned back to the bartender. "See? I don't need a ride. I've got a friend." She dangled her keys from her fingertip in front of the bartender. "I'm not stupid. At least not about this." She dropped the keys onto the bar and pulled a mint from her purse. "Why do they call it a Long Island iced tea? There's definitely no tea in here."

The bartender launched into an explanation about the controversy over the drink's origin. Something about Long Island, New York, versus some place in Tennessee during prohibition. She lost interest in the story when he started naming the original ingredients. He was pretty cute. Tall, like Jasper, but with dark hair and dark eyes. His accent was like Nia's, but stronger.

"I prefer the prohibition story myself—the veiled name and all," he said.

The deep amber-brown of his eyes struck her. She'd been so wrapped up in her misery and drama that she hadn't even looked into his face before getting drunk. Now her guard was down, and he was beautiful.

Penelope sat up straighter in the uncomfortable wooden stool and flashed him her best smile. "How long have you been working here?"

She forced herself to focus and listen to his story. He was an entrepreneur working on a start-up during the day and tending bar at night. He'd lived in Puerto Rico until he was fifteen and then moved to Atlanta. Penelope turned up her flirt game, surprised at how sober she could pretend to be. His name was Gabriel, and it sounded delicious when he said it. Penelope stood up and leaned over the bar, as close to Gabriel as the counter would allow. Aware that her tank and the position of her elbows on the bar offered him a show, she cocked a finger at him. He responded by coming toward her.

She lowered her voice, and he turned his ear to her. "What do you say I cancel my ride and go home with you?" Penelope pulled his earlobe between her lips and bit ever so slightly. The smell of his skin and aftershave made her want him more.

He leaned back, a wide smile on his face, and chuckled.

"Did it tickle?" she asked.

"Did what tickle?"

Penelope turned to see Nia standing beside her with her arms folded. "Oh, Nia, you're here! Meet Gabriel." She tried her best to pronounce it the way he did, but Nia's face told her she'd gotten it wrong.

Nia launched into a conversation with Gabriel in Spanish. Penelope didn't understand most of it. Sober, she could pick up a fair amount, but drunk, she was useless. The next thing she knew, Nia had paid her tab and hooked her by the elbow and was pushing her out the door. So much for the hot bartender.

Back at Penelope's apartment, Nia gave her two ibuprofen tablets and pulled her out of her tight skirt and into some yoga pants and a T-shirt. "If I wasn't so nice, you'd have quite a headache in the morning for that one. Do you realize how many of those Long Islands you had?"

Penelope was starting to sober up and wished she was having rebound sex with the bartender instead of getting a lecture from Nia.

"Why did you drink so much?" Nia sat down on Penelope's bed. Her tone was gentle.

She pulled the ponytail from Penelope's hair and ran a hand through it, her nails lightly scratching Penelope's scalp. It reminded Penelope of the night Jasper had broken up with her and Nia had come over with ice cream. Or that day almost three years ago, the very first time Nia had broken down about her infertility, curled up on Penelope's couch, crying.

"Jasper."

That was all she had to say. The single word was a code for how pitiful and sick she felt. One word for why everything was broken in that moment. Nia had been the first one she'd called after he ended it, and she knew all about it. What she didn't know was that Penelope had dipped a little white stick in a red solo cup and found out she was carrying Jasper's baby.

She swallowed, tasting tequila, and turned to face the wall. If Nia figured out that she was hiding something, she'd dig until the truth came out. She could sense when Penelope wasn't happy and was holding back.

But Penelope couldn't tell Nia, as much as she wanted to. The news would just hurt her. In the weeks when Nia was waiting for a positive pregnancy test, she usually became desperate and hopeful, always swearing she wouldn't get her hopes up but still thinking this cycle was finally it.

Penelope pushed the thought away and told herself it didn't matter. She wasn't keeping the baby anyway, so there was no sense in distressing Nia over it. Jasper didn't want her. He surely wouldn't want her with his unplanned child, living in a one-bedroom apartment in Grant Park, trading the kid for weekends, having to explain it all to his wife. Penelope wasn't going to let this accident ruin her life.

"Skipping work and drinking by yourself is not a healthy coping technique," Nia said. "I'm not judging, but I'm worried about you. Go to bed. We'll talk tomorrow."

Nia tucked her in, kissing her on the forehead and sighing with pity, before she let herself out of the apartment. Penelope thought about calling Jasper. But she had enough of her wits about her by then to realize that drunk dialing him would lead to disaster.

She took another sip of water, sank into her bed, and pulled her down comforter up over her shoulders. It wasn't cold enough for the down yet, but the warmth and weight of the blanket gave her security. She drifted off with her anxious thoughts flitting from Jasper to the hot bartender to the awful news about the pregnancy. She had a dizzy feeling when she closed her eyes and just wanted to hurry up and fall asleep so she could forget about it.

Chapter 9

The next morning, Nia pulled into the sloped driveway of her mother's bungalow in Gwinnett County after another negative pregnancy test. Nothing was private when you had a Venezuelan mother. That Nia expected to keep her infertility a secret was a reminder of how she'd become quietly Westernized.

When she was a teenager, her mother would give her the side-eye for bringing home too many white friends. "You're losing your Spanish, *hija*. Why you friends with so many *gringas*?"

And as a young adult, when Nia ate spinach salads and drank green smoothies, her mother would ask, "What are you eating? You've lost your butt. Let me make you some *arepas*." She would mutter under her breath about the way a real woman should look.

Her mother even knew when she'd lost her virginity. "Oh, hija, you look flushed. I see your innocence—it has drained from you. *Muchacha diabla*. Aye." And she shook her head.

Nia had feared the *chancla* would come off that time. She might have been a high school senior by then, but her mother was never above removing the sandal for a whack. The sting of the chancla had attached itself to several memories of her missteps during childhood.

Though she wasn't a child any longer, she felt she had no choice but to continue with a policy of secrecy. Nia's success at keeping her infertility, hopeful pregnancy, and adoption plans a secret from her mother was a feat that put her up there with the Venezuelan secret police.

Her mother's squat house sat on an uneven hill, and the driveway sloped where Nia parked in front of the one-car garage. She'd always thought the house looked like a face, two dormer windows staring like eyes and the stepped porch a gaping mouth waiting to swallow visitors. The predictable rhythmic beats of Oscar D'León pulsed through her mother's open windows, trumpets belting out over the percussion.

Nia gathered the grocery bags from the mercado. She didn't begrudge having to take care of Mamá. All her siblings shared in the responsibilities. Miguel was the *primogénito*, and while that gave him more responsibilities, it also came with certain privileges, like exempting him from the domestic duties. He was also the only boy in their family, which Nia often lamented. The patriarchy of her culture was not going to be overcome this generation.

After Papi had passed, Ana and Nia had taken a day each for weekly visits, on top of the supposed-to-be-weekly Sunday mass and lunch. Miguel had taken over Mamá's finances. Mamá refused to live with any of them, which was a relief. But Nia had warned Edward before they were married that the day would come when one of them would take Mamá in.

Barely a foot into the front door, Nia was greeted with "Oh, hija, you look pale. You getting sick? I can make you some *sancocho*."

Sancocho. It was the Band-Aid for any illness—the solution to a death in the family, a sour stomach, the flu, a bad attitude. You name it, sancocho fixed it. The thick, hearty cure-all stew, filled with meat and root vegetables, was one of Nia's favorite foods, but she wasn't about to admit that she needed the pick-me-up.

"No, Mami. I'm fine." She leaned down and kissed her mother on the cheek, still gripping the full shopping bags in both hands, and pushed past her to the kitchen.

Nia dropped the bags onto the counter and began unloading the weekly fridge refill. Mamá had finally given up on complaining about the groceries she delivered, in part because she knew Nia wasn't going to stop and in part because Nia had relented and now only shopped at the *mercado*, like Mamá preferred.

Lucía followed Nia into the kitchen and squinted up at her and then gripped her chin in her stubby hand and squeezed, turning Nia's face toward her.

The chin grab. I'm in for it now. Her mother's calloused fingers held her cheeks in a firm grip. It was futile to fight it. Once Mamá decided she wanted someone's full attention, there was no escaping.

"Are you pregnant? Oh, that's why you're pale! *Ay, Dios mío.* This is the best news. I didn't believe Ana, but she's right—you look so pale." She kissed Nia on the cheeks. "Little *nietos preciosos.* No more carrying the groceries. Sit." Mamá let go of her cheeks and turned.

The cheek grab was the ultimate lie detector. There was no backing out once Mamá had you in her grip, staring into your eyes and straight into your soul. Mamá didn't need Nia's confirmation or denial. Her mother moved to the stove.

"I'm not pregnant, Mami. But you're right—we're trying."

"I remember those first weeks carrying you. So pale. Not as pale as you. I never looked like a gringa. Manzanilla will do it. You sit." She started water on the stove. She would not be told no about the tea. Or the imaginary pregnancy.

Nia sat on the stool in the kitchen, letting her mother fuss over the tea. She couldn't have stopped her if she'd tried. "Mami, I don't want you to get too excited. We've been trying for a while and haven't been able to conceive yet."

Mamá nodded. Her usual aggressive tone had abated into a soothing singsong sweetness, like the way she talked to Ricardo, her oldest grandchild. It was not a tone she'd taken very often with Nia. "Mami knows. I know you don't yet. But I can see it. Maybe that's why *Viejo*'s family always called me *bruja.* I know things. You've got one brewing in your belly, hija."

The teapot whistled, signaling her mother's effort to soothe her. Nia held back tears. It was possible that her mother was right. She *could* be pregnant and not know it yet. Nia thought she might abandon that kind of wishful thinking months before when they'd finally given in and gone to the fertility specialist. Every month, she swore she wouldn't get her hopes up about being pregnant. Every month, she did it anyway. And every time, she was devastated. There was no reason to think the IVF would be any different.

Mamá served the manzanilla and talked on and on about her own pregnancies and Ana's three. Nia didn't bother arguing. Once her mind was set, there was no dissuading Mamá.

She sipped the earthy hot tea, enjoying the floral hints and crisp apple flavor despite her growing frustration. She wouldn't need the tea to "calm her belly," as her mother had said. She'd need it to calm her nerves from listening to Mamá get her hopes up. *What will she say when the pregnancy test is negative again? What will she think of me?*

Nia realized she'd been ignoring her mother for several minutes. "And if it's a son, Oscar. Viejo's great grandfather was named Oscar."

Her mother was trying to name a child she hadn't conceived yet. *Did that just happen?* "Mami, we don't need to talk about names yet. First, I have to get a positive pregnancy test."

With her lips flattened, Mamá held her knife, frozen, over a stack of potatoes and yuca. She was starting on the sancocho after all. It was going to be a long visit.

Nia stood and picked up a potato and the peeler. "And I'm not naming him Oscar."

"Well, you certainly don't want your Papi's name. He hated that name, God rest his soul."

"Ignacio isn't so bad."

"Not if you live in Venezuela. But you don't. Now you are *norteamericana*, and you have to choose a name you can say in English or Spanish. *Jesenia?*"

Her mother was the one who'd named her Jesenia. And now she used her own daughter's name to bully her. So typical.

Nia held the potato in her palm, slicing off the skin. If she was going to listen to her mother name her nonexistent child and tell more stories of her pregnancies, she might as well get some sancocho out of it.

Chapter 10

Penelope yawned. The previous night's drinks lingered—her rank, stale breath made her wrinkle her nose. The clock on her cell phone told her it was after ten, the big white letters announcing that she'd slept late after the long night. At least Nia hadn't turned on the alarm clock before leaving her apartment. That would have been cruel.

Nia. During the peak of her drunkenness, she'd wanted to tell her best friend the truth. It was simple. The embryo was a biological event at this point, not really a baby. Termination was the solution.

She sat up and swung her legs off the bed, and her feet landed in the discarded heap of last night's clothes. She picked them up, uncovering the four-inch heels beneath, and walked the wad of clothes over to the bathroom, the cold tile floor waking her further. The balled-up tank and miniskirt smelled like an ashtray. *Did I smoke last night?*

She threw the clothes in the hamper and licked her dry lips. They tasted like two-day-old Long Islands mixed with sleep and mold. And smoke. She opened the mouthwash and swirled it around her mouth to relieve the odious taste so she could brush her teeth without gagging.

Plopping back down into her bed, she dialed Edward's cell phone. Luckily, she didn't have to call his office. And she wouldn't risk talking to Nia, who would be with her mom that morning.

The trilling rang in her ear. Two rings. Three rings. "To what do I owe the pleasure?" Edward said. "You want to tell me about another breech hippie birth down at AMC?"

"Cute, but no, not why I'm calling. Nia's at her mom's, right?"

"How is it that you have each other's schedules memorized?"

She ignored the question. Edward was always teasing them. "Listen, I need an appointment, and I was wondering when I could come into the clinic... discreetly."

He flashed right out of friend mode and into concerned-friend mode, or maybe it was doctor mode. "What's the issue, Pen?" His tone had turned serious.

She let the nickname slide. No one but Nia called her Pen. Of course, that meant Nia probably used the name in front of Edward, and he'd picked it up. She hesitated. Edward was a professional, but he was also a friend. And her best friend's husband, from whom she was trying to keep her unwanted pregnancy a secret. But he would help.

"I need a termination."

"You okay? Want to talk about this? Does Nia know?"

"I'm not an idiot. I know she can't handle this."

"She told me she picked you up last night."

"Uh-huh," Penelope said vaguely.

"How's the hangover?"

"It's temporary." *Like my current condition.*

"I can schedule you. You want me to do it or choose someone else for you?"

"Choose someone else. But you know me, Edward. Don't choose someone I'll hate."

"Okay. I've got the schedule up. I can probably get you in with Richard... next week, it looks like."

"That's fine. I like Dr. B."

"You've got someone to come in with you?" he asked.

"Yes. When can I come in?"

"Tuesday. Two o'clock."

"Thanks, Edward."

"You want to talk about this, Pen?"

She swallowed, trying to fix her dry throat. "No." She pulled her blankets back over her legs, tracing the fleece with her fingers.

"I'm here if you change your mind. You don't have to talk to me, but talk to someone before the termination. Please?"

"Fine," she said.

"And I know this goes without saying, but please, don't talk to anyone who will tell Nia. I can't handle another breakdown from her, and this will just send her into a spiral."

"I know."

"We're right at the peak of another cycle, almost ready to test, so her anxiety is high."

"I wasn't planning on telling her. I can handle this, Edward." *And I already know exactly where you are in the cycle. She's my best friend.* "Anyway, thanks for this."

Hanging the phone up, Penelope sank back into the bed and pulled the blanket up to her chin. It wasn't the abortion that had her questioning herself. She knew it was the right choice. But she'd never had to keep something from Nia before. Her stomach twisted in protest. The lying shrank her, taking her back into her childhood, when she'd lied to her mother just to protect herself.

She wanted to at least tell Jasper, but the thought of that seemed comical. As if he would open his arms and hold her and tell her he wanted her to have his baby. A fantasy of walking up to his house and telling the truth played in her mind. It made her want to laugh. Jasper only cared about Jasper. She'd considered that his wife might have begun to suspect him when he ended their relationship.

What was I thinking? That he was going to leave his wife? That we were going to live in the suburbs, have two point five kids, and play tennis on the weekends? Delusional. No, she didn't want the baby. As much as she wanted Jasper, a baby would only complicate the mess that had become her life.

Penelope had been thirteen when she overheard the conversation. Pretending to be asleep was a common coping technique in those days, and Penelope would pull the thin blanket up and tuck it beneath her chin. *If she thinks I'm asleep, she won't try to talk to me. Hopefully, she'll just go to her room and pass out.*

She really had been asleep until her mother came banging through the front door like a herd of camp kids high on sugar. Her mother was surely high on something or maybe just drunk. Her laughter spilled down the hallway and penetrated the thin walls. Penelope was already frozen when she heard a deep bass rumble laughing along with her mother. She decided she would flip her lock once she heard the click of her mother's bedroom door. She thought of her little brother across the house, safely tucked away in the old converted garage room.

The laughter moved the other direction, and kitchen cabinets slammed. "I found us some glasses," the deep voice said. Penelope focused on the strip of light beneath the door. A single line of yellow light seeped in from the hallway.

"No need. I can drink from the bottle," her mother answered.

"This's a nice place you got here," the man said.

Penelope rolled her eyes. What a horrible compliment to try to get into someone's pants. And he was already there—it wasn't like her mother would say no. She thought Penelope didn't know. She thought Penelope never heard. But her mother's room stayed open—soft grunts and shallow gasping breaths penetrated Penelope's cheap hollow door.

"You sure your kids aren't gonna wake up?" he asked.

"They're heavy sleepers, even with noise. Probably from all that time I ran the vacuum when they were babies."

A thump sounded. Penelope imagined the man lifting her mother onto the countertop, leaning into her, scooting between her straddled legs as she wrapped around him. Her stomach turned. In the morning, her mother would ask if she'd heard her come in from work the previous night. Penelope would lie, like she always did.

No, she hadn't heard her mother coming home drunk. She hadn't heard her mother fuck a stranger. And before the man left and her mother began snoring, Penelope certainly hadn't heard the conversation turn to her.

"How old are your kids?" he'd asked.

"Thirteen and nine. Girl and a boy."

She pictured the man, tall and burly the way her mother liked them. Old. Probably had yellow teeth. Smokers. Men who drove motorcycles and bought scratch-off tickets at gas stations.

"Same dad?" he asked.

What the hell is wrong with this guy? Penelope saw herself flinging the thin blanket off, standing up, slapping her door open, and stepping into the yellow light. "Fuck off, man," she would say. "Fuck. Off."

But she didn't. She curled the blanket tighter under her chin. Her breath caught in her throat.

"No. The oldest kid was a big mistake. Worst man on the planet. I should've listened to my instincts and ended it. Now I've got a mouthy teenager. Changed my whole life. I might've made it in New York if I hadn't gone through with that. The other one, well, he's different. His dad was better. But he's dead now."

Penelope clamped her lips together when she realized she was crying quietly. The tears were cold on her cheeks, burning her. That was why her mother was so wretched to her. That was why her mother hated her. She'd never wanted Penelope. She'd wanted an abortion.

Penelope flopped over on the lumpy twin mattress and faced away from the door. She never turned her back on the door, but that night, she didn't care what happened. *Let it come.* She wasn't supposed to be there anyway. She wasn't even supposed to be alive.

Chapter 11

The familiar earthy smell of sandalwood incense filled Lotus's bedroom. Rob lit it every morning before starting his daily movement.

"I have a date tonight. What time are you going to be home from helping Penelope?" Rob straightened on the floor and looked up at Lotus.

She sat in the bed, nursing Blaze, both of them still in their pajamas, while Rob stretched in the open space in their bedroom. A date. Lotus hadn't been on a date since she'd become pregnant. After she and Mitch had broken it off, she just hadn't felt like it.

"I don't know. I mean, she's having an abortion. What do you want me to do, just drop her off and get back in time for your date? She might need me to be present."

"Why does she need *you*? I thought you two weren't that close." He leaned over into a forward bend.

Lotus pressed her lips together into a thin line. *Deep breath.* "We're family, and she needs me. That's what family does. And things have changed since the funeral. We are close."

Rob's head hung down in the dangling stretch, and he clasped his forearms with his hands. His long hair pooled on the floor. A muffled sigh escaped him. Lotus pretended not to hear it.

He stood again. "Do you want me to cancel my date? Is that what this about?"

Lotus gave a short, staccato laugh. "Is that what *you* think this is about?"

Blaze sat up and planted a wet kiss on her face. His sweet milky breath melted some of her anger. It reminded her that he needed her—he wasn't ready to wean. Then he flopped over in her lap and switched sides, paying no mind to where his knees and elbows landed as he repositioned.

She grunted, bracing herself against the stab of his elbow. "I don't care who you date. You know that. This thing with Penelope has nothing to do with you. I'm trying to be there for my cousin. I can't help if that interferes with your date. Maybe you can call Kendra."

She certainly wasn't going to call the sitter. If Rob had a date, then fine, he could make arrangements. But Blaze wasn't the easiest for a babysitter. Kendra was just about the only one Blaze would tolerate besides his parents. If Kendra wasn't available, it was going to be too bad for Rob and his date.

"Fine," Rob said.

"Her appointment is at two. Once the procedure is done, I'll take her home, make her some tea, tuck her in, and say goodbye. I'm sure it's not going to be much later than dinnertime."

He gave her a curt nod. She ignored it and went to the kitchen. Rob's date was not her priority. While they tried to accommodate each other's dates and childcare in their marriage, that day was about Penelope, and she wasn't going to give another second of her time to Rob's pouting.

Lotus entered the kitchen to find Jagannath standing at the kitchen island, whisking a thinned starter for making yogurt.

"Rob told me you're interested in working at the Garden?"

"If you need someone, that would be great."

She nodded. "I could use another hand there. Especially for opening and inventory."

"When do you want me to start?"

"Let me get through this week, and I can start training you next week." Lotus opened her laptop and plopped down at the kitchen table.

Twenty minutes later, Rob came in. Lotus didn't notice until the smell wafting in with him got her attention. The burnt-earth smell meant only one thing. Rob was high. Again.

"Wake-and-bake kind of day?" she asked.

He gave her a sheepish grin and pulled open the refrigerator. Knowing she didn't approve, he never smoked in front of her, but that didn't mean he wasn't doing it. She'd encouraged him to quit, especially once Blaze was born. It was different having a baby in the house. But he hadn't quit, and then she'd found herself making excuses for him. Usually, he stood at the bathroom window and blew the smoke out. He always lit incense while he did it because he was a thoughtful smoker. It helped his anxiety. It was harmless, hardly even a drug.

She shut her laptop and went upstairs. She needed some time alone. Yoga could always recenter her in times like this.

Lotus straightened out of warrior and moved into tree pose. She liked to close her yoga practice with balancing and told herself that it helped her steady her life. Her audible breath came slowly and deeply as she hissed in the back of her throat. After balancing both sides, she lay flat on her back on the thick yoga mat and closed her eyes. She let go, focusing on releasing her body into the floor, but it only drew her attention to the crick in her neck and the ache in her knee.

Despite her daily conscious practice, her mind wandered. *Did Rob remember to make the deposit? Did the shipment of floor pillows arrive from Indonesia? Are we low on incense?* She recognized the thoughts as a bombardment into her yoga practice and tried to push them aside and clear her mind.

She cut her Savasana short and hopped into the shower. Penelope needed her soon.

Penelope. Her cousin had gotten herself into it this time. Lotus chided herself for her making a judgment. She didn't mean to. That situation had happened to all of them—at least, the part about getting involved with the wrong guy and making stupid mistakes. The unplanned pregnancy, well, that had happened to a lot of her friends, though never to her. She thought about Jake, her big mistake. She could have easily ended up at the abortion clinic, wading through protesters holding signs with dead babies. Her college roommate had gotten one. And her closest friend from the yoga teacher training had had two. She didn't judge them for it. Still, she was glad she wasn't the one making that decision.

Chapter 12

The elevator opened on the eighteenth floor in front of Edward's ritzy Buckhead office. Penelope hadn't been there since he opened the private practice, but there was something about standing in his office that suddenly felt wrong and awful. Hiding her pregnancy from Nia was both easy and difficult. Easy because she was protecting her friend from pain. Difficult because Nia was her *person*, and this was a time when she needed her person to hold her hand.

"Ready?" Lotus asked.

That day, Lotus was her person. To be fair, Lotus had been there for her before. But she still felt odd without Nia.

Penelope realized she'd been standing in the hall outside the glass door, frozen. She nodded, and Lotus pushed the door open. A dozen women sat in the waiting room at one stage or another of pregnancy. There was a brunette in her forties with gray streaks in her hair, reading a parenting magazine and looking more than nine months pregnant. An Indian woman with an older lady, probably her mother, wore a sari and showed something on her phone to a toddler. A young couple, probably in their early twenties, held hands and spoke quietly about whether it would be a boy or a girl. Penelope tried not to look at them and went straight for the counter to sign in.

"I have an appointment with Dr. B," she mumbled to the receptionist.

Edward's place in the tower had been a great spot to start his practice. He had credentials at Northside and loved working in the "baby factory." Edward teased Penelope often about the position she'd taken at Atlanta Medical Center. AMC offered waterbirth, midwives, breech deliveries—the sort of births he didn't see at Northside. But despite her myriad of experiences with labor and delivery, she hadn't assisted at an abortion. She'd cared for patients be-

60

fore or after, in a couple of rare cases, but those were situations when the baby or mom wouldn't have made it.

"You still okay?" Lotus asked, putting a hand on her shoulder.

Penelope fought the urge to shrug it off. The overt comforting only made her feel guilty. Of course, thinking about work wasn't really helping the situation either.

"I need a fucking Valium or a drink," she whispered.

Lotus nodded and rubbed her back briefly then let her hand drop.

Good. Maybe she noticed with her "intuitiveness" that I don't like that shit. As soon as she thought it, Penelope felt bad. Lotus was nice enough to bring her to the office. *I'm so ungrateful. Some cousin. Some friend.* Her mood and attitude had nothing to do with Lotus being a crunchy-granola woo-woo hippie. To each her own—she truly believed that. Penelope just wanted this over with. Maybe the burning rage would leave when the baby did.

Penelope wanted the receptionist to fling open the door and lead her down the hallway to the back room and shut the waiting room out. The eyes of the rest of the pregnant women bored into the back of her skull. She could feel it. By the fish tank, a petite blonde with a belly the size of a basketball read a pregnancy book. A frizzy-haired brunette drank coconut water from a boxy cardboard bottle and played a game with a preschooler on a tablet. The women who waited wanted to check on their babies—see them on ultrasound or hear the heartbeat. They wanted to talk about scheduling their inductions or report on their swelling ankles.

Heat pulsed up her chest and neck and threatened to suffocate her. The abortion clinic would have been better than this. No Anne Geddes art staring down from the walls. No rooms full of pregnant people rubbing their bellies and navel-gazing. Just protesters and women who knew why you were there. At least that choice would have been an honest one. Instead, she'd chosen to hide in plain sight.

She stood at the counter in front of the receptionist, who might be the only one besides Lotus who knew she was there for an abortion.

The receptionist slid a clipboard and paperwork across the counter to her. "Just fill these out."

She sounded bored. Or maybe patient. The kind of tone people used when they were trying to remain neutral and hide what they really thought. Penelope could see it in her eyes. Her stare said, "What has that baby ever done to deserve this?"

At least at the abortion clinic she would have been expecting that stare, if not from the employees then on the way in and out. She took the clipboard numbly in her hands. She didn't deserve anonymity.

"Is Edward here? I mean, Dr. Simmons?" Penelope asked.

The receptionist narrowed her eyes as if she was trying to figure out what made Penelope and Dr. Simmons so familiar. "No, he's been called to the hospital."

Penelope nodded and turned with the clipboard, holding back tears, trying to stop the shaking in her hands. The desert in her mouth forced the words down. It was too late. She had to stay. Reason for visit: abortion. The clipboard was a giant sign of a dead baby waving above her head. And it told everyone that she was there not to listen to a heartbeat or complain about hemorrhoids but to get rid of her unwanted baby.

"You want to sit?" Lotus asked.

Penelope realized she was standing a step away from the receptionist counter, clutching the clipboard, her breath coming faster than normal. She nodded weakly. Lotus slipped her arm in Penelope's.

Then the glass door swung open, and there stood Nia. She held a bouquet of pink and blue balloons in one hand and a small silver rectangular box in the other. She had a mischievous glint in her eye.

When her gaze settled on Penelope, her face broke into a white full-toothed smile. "Oh my God, Pen, I didn't expect to see you here!

I wanted to call you so bad. But I had to tell Edward first. Isn't it great? I guess the balloons give me away. I thought it would be cute—pink and blue. Is he here?"

Penelope shook her head weakly. "At a birth." The words came out more like a croak. She tried to smooth her face, forcing herself to relax under Nia's watchful eyes.

"Oh, dang. Well, I guess I'll have to catch him after." Her shoulders slumped slightly. "Small world, seeing you here. What are you doing here, anyway?"

The innocence and perkiness of the question startled Penelope out of her head. If the clipboard and the happy pregnant women all around her weren't enough to make her feel out of place, her best friend standing in front of her, all balloons and smiles, was.

"Nia," she said in a near whisper. "I'm here for an abortion."

Chapter 13

Nia stared at the photograph on Edward's desk. It was the two of them on their wedding day. Her mother had wanted her to have a big wedding in the Catholic church. Four months before the event, when the stress of wedding planning and pleasing her mother landed Nia in the hospital, she canceled the big church ceremony.

She and Edward flew to the Dominican Republic and got married on the beach. She wore the dress. The photograph didn't reveal how hot it had been on the beach in June. It didn't reveal the itchy sand sticking to her skin, rubbing like sandpaper. Nia's makeup and smile didn't tell how frail she'd been, recovering from the anemic episode.

In October, she married Edward in the church. Just immediate family and the two of them. No reception. But the sacrament was important and had to be made in the church before God.

The silver box lay open on the desktop, its lid off, the pregnancy test nestled in shredded confetti paper. Stupid. It had been stupid to come to the office like this, carrying the pregnancy test like a gift, holding balloons like a clown at a birthday party. She hadn't expected it to be positive. They were finally on the list to adopt, and she was pregnant. Sometimes she went over the top. She knew that about herself. But instead of finding Edward and revealing her big news, she was the one who'd been surprised.

Penelope still hadn't come out of the bathroom. Embarrassed or ashamed, maybe both, she'd taken refuge away from the crowded waiting room, away from the staring faces. Away from Nia.

They were supposed to be best friends. She'd thought they could tell each other anything. But Penelope had hidden this as if it were a little white lie, when it was probably the most important thing that had happened to her since her grandmother died.

The door to Edward's office opened with a creak, and Penelope stepped in, her cheeks flushed. "Sorry."

Nia stood and went to her. "Don't apologize. I'm sorry. I was just shocked."

She hadn't reacted well, dropping her silver box on the floor, her mouth agape. She could just picture herself—eyes wide, her lips moving faster than her brain, saying, "What? You're pregnant?"

Lotus had shushed her and escorted Penelope to the bathroom. Penelope's puffy eyes and the splotchy redness of her skin showed how well the whole thing had gone over.

Nia pointed to a chair. "Want to sit?" They had Edward's office to themselves, and she didn't want to leave without talking.

Penelope took the seat in front of the desk, clutching her purse in her lap. "So, you're pregnant finally? That's great news."

There was an airiness in her voice that made it sound like she was genuinely excited for Nia. But she looked miserable. Penelope sat with her shoulders slumped, like she was too tired to hold her upper body straight, and she looked pale and ashen. The postcry splotches on her fair skin added to the effect.

But Nia wasn't going to let her turn this on her. Penelope had lied to her. "You don't give me enough credit, you know. I could have separated your issue from my own. It's not right to go through this stuff alone." Nia wanted to believe it was true. But she might have only said it because she was finally pregnant. *Could I have said it a week ago and meant it?*

"I'm not alone," Penelope said. "I have Lotus."

"Your hippie cousin?" Nia asked.

Lotus had gone back to the waiting room, offering to give them some space. Nia wasn't being fair. Lotus had come, even carrying her own baby bump, from what Nia could tell.

"She's really been here for me. I wish you two would give each other a chance. I don't know why you don't like her."

"She's fine. I get it, and that's great that you have her. But I'm your best friend."

Nia fought the voice that told her she sounded like a middle schooler in a whiny puberty-induced sulk, complaining, *You hung out with Lotus instead of me.* She was Penelope's *person*, and she could have handled this. But a voice inside told her she was a liar, and there was no chance she could have stood there, barren and desperate, while Penelope had an abortion.

"That's exactly why I *didn't* tell you, Nia. I didn't want to hurt you. Here you are, struggling to have a baby, doing everything you can to make that happen, in the middle of hormone injections and an IVF cycle, and I just turn up accidentally pregnant like 'Oh by the way, knocked up on accident, heading for an abortion.' That doesn't sound cold to you?"

"I just—"

"I get it—you're mad that I didn't come to you. But fuck, Nia, Edward would've killed me, and besides, it's all going to be over soon anyway. It's not your problem. It's mine." The redness of Penelope's skin seemed to pulse with every word, the splotches getting angrier as her voice rose.

Nia was quiet, waiting for Penelope's anger to dissipate. "I'm not mad. I'm hurt. Don't you want to talk this through? I mean, don't you want to consider your... options? This baby could go up for adoption. Or we could raise our babies together. They'd be the same age."

She might have pushed it too far. But Penelope had to think it through. Nia had been there immediately when Jasper broke her heart, even though she'd known that relationship was doomed from the start. She'd brought her ice cream and vodka and let her cry and rage about it. She'd been there after Pen's Gram died, listening to her vent about her mother and the missing dolls from Gram. And Penelope had done the same for her, talking through every negative pregnancy test. So Nia needed to be there for this crisis, too, talking it through.

Penelope raised an eyebrow. "I *have* considered my options. I'm not stupid enough to have a baby I don't want and can't take care of right now. You think I want a kid growing up knowing I never wanted her in the first place? Trust me, it's a shitty way to parent. Don't you think I recognize the paradox of the person I am? I don't care. I'm not having a baby I don't want in order to save face with the L and D nurses. And I'm certainly not having a baby I don't want just so I can force a relationship that doesn't exist between me and Jasper. And I'm sorry about your infertility, and I'm glad you're pregnant now, but I'm not keeping a baby I don't want for you either."

Nia stood up. "So, I'll pick up the pieces from your breakup, and I'll come to the bar to pick you up and drive you home when you're too drunk to walk and when you're about to fuck a random bartender, but who am I? You don't have to tell me anything. Just call me when you need a favor."

Penelope looked like she'd been slapped. Her mouth hung open, and her eyebrows drew in. She grabbed Nia by the hand. "Don't make this about you," she said quietly.

"It's not about me. It's about you thinking only of yourself."

Penelope stood. "I didn't want to hurt you. That's why I didn't tell you. Trying to get pregnant has been so hard for you. What does it feel like to hear your best friend is pregnant and having an abortion? Imagine if you weren't pregnant right now—how that might feel." Penelope looked angry, but her voice was soft, and she blinked fast.

A knock on the door interrupted them. "Penelope?" The nurse cracked the door and poked her head in.

"I guess it's your turn," Nia said.

"I'm not going." Penelope turned to the nurse. "I'll have to reschedule."

The nurse offered to reschedule her at the desk then excused herself from the office.

"Now you don't want to do it? What about all that ranting about how shitty it would be to keep the baby?" Nia asked.

Penelope looked down. She didn't answer right away, but when she looked up there was fire in her eyes. Determination.

"I'm still having the abortion. But I'm not going today and doing it like this. I don't want to fight with you. And I certainly don't want the day you announced your pregnancy to be the same day I aborted mine. I have to go." Her hands shook as she grabbed her purse from the chair.

Penelope pushed past her out of the office. Nia closed the silver box and put it in the center of Edward's desk. She tied the balloons to his office chair, two on each arm. He'd see it when he finished at the hospital. By the time she reached the waiting room, Penelope and Lotus were gone.

Maybe Nia was wrong. Maybe she was being petty. *But if Penelope can't tell me about the most important thing going on in her life, what kind of friendship do we really have?*

Chapter 14

The sound of the light rain and the swishing of the windshield wipers didn't fill the empty silence that blanketed the car ride. Lotus focused on her breathing as she drove, turning and stopping, accepting the quiet from Penelope and ignoring the elephant in the car. Penelope had too much depth to deal with someone like Nia all the time. She wondered why it was that such a shallow, narcissistic woman had become Penelope's best friend. Probably because her own mother was so shallow and narcissistic. Maybe it was a Freudian-type regression or something.

She exhaled a sharp *ha* when she caught herself in a spiral of thoughts. Penelope looked over at her, and she smiled. Of course she'd noticed the breath, but she wouldn't ask Lotus to explain, and they both knew it. Lotus repeated her nonjudgment mantra to herself and exhaled sharply again. Her yoga teacher had taught her that in an intensive. She used it to expel the judgmental energy.

"Want to talk about it?" Lotus asked. She could feel the distance between them. Penelope was holding back.

"I know I can't say this to her, but Nia's abortions are not my fucking problem. You should have seen how hopeful she was when I canceled my appointment. Thank you for staying. I wasn't sure what I was going to do if I came out and you weren't there."

"Her history is hers to carry. I'm glad you felt strong to say what you needed. When are we going back?"

Penelope looked out the window.

Lotus glanced sideways at her. "You didn't make the appointment."

Penelope shrugged. "I was flustered. I just had to get out of there."

Avoidance. A natural response. Penelope would have to come to it in her own time, on her own terms.

69

"I don't want to talk about it. How's it going with your new roomie?" Penelope asked.

Frustration rose in Lotus's chest. "I'm trying to be cool. Apparently, he's going to be staying for a while."

"And you're okay with it?"

"Not really. He hurt Rob a long time ago, and they both pretend like they're still friends. Rob was in love with him."

She could see Penelope trying to stuff her surprise and keep her face neutral, but it wasn't very convincing.

"I know," Lotus continued. "It's unconventional to have a former lover staying with us. Rob and I are open, though—you know that. Either one of us can take a lover or boyfriend or girlfriend as long as we are honest with each other about it. I just don't want it to be *that* guy. I met Rob just after their breakup, and he was pretty messed up over it for a long time."

She hated explaining herself to Penelope. Penelope was in no position to judge, but still, as matter-of-fact as Lotus was about their polyamory, she was always left feeling like she had to explain. *No, we don't have sister wives. Yes, he's bisexual, but we prefer the term* pansexual. *No, I don't think it's harmful for Blaze to be exposed to more love or to have polyamorous parents and others in his life who love him. No, we aren't jealous all the time. Of course we sometimes experience jealousy. We just have more tools in the toolbox to process the underlying insecurity. Yes, we still love each other. No, we aren't considering divorce.* And on and on.

But even if one of them had a boyfriend or girlfriend, they didn't start living with the person. Jagannath wasn't a stranger or just a friend—he'd broken Rob's heart, and Lotus had mended it. She nearly hadn't dated Rob because of it. He was too messed up. But he hadn't been entirely honest about just how fresh the breakup with Jagannath was at the time. Only later did Lotus realize that his idiosyncrasies were all leftover scars from Jagannath. If she was honest with herself, her own grief had also been a factor when they met too.

"Have you told Rob how you feel?" Penelope asked.

"How can I? He swears that he's just being a good friend because Jagannath needs a temporary place to stay. He told me I could put Jagannath to work in the store so he won't be completely freeloading."

Penelope nodded. "So, what are you going to do?"

"What can I do? Keep an eye on things and hope I don't see the rose-colored glasses descending on Rob's face? I don't know."

"But isn't your whole philosophy on love about openness and transparency?"

They reached the parking lot outside of Penelope's apartment building. Lotus felt a shift. "You're right. It is. I'm going to stay present about it. Doesn't that seem right?"

"I think so. Just trust your gut." Penelope leaned over and hugged her. "Thank you for coming today. It meant a lot to me."

For Penelope, that was a big show of affection, and Lotus was reminded how important it had been for her to accompany her cousin that day. She started through the rain toward her Inman Park home, hopeful that Penelope would ignore Nia's opinions and do what was right for her.

Rob's car was gone when Lotus returned. "Rob?" she called as she stepped into the foyer. Maybe he'd let Jagannath borrow his car. Although Jagannath mostly used the bicycle.

"We're in here."

Jagannath. She rounded the corner and found Blaze and Jagannath sitting in the floor, playing with the wooden trains.

"Mommy," Blaze squealed. He dropped a train into the pile on the floor, ran over to her, and hugged her legs.

"Hi, baby. Are you having fun?" She reached down and rubbed his back as he buried himself in her skirt. She dropped her boho sling bag to the floor. "Show me what you built."

The wooden train tracks snaked the playroom. Jagannath sat on the floor, cross-legged, in loose linen pants and a T-shirt. He smiled up at her.

Blaze ran back to Jagannath and plopped into his lap. "Joggy taught me to build under." He pointed at the tracks crossing over each other.

"That's really great," she said. "Jagannath, can I talk to you for a minute?"

"Sure." He set Blaze next to him and put another train in his hand then stood. Lotus left the room, and Jagannath followed.

"Where's Rob?" She folded her arms, trying to keep her voice even but unable to hide the tension.

"On his date. He said you knew." Jagannath looked at her questioningly.

"I knew he had a date. I also told him I might be late getting back. What the hell?" She turned her back, looking out the window.

"I'm sorry, Lotus. I offered to keep Blaze when he said he had to go. I thought it was cool. I didn't mean to overstep."

"Yeah? Well, you did." She kept her arms folded. Part of her could see that she was pouting. The other part told her she was right. Rob wasn't supposed to leave their son with anyone without discussing it first. "What happened to Kendra?"

"She was busy. Rob had been counting on using her. I stepped up when she couldn't, that's all. I honestly thought I was helping."

She turned back to face him. "Okay."

"Okay? Are you sure? I want to know your rules and respect them. I'm here now, and I appreciate you letting me in. I want to help."

Blaze darted into the room, carrying a train in each hand. "Race time!" he yelled at Jagannath. Blaze liked him, at least.

"Thank you," she said to Jagannath.

It wasn't Jagannath's fault. It was Rob's. Lately, it seemed like whatever he wanted came first.

Chapter 15

"I was kind of a jerk, I guess, but I had every right." Nia paced the kitchen, Pixie feverishly following at her heels.

"So, make it up to her," Edward suggested, as if it was just going to be that easy to fix things. Sometimes he was so simple.

"I mean, I was in shock. I wasn't trying to be a jerk, but she didn't even tell me. Can you believe she didn't tell me?"

He gave her a patient stare. She hated that practiced look of calm that he turned on her. She wondered if they taught that in medical school.

"Yes, I can believe it. She was trying to protect you."

"Maybe I don't need protecting!"

"She cares about you. She knew it would be hard for you to hear."

Edward sat at the island on a barstool. She stopped in the center of the kitchen, leaning on the granite counter. "You ruined the surprise, you know," Nia said. The fire had gone out, and she could hear the lilt of disappointment that had crept into her voice. Pixie stopped mocking her and curled into a ball at her feet as if exhausted from the back-and-forth kitchen trot.

"Emergency surgery waits for no one. I was supposed to be at the office, not in the hospital. I was checking on a patient when that abruption happened, or I wouldn't have been there at all. But you don't want to hear about that." He shook his head and reached for her hands. She let him draw them up in his, and he ran his finger along her palms and fingertips. "I know it's tough for you to watch. We haven't even gotten to the hard part yet."

She looked at him, her eyes doing the squinty thing that happened when she was mad. "You are complicit, you know. You lied to me too."

"Ah, but I have to hold patient confidentiality. Legally, I couldn't tell you."

74

Nia pressed her lips together. "It's not funny."

"Babe, think it through. Your best friend called me for help. But she's also a colleague, and she needed someone she trusted. Did you want me to send her to the abortion clinic?" He leaned toward her as he asked the question, his tone calm, trying to smooth Nia over.

Nia wanted to be supportive, but Penelope didn't understand what she was doing. Nia hadn't been very forthright about her abortions either. Comments like "He was abusive," or "I was so young" took the edge off and played on people's sympathy. The whole truth, though, included Nia's own part in the pregnancies and the abortions. She hadn't shared those details with anyone. Not even Edward. So of course Penelope couldn't understand the horror of the abortions or the regret that lived deep in Nia's bones.

Penelope had no way of knowing that every year, the dates would haunt her. And not just the date she found out she was pregnant or the date she had the abortion. There would also be a due date, the mythical birthdate that her baby would never celebrate.

Everything Nia had told herself to get through those abortions—*It's what's best for them. It's what's best for us all*—was a lie. They were still her children, and she had killed them. Sister Mary's face haunted her. She could picture the black-and-white habit like a halo around her wrinkled face.

"No," Nia said. "I didn't want you to send her to the abortion clinic." She scooped Pixie into her arms, petting the soft, freshly groomed Yorkie. "But now I've upset her. I just wanted her to hear me out."

"Babe, it's okay. You can fix this with Penelope." Edward took her face into his hands, rubbing away a tear that had slipped down.

What would he think if he knew what a cold monster I really was? He would see that her infertility was a punishment. He thought she cried for Penelope's friendship. She wanted to, but those tears were for her babies. She would cry for them and for Penelope's baby too.

Eventually, she stopped the thoughts of her lost children and put them back into the dark place where she kept them, and her tears dried. "You're right. I can make this right with her. She didn't go through with the abortion."

Edward raised an eyebrow. "Really?"

"No. She said she didn't want our news to be tainted with her abortion, so she rescheduled."

Edward let out a breath. "Reach out to her. You need each other right now. She's a good friend. The best, I hear. Don't let this become a wedge between you." Edward kissed her on the forehead.

"I won't," she promised.

Nia vowed to support Penelope. Even if she didn't agree. But she would not let her friend go into it without knowing the truth. All of it.

Chapter 16

Penelope ran her fingers along the soft infant beanie she'd knitted for Nia's baby. The rows of angora wool bled seamlessly from pink to blue. The tiny scraggly ends of the yarn had been woven in and hidden among the precise identical stitches.

I'm excited for you and your baby. She needed to say it somehow. Her own situation would not cloud her happiness for Nia. She wouldn't let it. Nia and Edward desperately wanted their baby.

After she finished the hat, she hadn't seen Nia all week. There was a relief at letting her friend in on the truth. She'd done enough lying through her childhood to last a lifetime, and she hadn't wanted to lie to Nia. She'd just needed the problem to go away so things could go back to normal. But now that Nia knew, there had to be some way to separate it from Nia's pregnancy—to celebrate it while Penelope let go of her own.

The beanie sat on the edge of the kitchen counter, flanked by the half-burned lavender candle Lotus had given her for Christmas—or maybe for Yule—and a half-finished copy of the latest book-club read. She'd considered wrapping the beanie or putting it in a little gift bag. No, she didn't want to make a big deal out of it. Just a small gesture. She left in on the counter.

We could raise our babies together. They'd be the same age. Nia's words sliced through her chest and settled heavy on it. She couldn't breathe with the weight of it pressing into her lungs. She had to go through with the abortion. She could never give this baby what a mother was supposed to give a child. Loving it, or even just the idea of making it work, it just wasn't going to be possible. Maybe someday, on her own terms, she would be a mother. But not like this. It would be cruel for her to bring a baby in the world. The idea was a crazy fantasy, the kind her mind sometimes entertained, like feeling the urge to drive off a bridge or to punch her boss in the face. Fleeting, not realistic.

The thought of looking down into a child's eyes and seeing Jasper's haunted her. She couldn't spend the rest of her life being reminded of Jasper every day. Maybe to him, she had just been a fling, but Penelope felt something between them she couldn't quite describe. He'd been the one. Forever, he would be the one who got away. The thought made her want to roll her eyes at her own cliché.

She hadn't meant to fall in love with him. It had happened by accident, as those things did. She sank into the memory of falling for him. Reliving moments with Jasper was all she had left of him.

"My aunt died," Jasper had said.

Penelope had snapped up from her position tucked into him on the couch. He'd come over after a multiday shift at the firehouse. "Oh, I'm sorry. Why didn't you say something?"

He shrugged. "I don't know."

"You didn't have to come, Jasper. I'm sorry. I didn't know."

He pushed a long strand of hair out of her face. "I wanted to come. I needed to see you."

"How can I help?" Penelope asked.

She didn't know much about comforting the grieving. She hadn't been much help to Lotus when Stone had died. And she'd been so caught in her own grief when Gram died. In Penelope's mind, she was the last person anyone would go to for comfort.

His lips parted, and he reached for her and placed a gentle kiss on her mouth. She opened it and let him in. His warm breath gave her goose bumps. "You make me feel alive."

Penelope returned the kisses to his neck, his unshaven face rubbing gently against her. The sandpaper friction was so different from the gentle, warm feel of his mouth, and she collapsed into him.

They left the light on—not intentionally, but they were both wrapped up in the moment together, and neither bothered to flick it off. For a moment, Penelope considered how long it had been since she'd last been to the gym. *Does his wife look better in a bikini than I do?* Penelope wasn't petite. She'd always had heavy breasts with hips and an ass to match.

But his eyes roved over her body, and when he said, "God, you are beautiful," she believed him. He'd passed over every little spot she second-guessed on herself. He only saw what he wanted, which was evident in the way his body responded to hers.

Jasper opened his eyes and stared at her. She closed her eyes, trying to let go, but when she opened them again, his gaze was still fixed on her. "Look at me, Penelope."

His voice was low and deep. She did as he asked, fighting the urge to squeeze her eyes shut and throw her head back. Only after she shook, clutching him, did he let go.

After, he collapsed into her, pulling her close until she was back on his chest, curled against his sweaty bare skin. Jasper didn't say anything, but the heat rolled off him and invaded Penelope.

Sex with him had never been like that before. It was not the meaningless fun they usually had. Penelope remained still, waiting for his breathing to slow. After ten minutes of silence, she started to peel herself away from him.

"Stay," he said. "Stay here. Please." The *please* was so quiet she wasn't sure she'd heard him right.

She curled back into him. She wanted to go wash up a bit or at least grab a tank top and panties, but a force connected their bodies, and it held her there with him.

"You're amazing, you know that?" he said.

"Me? You were the one with all the moves tonight." A weak attempt to see what the hell was going on, but it was all she had.

"I wanted to make love to you."

Just hearing the L-word from his mouth freaked Penelope out. *What the hell is he talking about? He's my fuck buddy. Fuck buddies don't make love. We call each other when we're horny, and it's nothing more than that.*

"Well, it was really good." She pushed away the thoughts of what *making love* might mean.

"It was lung cancer," Jasper said after a few minutes of silence.

"Oh, that's a bad one."

"She was so young. I didn't think it was going to go like that. It spread so fast."

"Were you close to her?"

"She was my favorite. Used to take me to the theater all the time when I was a kid. Once I became an adult, it was the other way around. She's the reason I love a good musical."

Penelope chuckled at the idea of this six-foot-four Greek god of a man sitting in a musical with his aunt and the rest of the theater nerds.

"What? You think that's funny? That I like theater?"

"It's just... unexpected."

"Maybe I'm full of surprises." Then his light tone turned serious. "Have you ever lost anyone close to you?"

The whole night was filled with him catching her off guard. "I sure have. My grandma Hattie."

"Tell me about her."

So she did. Penelope told him about Gram teaching her how to knit. She told him about her love of tea. She told him about playing bridge with her friends when she moved to Palm Coast. She talked about their visits and the trip they took to Niagara Falls the year before she died.

"It was cancer too," she said.

She never really talked about Gram to anyone outside the family except for Nia. She wiped a tear from her eye and pulled back from his chest. In his face, she found openness and understanding.

"She sounds really special." He kissed her then, not in the way that was going to lead to another round but in a way that showed he cared for her.

They stayed up until five, talking about life. Gram, his aunt, his parents' Christmas traditions. He stayed away from mentioning his wife. The truth was, she didn't care that he was married—she wanted it that way. After that first night at the masquerade ball, she'd wanted him again only after finding out he was married. There was no expectation. No commitment. She didn't have to worry about losing herself or him breaking her heart. She'd willingly be the girl on the side.

But he wasn't supposed to stay all night. They weren't supposed to talk and laugh and cuddle. They weren't supposed to have coffee or breakfast in the morning. And he wasn't supposed to look at her like she was more than they'd agreed on.

The next day, flowers arrived at Penelope's house. Three days after that, he asked her to go to the theater. A week later, Jasper showed up with Chinese food for lunch and rubbed her feet after a particularly bad shift at the hospital. He told her about the little boy he'd saved from a house fire at work the night before, his eyes shining with pride. They stayed in sweatpants and watched *Survivor* together. He never tried to fuck her. She even offered him a blow job, and he refused.

The next time they were together, they made love again, and it scared the shit out of Penelope. She felt the words on her tongue. *I love you.* Or *It's over.* She couldn't say either. She didn't want to love Jasper. He was bound to get tired and move on. There was no future. She told herself all the reasons to end it.

But when she opened her mouth to say it, he put a finger over her lips. "Shhh. This is perfect. Just let it be."

And that was what she'd done.

Penelope fingered the beanie, stroking the yarn. She turned away and busied herself in the kitchen. Nia would be there soon. Her favorite teapot needed a good scrub. Her grandmother had given her that one, a gem she'd found in an antique store. *Is Nia drinking caffeine now, or should I make herbal tea?* Magnetic tin canisters clung to the sheet of metal on the wall of the kitchen, each one holding a different loose-leaf tea. The clear lids revealed the tea inside, only slightly obscured by the tiny white printed labels. She opened a lemon black tea and inhaled. She closed the lid and opened the lavender tulsi tea. They all smelled like safety. They reminded her of her connection to Gram.

She picked up the blueberry white tea. Regardless of what Nia drank, she wanted her favorite that day. No caffeine for Nia. Yes, she'd serve Nia the orange cinnamon.

Despite the dread growing in her belly, Penelope couldn't keep Nia away. It would be fine as long as Nia wasn't coming over to talk her out of the abortion. And as far as Nia knew, Penelope might have already gone through with it.

Chapter 17

The Lotus Garden shop was nestled between Coyote Trading and the Hookah Hookup right on the corner of Moreland Avenue and Euclid. On Lotus's side of the street, the bricks were yellow-gold, and the inset signs for each store differentiated one establishment from the next with varying colors and fonts. The storefront faced the garish red sidewall of the Clothing Warehouse, a shop that extended beyond the Hookah Hookup, the Lotus Garden, and Coyote Trading all combined. Lotus often wondered what it might be like to be positioned across the street or on a different corner, but the blocks weren't very long, and people hanging out in Little Five Points would eventually make their way down to her. Proximity to Charis Books, just across Euclid, had been enough to anchor her onto the corner, even if it meant settling across from the clothing giants and vintage sellouts.

Lotus counted the till, started the computer, and opened the point-of-sale system. She lit some incense and flipped the sign on the door so *OPEN* faced outside. Not that the burnouts in this neighborhood would be out shopping at eight in the morning, but maybe she could get some tourist traffic. Hippies, hipsters, and punks of all ages flocked to Little Five Points when they were in the city. She carried the incense around the store, tendrils of smoke curling off the thin stick and permeating the room as she made her usual round, flicking her wrist in a half-moon shape to bless the space.

Eight fifteen. Jagannath was supposed to be learning how to open the store with her. She'd left without him intentionally. *Let's just see if he can be where he says he will be.* He had the bike Rob had loaned him, but even a walk would have only taken him fifteen minutes.

Rob. Lotus had already fallen asleep when Rob returned to the house smelling like Chanel and honey bourbon. She woke when he

came to bed but didn't stir, tamping the anger back down until his
soft snoring told her he was asleep. She couldn't deal with a drunk
and probably high Rob in the middle of the night. In the morning,
by the time she got out of the shower, Blaze had crawled into their
bed, and he and Rob were snuggled up and back to sleep. So she left,
packing it away for another time.

By eight thirty, Lotus had lost her grip on her patience. Jagannath was supposed to be there to train. *Wasn't it his idea to help out?*
That was the deal they'd made. As much as she was starting to appreciate the way he played with Blaze or helped around the house, she
couldn't deal with another person strolling into work whenever he
felt like it. It was the same as Rob leaving on a date despite what the
rest of the family needed.

Lotus stacked the round zafu meditation pillows, roughly
pounding each one on top of the next. The bells on the front door
tinkled, and she turned to see Jagannath striding through the door,
eyes sparkling, a cheerful smile spread across his face.

"Good morning." He wore a T-shirt screen-printed with a blue-
skinned Krishna holding a flute—Rob's shirt, a design they sold in
the store. It looked like it belonged on Jagannath, with his mostly
shaved head and tuft of remaining hair, which she had since learned
from a Google search was called a *sikha*.

She took a deep breath. "You were supposed to be here at eight
to learn how to open the register. It's finished now."

Jagannath responded by pulling a book out of the man purse
strapped across his chest. "I know. But I forgot this at Charis last
night, and Norah held it for me at the desk, so I went back to get it
this morning."

He handed the book to her. It was *We Should All Be Feminists* by
Chimamanda Ngozi Adichie. Lotus looked down at the thin book,
puzzled.

"Open it."

She opened the cover and found it was inscribed to her and signed. "How did you get this? Wh-Why?"

"To say thank you. You've been so kind to me, and I know you adore her."

"Wow. This is so generous. I never expected—"

"That is the nature of gifts. And I hope you don't mind—I read it myself. 'Culture does not make people. People make culture. If it is true that the full humanity of women is not our culture, then we can and must make it our culture.'"

Lotus could feel her mouth hanging open as he quoted from the book. Generosity of spirit—not what she'd expected before he'd come to stay with them. "Thank you." She could hardly get the words out through her shock.

"You're welcome." He smiled a boyish grin at her and dropped his bag onto the counter. "Now, my apologies for being late. Where shall we start? I'm all yours."

Chapter 18

Nia was fifteen minutes late to Penelope's apartment, which was right on time for Nia. Penelope had learned to pad the time whenever she invited Nia to do anything.

"Sancocho," Nia said, setting the lidded bowl on the counter. "I thought you might need some."

She turned and wrapped Penelope in a hug then released her and stepped back. "I'm sorry I was an asshole."

Penelope hadn't been expecting that. "It's not an easy situation. I get it."

"No, I don't think you do. And I need to fix it. I don't want you to experience it like I did." She reached out and grabbed Penelope's hand. "I want to go with you. I'm your *person*. And it broke my heart that I couldn't be there for you. That's what I've been thinking about this past week. What kind of friend am I?"

The knots in Penelope's stomach dissolved. After all Penelope's fussing over the beanie and the tea, Nia had forgiven her for not sharing her news.

"I'm sorry I didn't tell you," Penelope said. "I was trying to spare you."

"You don't owe me an explanation. This is your life and your choice. And I get it. You didn't want to hurt me."

Penelope handed Nia the beanie. "I made this. For your little one."

Nia fingered the tiny hat, her eyes shining. "You did? Thank you."

"I need you to know that I'm okay. I'm happy for you and Edward. I'm happy you're pregnant."

Nia ran a finger around the edge of her eye, wiping the moisture away without smearing her makeup. She nodded and didn't say more.

Penelope led her farther into the small apartment. She poured the tea she'd debated over. "So why did it take us a week to get together?"

"Because until now, I didn't have the courage to tell you that I could be there no matter what." Nia took the mug in both hands and went over to the sofa.

Penelope poured her own and sat in the chair opposite. "Okay. And you're going to be okay? Seemed like this was sort of triggering for you."

Nia took a sip of her tea. Then she took a deep breath and looked directly into Penelope's eyes. "I don't want to make this about me. And I don't want to talk about my abortions. I just don't want you to feel like you're alone in this. I also want you to know that I get it. I was in no position to keep a baby when I was barely eighteen and heading to New York for a modeling career. And I did what I thought was best. I was a baby myself back then. But I didn't let anyone help me—either time. And I regretted that later."

Penelope nodded slowly. "I would love for you to be there for me. I just don't want to put you in a position to deal with something you might not be ready for. Especially now that you're pregnant."

"I think that my being pregnant is helping, actually. All this time, I've been wondering if I was being punished or something. I know, it's illogical to you, but I'm Catholic."

"I don't think it's illogical," Penelope said, though in the back of her mind, she wondered if she might feel differently if she was religious.

"But it's in the past. And we're here now, dealing with this situation for you. And I'm here. That's the most important thing to me. Not hiding from my past. Not refusing to deal with it or seeing your situation as mine but standing by you and holding your hand and being there for you. That's what matters."

"It might be hard to see me go through it. You don't have anything to prove, you know."

"I know. But I was an asshole to you. You were just doing the same thing I had to do. I hid everything from my family because I was ashamed. Catholic girls don't get abortions."

"I wasn't ashamed," Penelope said. "I just didn't want you to have to deal with it." *And I didn't think you could handle it.*

"I know," Nia said.

"I would love for you to take me. It would mean everything to me."

After the way Lotus had handled the last office visit, Penelope honestly wanted Lotus to be there. But Nia was facing down her past. The sacrifice Nia had offered up to be there for her felt important. Lotus would understand. She always did.

Chapter 19

Nia dropped her purse in the chair in Edward's office. "She's doing the urine sample, then she'll be ready." She felt a bit nauseated, but now that she was pregnant, she chalked it up to that and pushed the feeling down.

"You sure you can handle this?" Edward crossed his arms over his white lab coat. His scrubs and coat made him seem like a different person. At home, he was her husband, her lover, her confidant. In the office, he was the boss, the doctor, the authority.

"Don't cross your arms at me." Nia smiled at him, hoping to allay his concern. "And for the fifth time, I'm fine." She dragged out the word *fine*. "You were right. She's my best friend. I have to be here for her. This is the stuff that matters in life. Who shows up when the shit hits the fan?"

"I know you do."

Edward and Penelope both hadn't wanted her to know about the pregnancy. But she wasn't a weak little pretty girl who couldn't deal with things. She would show them. She'd been through worse shit than this. *Like being the one on the table.* No matter what was going on in her head, Nia knew she could handle it. Nia *would* handle it. And if she couldn't, she was sure she could make them believe she was fine.

Edward kissed her on the forehead. "You can go out at any time if you need to."

"I know." Nia had no intention of deserting Penelope or reinforcing their perception of her as fragile.

Penelope came out of the bathroom. The nurse opened the cubby door from the outside of the restroom to collect the urine sample and verify the pregnancy. *Not much point in that.* Nia took Penelope's hand and led her back to the room. She would stay no matter how hard it was. Her poker face would get her through. She'd bluffed her way out of fights, and she'd faked her way into night clubs at sixteen. She'd be able to stay neutral, no matter how hard she was praying for Penelope's baby.

She started her prayer for the baby silently. *God our Father, in company with Christ, may those who die rejoice in your kingdom.* She skipped verses about life. She skipped verses about God's will to return them to dust. This was not God's will. But she wanted the baby to go up with her prayers. The baby was innocent, and God would cradle the innocent child in heaven right next to Nia's own innocent children. The thought of her own babies made her eyes well with tears. She forced them back, blinking them away. This was not her abortion. This was not her choice. She could only stand aside as Sister Mary had done, praying for her.

Nia sank into the prayer and into her own mind. She'd never heard the heartbeat of her unborn babies. Not the first time or the second time. She didn't have the privilege of a doctor friend to call for her abortion. She hadn't even had a friend to hold her hand or drive her there.

She saw the clinic in her mind as if she were walking into it again. The paint peeled off the sides of a building nestled in the corner of a strip mall. She got out of the yellow cab, all of twenty-three years old, and approached the clinic, glancing left to see an overweight woman scowling at her as she walked up to the vitamin store. She glanced right and saw a bearded man's eyebrows draw in as he walked toward to the DMV. *What a horrible location for an abortion clinic.*

There had been no protesters. Not that she feared running into anyone from her parish, but she didn't want to see anyone at all—not the strangers going about their errands or the hateful, condemning protesters. She had been one of those once just after confirmation, when she was fourteen. Saint Catherine's youth group had gotten wind of the pro-life demonstration. She'd never protested before and thought it might be fun. They weren't invited to go with the adults, but Brad and Victor both had cars, and she and Izzy piled in and crashed the demonstration. The adults in her parish had been too proud of them to turn them away. Instead, they handed them signs, and Nia stood on the street in front of that clinic, shouting about God's will.

It had been a different clinic that day. But the same.

The woman behind the desk in the Emergency Pregnancy Services clinic wore her gray-blond hair in thick curls sprayed in place atop her head. Only grandmothers in the South wore their hair like that. The tackiness of the clinic momentarily froze her. Nia walked on runways. She had worked for Calvin Klein, Christian Dior, and Dolce and Gabbana. She didn't belong there.

The woman behind the desk repeated a question, and finally Nia said, "Jesenia Menendez. I have an appointment at ten."

Maybe it was the pregnancy-heightened sense of smell or the way memories seared a certain sensation into her, but Nia would never forget the odor of that place. Stale smoke covered in bleach. The awfulness of it sank into her skin. She could smell it later when she was back home.

As for the abortion she'd had at twenty-three, she remembered it in fragments. The white lights above blinding her as the doctor turned on the spotlight before beginning the procedure. The nurse's thick ankles clad in white tights and stuffed into stocky white shoes as she stood next to the wheelchair where Nia sat on the curb, waiting for the yellow cab to arrive to take her home. The soreness after. The days of bleeding. The lingering pregnancy symptoms, nausea, and bloating. It all hung over her, reminding her of what she'd done. Of what had been done to her. Lance, her manager at the time, hadn't raped her. He probably would have stopped if she'd said no. Maybe she hadn't been in the best state of mind. Maybe she'd said yes for the wrong reasons. But she'd still said yes.

Nia held Penelope's hands, willing the tears away. She didn't cry, but they welled in her eyes. She wanted to make the pain go away for Penelope. She wished the procedure could be done while Penelope slept. Then the memory would go away. But no, she'd still see the peeled paint, smell the bleach and smoke, and remember the puffy-haired receptionist.

This wasn't Nia's abortion. Penelope had to make her own choice. Nia shut the thoughts of her past away and focused on her prayer. It was time for the Hail Mary.

Chapter 20

Penelope folded her hands in her lap, trying to keep as covered as she could in the paper office gown. Every time she moved, the paper beneath her would crinkle loudly. *You'd think they'd get some cloth ones for a procedure like this.* At least the metal stirrups were hidden from her sight, tucked under the bed.

Nia rubbed her arms. *Is she cold?* Penelope was the naked one, and she wasn't cold.

Edward entered the room after a knock, and behind him came a skinny nurse, probably in her forties. "Penelope, I need to just do an abdominal ultrasound before we begin the procedure. Kyla here is about a hundred times better with the ultrasound machine than I am."

He didn't make eye contact with Nia, and Penelope could feel the intention of his diverted gaze. She wondered what had transpired between them. He hadn't wanted Penelope to tell Nia, but it was too late to worry about that. If there had been an argument, Nia had clearly won.

Kyla wheeled the cart of equipment over to the bedside and typed a few strokes on the keyboard, bringing up the ultrasound software. She warned Penelope about the cold gel, but Penelope barely heard her. She'd been putting that gel on pregnant abdomens herself for years. She knew it was cold. Penelope didn't look at the machine. Kyla had the monitor turned so Penelope couldn't see it. There was no sudden shock of a heartbeat—the nurse had the sense to turn the sound down. No rhythmic thump of life, just palpable silence. When no one said anything, Penelope looked up to find Edward frowning at the monitor.

"What? I know that face." She'd worked with him long enough to recognize a problem, even if it had been a while since they'd had deliveries together. Learning to read each other's nonverbal cues was like a secret language between doctors and nurses. Sometimes, in the delivery room, there was no way to speak in front of a pushing mother-to-be. The slight change in the eyebrows and knowing looks were all they had in those moments.

"How far along did you say you are?" he asked.

"I think about nine weeks now."

Edward put a hand on his hip. Penelope used to tease him for standing like that. His brows drew in, and a crease formed between them.

She stiffened beneath the paper gown. "What is it?"

He shook his head slightly. "I'm sorry, Penelope. That's not what I'm getting."

Edward hesitated.

"Come on, then. Turn it and show me," she said impatiently.

He stood frozen for a moment and then swiveled the monitor, and the black-and-white fuzz on the screen coalesced into a baby. No mistaking that little fluctuation in the center. The heartbeat. Kyla moved the wand on her abdomen, pressing in and making a hand appear, then a foot. The software used the measurements and computed them into an estimated gestational age. The measurements drew her attention. She didn't know much about ultrasonography as a technician. She could see the anatomy of the fetus, but she couldn't have taken the measurements herself. Still, the white-on-black text in the right side of the window told her before Edward had a chance. In small white letters, the gestational age read *14w3d*.

Fourteen weeks and three days. She tried to swallow to bring saliva to her dry mouth. Impossible. She couldn't tear her gaze away from those numbers. *14w3d*. But she was only about nine weeks. She recounted her time with Jasper then calculated when she'd missed her cycle and realized she was pregnant.

But what about the cycle before that? It had been light, different from her other ones. But it had been there, and nothing out of the ordinary had happened to give her cause for alarm. Except now she was pregnant. She'd never had her numbers checked. There had been no need for that. She hadn't planned on prenatal care, just the abortion. She'd left the last office visit without an appointment or even confirmation of the pregnancy. She was a nurse. And in Labor and Delivery, of all places. She didn't need confirmation. And she was in the second trimester and beyond the point at which she could have a normal D&C.

Nia was speaking to her, but it sounded like she was talking through mud. Penelope was in a far-off place, away from them, away from the clinic, away from the crinkly paper on the table and the silent heartbeat of her overgrown fetus. It was too late.

It was too late.

Chapter 21

Nia held Penelope's hand in the silence. Edward and Kyla left the room. Kyla mercifully took the ultrasound machine with her. Penelope had a sick desire to look at the baby again—to turn up the volume and hear the rhythmic thump of the heartbeat.

She had decided she was going through with termination. *But a second-trimester termination? Do I have that in me?* In Georgia, the law allowed for second-trimester abortion. But second trimester was an entirely different procedure. It required her to go to the hospital. It required IV sedation.

The hospital and sedation didn't scare her. But the idea of removing an early fetus versus a developing baby tore at her chest. She hadn't attended a late-term abortion as a nurse, but she'd done early deliveries with fetal demise of babies who were not much older than hers. It was too late.

Nia sat quietly next to her. To her credit, she didn't cry. She held Penelope's hand, embracing the silence. Embracing the shock. This was going to be even harder than she'd anticipated. She couldn't keep this baby and raise a child she didn't want. She was sure Jasper didn't want this.

"I don't want to have a second-trimester abortion," she said quietly. "I can't." She choked on the words, refusing to cry. But there was a desperation inside her, a sinking feeling of complete loss of control.

"Maybe there's something else that can be done. Or do you want to keep the baby?"

Penelope looked into Nia's dark-brown eyes. They held a glimmer of hope.

"No." But maybe the gestational age was a sign. Maybe it wasn't right for her to have the convenience of moving on. Maybe it was happening like this because there was some couple out there who needed a baby—the one she couldn't keep. Nia held the silence with her and let it stretch.

The stiff paper broke the spell as Penelope sat up and swung her legs off the side of the table. It startled Nia, who let go of the sweaty grip.

"Adoption." Penelope's voice sounded calm, like it was coming out of someone else's body. She was sure. But anguish, despair, and guilt tore through her. Penelope nodded to reassure herself. "Yes. Adoption. I can give this baby to a family who wants it." She looked up to find Nia's eyes filled with tears. Maybe she was happy for her. Penelope couldn't worry about it at the moment.

She threw off the gown and began dressing. Imagining herself going through the pregnancy made her chest hurt. She would have to do it. She would have to carry the baby and deal with the consequences. The thought of raising the child herself felt even worse than giving it up.

Nia offered a stream of consoling words. Yes, adoption was a great idea. There were plenty of people who could love this child and raise it. Penelope just knew she wasn't one of them.

Chapter 22

Lotus had fallen in love with Rob on the Appalachian Trail. But in the past few months, something was growing between them. Something dark and menacing. The store, Blaze, the pregnancy—they were all justifications for ignoring the dark cloud. The truth was, she was growing to resent him. She resented his lack of help and his attention to himself, to his other partners, and to whatever was in his orbit that pulled the focus away from her and their family.

In the space that grew between them, there was a pressure on Lotus to find out how things had devolved into the current state. They'd been so different when they met on the trail. *Who were we as we discovered one another and fell in love?*

Her mind rolled, and she took another look back at her younger self again, hunkered in the corner of the lean-to just as the rain started. Her feet were stretched out before her, and her sleeping bag and backpack were inches from the next hiker. She'd wiggled her toes, enjoying the moment of freedom from her boots. Dressed in a fresh shirt with a bowl of rehydrated freeze-dried pad thai in her belly, Lotus curled into her sleeping bag. The snoring a few bodies over reminded her why she preferred her tent, where there was no snoring—except maybe her own—no space limitation, and no shelter mice.

She'd hoped, before the trek started, that the air out there would fill her lungs and remind her how to breathe again. Ever since Stone died, she couldn't seem to get enough space. But even on the Appalachian Trail, alone every day for miles and miles, nodding to other hikers and listening to the creek run through the woods, she still couldn't get far enough away.

Another hiker appeared in the doorway of the already crowded shelter, a pair of hiking poles in one hand. Raindrops slid down the side of his square jaw. He had the look of an unmanicured thru-hiker, but his hair was just a little messy, and he sported a week-old shadow instead of a gnarly beard. She'd seen him before. Maybe they were leapfrogging each other on the trail, passing each other by whenever one of them took a zero day.

Despite the already full shelter, the hikers closest to the door let him in—the people she'd met so far all had hearts of gold, fitting the cliché of thru-hikers. Everyone in the shelter slid a few inches this way or that to make room for him. Somehow, the biggest space opened up near Lotus, and the newcomer made his home beside her.

He stuck out a hand, offering his dirty hiker's shake. "Origami," he said, offering his trail name. "Thanks for making room."

She shook his hand. "Lotus."

"Nice. How'd you get that one?"

"Grew up in a commune with hippie parents."

"Oh." He dropped the flap on his gear bag and looked up. "I thought you were giving me your trail name."

It wasn't the first time she'd heard that. Lotus wasn't exactly a common name. "Nope. I don't have a trail name yet."

He smiled at her, his eyes lighting up. "Oh, fun. So you need one!"

This was a guy who clearly delighted in being creative. It took guts to hand out trail names. She'd considered what she wanted in a trail name before starting her hike. Something bold. Something original. Something that summed her up in a few words. But with Stone dead, she hardly knew who she was anymore. There was a constant hollow feeling, like one of Grandma Hattie's famous jewelry pieces missing the gem, a metal claw clutching at nothing.

Still, she smiled at him. "How'd you get yours?"

Origami continued to dig around in his bag. At that distance, she noticed the buff covering his temples and forehead. Beneath it, a mess of long, thick hair was collected into a band at the base of his neck. He leaned over his pack, continuing to dig for something.

Mesmerized by something magnetic about him, she kept her eyes on him. Finally, he withdrew from the bag with a paper between his fingers and handed it to her. It looked like the wrapper from a Hershey's chocolate bar but was shaped like a butterfly.

"Well, that's a new way to handle *leave no trace*," she said.

He chuckled and flopped out his bedroll. "It's yours," he said when she tried to hand the butterfly back. "You want to stay by the wall?" His eyebrows were raised, a look of doubt on his face.

"Sure, why not?"

He shrugged. "I just didn't think you'd want to be in the path of the shelter mice."

"In their path?" One more thing she hadn't researched enough before starting her trip.

"Mice tend to follow the walls. It's the worst place to sleep. Have you not stayed in a shelter yet? Did you start at Springer?"

All the questions made her feel like the noob she was. *I'm fierce. I am woman. I'm on the trail, thru-hiking the AT alone.*

"Honestly, I prefer my tent. But with the pounding rain, I figured the shelter was the better option tonight."

"You made it pretty far without staying in a shelter. This is my third already. I started at Springer."

"Me too. The last rain was on my zero day, and I went into town at Hiawassee. Have you thru-hiked before?"

"Not all the way. I've had a couple of false starts. This time, I'm going all the way to Katahdin. You hiking with a bubble?"

My bubble. The hiking group that she started with at Springer. At least Lotus understood that. "My bubble sort of split up. There weren't many of us, and not everyone took the zero day together. One girl sprained her ankle and left already. You?" The truth was, she hadn't gotten attached to them and hadn't cared when they split.

"I fell behind my bubble. Got sick and took two zeroes in a row, but I wasn't going to leave this time. I stayed in a hostel at Hiawassee and then got back on."

Hiawassee. That was where she'd seen him. On her zero day.

As interesting as Origami was—she hadn't learned his real name—the rain thumping on the roof and fatigue from the day's miles were enough to send her to sleep. But she already had a suspicion a new bubble had formed, one that included a creative long-haired origami-making guy.

In the morning, after an oatmeal packet and instant coffee, Origami and Lotus started out on the trail together. A couple of other hikers kept pace, and within a few days, they had a new, naturally formed bubble. Everyone else had a hiking name. Banana Split wore gaudy yellow pants poorly reseamed in the butt where he'd torn them on day one and earned his trail name. As much as Lotus envied that they all had trail names, she didn't want to end up with a name like Banana Split from doing something stupid. HotMama was the oldest in their little bubble and had decided to jump on the trail after her youngest kid left for college. She had a bright smile and sad eyes.

Lotus stuck close to her new friend, noticing all the little quirks about him. When he exchanged more than a nod with someone, he handed out origami. He answered honestly without making her feel like an idiot when she asked him how he cared for his long hair in the woods. They took their first zero day together, and he ordered a chai at the coffeehouse and told her a story about drinking it in India.

That evening, as she struggled to hang her bear bag, she caught him looking at her with a half smirk on his thick lips. She stopped midswing in her struggle to get the rope to the right branch. "Are you amused?"

"Maybe a little," he said.

"I don't see you over here offering to help."

"I know you wouldn't let me anyway."

He was so frustrating. And right. But it was more than that. At dinner, his arm brushed against hers as she passed him the salt. Her skin broke out in goose bumps.

When Origami hiked behind her, she thought about the way her ass looked in the skintight hiking pants and wondered if he thought of her as trail candy. As dirty as they were from the trail, she thought about his sweaty body pressing against hers. Up against a tree. Down in the dirt. Hidden inside the tent, the noises echoing out to the other hikers. But she liked her bubble and decided it was better not to make a move on this interesting guy. Not yet.

Chapter 23

Sunday following Penelope's almost abortion found Nia and Edward at Mamá's house after mass. Edward wasn't Catholic before they were married. Once they'd decided to marry, he'd taken the classes to "become" Catholic. But he wasn't really Catholic. His beliefs rested somewhere between agnosticism and Buddhism.

When Edward wasn't on call, he did his duty and showed up for Nia and her family. The news of Nia's pregnancy had spread to her family before it was even confirmed. Mamá couldn't keep her suspicions to herself. The story was already big enough to become one of those that Nia knew would last and penetrate her family's mythology. "And I knew you were in your mami's belly before she did." Nia could practically hear her mother telling that to her child.

"Nia, the flan is perfect. Just like Mamá's," Ana Sofia said.

"Thank you." Nia didn't tell her she'd thrown the first one out. This one was smooth and perfect. She'd caramelized the sugar a bit too long, just the way Papi used to like it.

Ana occupied herself with a never-ending stream of questions about the pregnancy, and Nia soaked it in. "And the nausea hasn't been too bad?" Ana asked.

"It's definitely there. I keep crackers on the nightstand now. And I never let myself get hungry. It makes the nausea much worse."

"Drink the manzanilla," Mamá interjected.

Nia smiled sweetly. "Of course, Mami."

Once Ana had exhausted her list of first-trimester symptoms, she recounted her own pregnancies in detail. Edward, Miguel, and Hunter, Ana's husband, went out to the back patio with cuba libres in hand, ice and lime wedges bobbing on the surface of their drinks.

"You'll have to get over your obsession with your body, you know," Ana said.

Nia narrowed her eyes at her sister. "Seriously?"

"I'm just saying, you see mine and Mami's. That's what it's like after children." Ana pointed to her middle.

She wasn't round like Mamá. Even Mamá didn't look fat so much as thick. Sturdy. Ana was mostly thin, with skinny wrists and knobby legs, but there was a paunch that hadn't been there before. And her butt was bigger, but that was because of her body type rather than from bearing children.

"You look good, Ana. Don't say that about yourself. And I'm not *obsessed*. But I do take care of my body and will continue to do so. So don't talk about it, if you don't mind." Just because Nia had modeled in the past and taught spin classes and liked exercise didn't mean she was obsessed.

Ana and Mamá exchanged looks, as if to say, "See, she's obsessed." Her sister's only cardio was pushing a stroller, and her only lifting was picking up toys discarded on the floor, but that didn't mean it was wrong for Nia to exercise. She certainly wasn't going to discontinue it, not during pregnancy or after the baby came. Ana had never liked exercise, and the kids were just an excuse for her inactivity.

Nia wouldn't be like that. She'd still work out because it was ingrained in her lifestyle. And no matter what the baby did to her body, she'd deal with it. Things would stretch. It would be fine. She was more worried about the flaps of loose skin she'd heard about from her message-board moms than becoming fat. If she became overweight, she could work it off at the gym, but loose skin would have to be fixed with surgery. In spite of the years she'd spent focused on looking perfect because it was her job, she wasn't a big fan of elective surgery.

Miguel's wife showed up right as they were about to leave, mumbling about her law firm and whatever important thing had kept her from mass and family day. Edward and Nia finally made it out the door after kissing cheeks and high-fiving the nieces and nephews. Mamá walked outside, trailing Nia to the car.

"Don't listen to Ana Sofia. You were not blessed with her round behind, and you won't look like her after this baby. You take after your father's side." Papi had been thin and tall for a Venezuelan. Only later in life did he develop a round belly, which was likely because of imbibing more than anything else. His arms and legs had remained fit and strong.

Nia pulled open the door and set her purse on the seat then turned back to her mother. "Thanks, Mami. I'm not taking it to heart." She kissed her mother on the cheek.

Ana trotted out of the house, carrying the washed flan tray, with a dish towel flung over her shoulder. "You forgot your pan."

She put the dish into Nia's hand. Maybe she'd noticed that Nia had been hurt by her comments. Maybe not.

Nia turned and shoved it into the car, knocking over her purse. The contents spilled, tumbling not onto the floorboard but out of the car and into the driveway. Nia dove for the bag, not wanting it scratched or dirtied by the asphalt. She scooped it up and brushed the dust off, not bothering with the contents as much as the bag itself.

"Oh." Mamá fussed over helping pick everything up. It had been a while since Nia had cleaned the purse out.

When the contents were wiped of dust and placed back into the open-top tote, Nia turned to thank her mother.

"What's this?" Mamá asked, holding a pamphlet in her hand. *The Cradle of Love Adoption Agency* sprawled across the top of the page in gaudy pink lettering. Below it was the corny logo of a baby's cradle filled with an overflowing heart.

"It's nothing. We looked into it."

"A baby that isn't yours? That isn't Menendez? How?"

"Don't be so old-fashioned, Mami. Lots of people adopt."

"But—"

At that, Edward appeared at her side, taking the pamphlet from her mother's hand. "Thank you, Mamá, but we have it handled. You don't need to worry about it."

"But, Edward," she began. She pronounced his name funny, like it was two words. "You are a man. Don't you want your baby to be your own seed?" The look on her face was one of confusion mixed with a frown of disapproval. It didn't matter that Nia was pregnant and her mother had known nothing of their adoption plans. She disapproved of adoption on principle.

"Mamá, please," Nia said, imploring her mother to drop it.

Mamá shrugged. "I just don't see how he can be Menendez if he is just some borrowed child. You have no idea what you are getting. *Ay, Dios mío*. Thank God you are pregnant and didn't have to go through with that." She crossed herself as if to thank God but also to ward off the evil of adoption.

Edward came between Nia and her mother. The expression on her face must have alarmed him. He held the door, gesturing for Nia to get into the car. She did, looking back at her mother, unable to hide her rage. Edward shut the door, shut out her mother and got into the driver's seat.

He pulled away from the house as Nia crossed her arms and stammered, "She has no idea what's she's talking about." Maybe it was the hormones, or maybe it was the overwhelming feeling she sometimes got from being around her big family, but she couldn't stop the tears.

"Don't listen to her, Nia." Edward put one hand on her leg and drove with the other. "You're right—she doesn't know what she's saying."

"And it's not Menendez anyway. It's Menendez-Simmons, and no matter where our baby comes from, that will be the case."

"I know."

"And I never took us off the list," she said, the words coming out in a rush.

"You didn't?" Edward glanced sideways at her as he drove.

She shrugged. "I don't know. It seemed like bad luck. Besides, after everything we did to get on the list and wait for a baby, after all the trauma of the last three years trying to get pregnant, I didn't think the IVF was going to work. Especially not on the first try!"

"So, what are you saying?"

"I'm saying, it takes years to get a baby. And just because we got lucky on the first IVF doesn't mean it'll be easy to get pregnant with the next baby. We already decided we wanted to adopt. What changed?"

Edward nodded. "You're right. It makes no difference to me if the baby is 'from my seed.'" He said it in a mocking way. "I love you, Nia. You're going to be a great mother."

She put her hand in his, lacing their fingers. Edward was the best thing that happened to her. He put up with her, and he put up with her stubborn, intrusive family. He was going to make a great dad—to the baby in her womb and to the baby that needed a family through adoption. And her mother was going to have to find some way to work through her bias.

Chapter 24

Penelope cleared her throat. She'd expected to have to relive the situation at least a few more times. She would have to carry this baby to term and put it in a deserving mother's arms. The reality of that was not the problem for her.

She crossed her legs the other direction. Maybe calling someone Lotus knew was not the way to go, but Lotus had sworn this attorney would be a great choice, so Penelope sat across from the woman, all business, ready to start the process of finding adoptive parents. Marianne wasn't some curious old lady at the grocery store who wanted to know about the pregnancy. She was a professional, and she sat erect in her chair, hands folded. While Penelope knew it wasn't the right choice to keep the baby, she still felt the judgment shooting out of Marianne's eyes and stabbing at her.

She cleared her throat again. "I'm looking for an adoptive family. This was an unplanned pregnancy. I was going to terminate until I realized I'd gotten the due date wrong and was already in the second trimester. I'm a nurse. Maybe I know too much, but I couldn't go through with a second-trimester abortion, and I'm looking for adoptive parents now." She could hear herself rambling.

Marianne nodded and scrawled notes. Penelope tried to fill her in, but she really wanted to hear how the adoption worked. And the longer Marianne let her go on, the more she felt like she was revealing information that wasn't relevant.

Eventually, Marianne interjected with the dreaded question. "And the father?"

"He's, um... not in the picture."

She nodded patiently, and her pen stopped moving. "But you do know *who* it is?"

"Yes."

"And you know how to locate the biological father?"

Penelope swallowed. "Yes, but—"

"The State of Georgia statute nineteen requires the father to surrender his rights in order for the child to be placed for adoption." She said it all in a kind tone, but that didn't stop the sting.

Penelope folded her legs again, heat rising in her face. "But I don't feel like we need to involve him. I wasn't involving him in the abortion decision. I was allowed to do that without his consent. Why is this different?"

Marianne's voice remained kind. "This is a child—a child who is *his* too. By law, we can't go forward with an adoption he doesn't know about."

She paused, and Penelope tensed. She could feel a blow coming.

"He could decide he wants to keep the child and raise it. That is his right."

Penelope sank into the leather chair and let her head fall back. She closed her eyes, squeezing back tears. It was logical. Had she allowed herself to explore the possibilities in her mind, she would have figured it out on her own.

"I'm sorry. I know that isn't what you wanted to hear. But I have my limitations. I have to work within the law."

A quiet moment stretched between them as Penelope stared at the canister lights in the ceiling. Marianne had clearly done this before and was giving Penelope time to process the information.

"When does he have to sign?" she asked with resignation.

"Both of you will have to sign to relinquish rights after the baby is born."

Penelope sat up. "Okay, so I have the rest of the pregnancy before I have to get his consent?"

"It's customary to know you are both on board before finding adoptive parents. It's difficult in these situations when we don't know how the father will feel or react until such a late date. That can be very painful for everyone involved. We generally like for both biological parents to sign affidavits of intent before matching with potential couples."

"I understand." The heaviness in Penelope's chest felt like ten hospital beds piled on top of her.

Marianne's face softened. "There are many, many more adoptive parents than there are biological parents. The wait list for couples in line to adopt is two years, and my office has a reputation for being one of the faster ones in this area."

"Okay, so what does that mean?"

"I'm saying there are *always* parents ready for a child. But less often, there are children ready for parents. Talk to the father. He may want this as much as you do. You know your situation. You know what's best. And it sounds like you haven't come to this lightly. But you can't do it alone. You have to have his consent."

They stood, and Marianne extended her hand over the desk. Then Penelope let herself out and drove home in silence. She left the radio off. It had been too easy avoiding telling Jasper she was pregnant and about the abortion. And she'd let herself believe the adoption was going to be just as easy. Now she had to face him and tell him the truth. Her only option was to hope he was on board with the decision. She prayed to a God she didn't believe in.

Chapter 25

The yoga instructor knew her audience. Even if she'd wanted them to intone a nice long *om*, she wouldn't have asked it from the crowd of pregnant women crammed into the studio. Lotus might be the only one in there who didn't think a nice long *om* would be weird.

Picture windows opened at the back of the studio to reveal a wedge of trees surprisingly not mowed down for the commercial space. The room smelled of lemon and lavender. It had probably been started by some bored Buckhead housewife whose husband funded it. At that, Lotus glanced at Nia and pushed her judgmental thought out. *Ha.*

Nia gave her a sidelong glance, and Lotus pretended not to see it. Lotus had been surprised at the call from Nia and the invitation to the class. She'd been reluctant about the one-on-one encounter with her, but after the missed-abortion situation with Penelope, she figured Nia needed a place to celebrate her pregnancy and someone to celebrate it with.

Lotus's assessment of the fitness moms in the class turned out to be not entirely true. A mom in the corner did loud *ujayii* breaths the same as Lotus. Apparently, she was a yogi too.

Lotus was more about her connection to her root chakra than about the size of her hips and butt. When the instructor had them in *marjariasana*—the cat-cow pose—she didn't instruct them to lift their root chakras. *Am I the only one doing it?* She decided to tell Nia later. No, she'd ask the instructor about it first. She admonished herself for not looking up the instructor prior to the class. Lotus should have reviewed her credentials.

The class ended with Savasana, except the instructor gave them all bolsters to support side-lying a position. Instead of her usual corpse pose, flat on her back, spread, she curled on her side, saying something about protecting the veins so the weight of the baby didn't compress them. Lotus remembered it as the more comfortable pose in late pregnancy.

Open. Open. Lotus gave it a real effort to open her mind and to let go of her judgment. She attributed her decent first labor to her yoga class during pregnancy. But her teacher had moved away, and she knew her sense of detachment from the group classes was because she missed Shree.

The instructor went quiet after guiding them to release into the mat. Soft flute music playing in the background was the only sound, disrupted periodically by a participant adjusting position.

Lotus's mind drifted to Blaze, to Rob, to dinner that night, to Jagannath, to the gift he'd given her, to her pregnant body, to her hopes that she was carrying a girl, to admonishing herself for wishing for a specific sex. It jumped to sex and back to Rob again then back to Jagannath.

He'd only been out of the picture with Rob for a short time before Lotus had entered. Sitting by the fire that night on the trail, being honest in a way she hadn't expected, had opened her to Rob. In proper hiker etiquette, she and Origami kept their voices low. The warmth of the fire and heat between them kept her planted across from Origami, watching the shadow of flames on his face.

"Why now? What made you decide it was time?" Origami asked.

The question. Her stomach flipped. She'd practiced answering that question before coming onto the trail. She had a safe answer ready to keep the other hikers at a distance. It had never failed her, but in this moment, her carefully crafted answer remained dormant on her lips.

"My brother died." It was the first time she'd said it out loud. A swell of nausea rolled over her. Tears welled, but she swallowed them back.

"I'm sorry," he said quietly into the fire.

She mumbled a quiet thanks but didn't elaborate on Stone. "What about you? Nothing so drastic, I hope."

"Well, I always wanted to hike it, and I section hiked some. Tried a few times and quit. But I have a real answer to the *Why now?* question too. I just went through a breakup."

Of course. Freshly dumped. That made this guy worse than Jeff, the over-the-top mama's boy who had let his mother do his laundry, though maybe not worse than Steven, the sociopath from college. But still, Origami was on the rebound.

"Sorry to hear that." Her words sounded hollow.

He shrugged. "Probably for the best. We wanted different things."

Did his girlfriend want a commitment? Did she wanted to get married? She wondered what kind of things would warrant dumping him. Lotus's questions were less about what had happened in his past and more about figuring him out. If the tension between them was purely sexual, then so what if he was broken?

"I see the wheels turning."

There was heat in her cheeks, but she decided to ask anyway. "What did you want?"

"I wanted to be open. Free to explore whomever I feel connected to, drawn to."

Commitment. She tried to imagine the girl who'd wanted him all for herself, unwilling to let him wander and follow his lust. "Did she want to get married or just to be monogamous?"

"He. And just monogamy. *Just.*"

She barely noticed what Origami was saying because the "he" was clenched in the middle of her chest like the cramp she'd had at the top of Mount Cammerer. *Gay? How did I not see it?*

He'd flirted with her. She scanned back through their time together, searching for evidence. She thought about the way he'd touched her hand, how he'd filled her water, and how he'd offered to share his last bit of jerky before the next refill stop. *But wasn't he look-ing at my ass? Smirking at my struggle for the bear bag, watching me try to snag that branch?*

Yep, he was worse than the sociopath. Unavailable in the most basic way. In the I-prefer-the-company-of-men way. She silently chas-tised herself for misreading the situation and for being judgmental.

"Thanks for being open and sharing," she offered feebly.

"Sure," he said, and silence followed, signaling the end of their conversation.

That night, alone in her tent after reviewing all their interactions a third time and still not finding evidence of his gayness, she fell into a fitful sleep. But despite her feelings of rejection and confusion, their bubble was solid, and they stayed together in the weeks to come.

"So, what's your real name?" Lotus asked. They sat on a rock at an overlook. Their last five miles had consisted of a fairly steep hike. Lotus's feet were braced by the rock, her arms wrapped around her bent legs.

He finished a bite of beef jerky and looked at her. "It's not as in-teresting as Origami. Or Lotus for that matter."

"You don't have to tell me if you don't want to."

His dark-brown eyes met hers. The tension was there again, and she looked away, like she'd crossed a boundary or something.

"It's Rob."

She nodded, and he passed her a piece of jerky. His name might not have been a big deal, but his sharing it felt intimate.

Rob. He slept next to her every time they stopped in a shelter, giving her the wall and trying out the trail name Minnie—as in Mouse. It didn't stick. He pitched his tent by hers. He sat next to her at the fire. She couldn't stop thinking about how stupid she was for wanting him.

Another thunderstorm greeted them as they left North Carolina, and Lotus was starting to think she'd never have a real trail name. They stopped in Erwin, Tennessee, to see Split's friend, a section hiker who wanted to give them a break. And a real bed. Banana Split insisted the offer was for the whole bubble. All of them could use a bit of trail magic.

Jason, Split's friend, picked them up from the mountainside at a trail entrance frequented by day hikers. He drove a minivan, and Banana Split reminded him about the Jeep he used to own and teased him for becoming a "soccer mom." Jason laughed and accepted the gentle ribbing while he drove them to his home.

"I thought you'd all like to shower first. And then, there's a great brewery in town that I think you'll love."

Jason's home looked like a cabin from one of those vacation-rental websites. It was an odd cross between kitschy and inviting. A plaid blanket rested on the back of the sofa that reminded her of lumberjack flannel. Their son, who was probably not yet old enough to play soccer, lay on his belly on the floor with a picture book, flipping pages too fast to be reading. The space where he "read" contained a sheepskin rug positioned between a miniature wooden kitchen and a wooden playhouse with rainbow silks. Lotus was grateful to be out of the rain, no matter how Jason's house was decorated.

After showers for everyone, Jason drove them to the brewery, introduced them to the owner, and recounted his story of attempting a thru-hike. By this point on the trail, they'd told each other so many stories that it was refreshing to hear from someone outside the bubble. But Banana Split couldn't help himself after two beers, and he entertained everyone with new stories of his carnie family. It was debatable how much was real and what he'd made up, because he never wiped that goofy grin off his face. But everyone was downing their beers and laughing, even HotMama.

By ten o'clock, they were all back at Jason's, warm around his coffee table, continuing to drink and laugh. His wife, Tessa, participated, too, now that their son had gone to bed.

"So then I told him if he had a twenty, I'd teach him the trick," Banana Split said.

The beer made Lotus sleepy, and she excused herself for the night. After brushing her teeth and switching into pajamas, she opened the bathroom door to find Rob standing there.

"You could probably drink me under the table, you know," he said.

Lotus smiled at him, wanting to tug his strands of long hair down to her face and take a bite out of his juicy bottom lip. "Is that a challenge?"

"Not at all. I'm just saying, you kept up with the guys tonight. I didn't know you were such a party girl."

"Oh, I *am* the party, mister. Too bad you'll never know about that." She stepped toward him, expecting him to move aside as she left the bathroom, but he stayed, not budging.

"Is that right?" he asked.

She stood inches from his chest and had to look up to meet his eyes. He stared at her. That ethereal tension between them was coupled with her lack of reservation.

"That's right," she whispered.

In an instant, she was on her toes, pressing her lips against his. Warm and salty, he tasted like Porter and peanuts. At first, she was just fucking with him, planting one on him for the shock value. But it quickly turned from a joke to a real kiss as his tongue snaked inside her mouth. She reached around the back of his neck and pulled him desperately into her, letting her tongue slip into his mouth, releasing him, and kissing down his neck. Lotus pushed against him, and he backed up. They continued to kiss as they made their way down the hallway and fell through the doorway of her assigned room. She was sober enough to know better and drunk enough to disregard it. She couldn't get her clothes—or his—off fast enough.

Afterward, she flopped down beside him in the bed, trying to catch her breath. He put a hand on her stomach and ran his fingers lightly along her skin.

Lotus turned toward him, trying to get a sense of how he felt. "You okay?"

"Haven't been this good in a long time."

"I mean about... this. About me, you know, being a woman and all."

He looked confused, the skin around his eyes tightening. Then a hearty laugh burst from him.

"What's so funny?"

But Lotus couldn't get an answer from him because he continued the loud guffawing.

"What?"

He wiped a tear from his eyes. "You thought I was gay?"

"What? Of course I did. You're gay. You just had a breakup with your boyfriend."

He sat up on his elbows and looked at me. "Did that sex seem like I'm gay?" There was a look of arrogance on his face.

"I mean, I just thought, the way you talked about your ex..."

"Just because I also like men doesn't mean I'm not into women. I thought there was something between us, or I never would have come on to you."

"I kissed you! It was kind of just a joke at first. I mean, I wanted to. But I didn't think anything was going to happen."

"Regrets?" he asked.

Lotus sat up and put a hand on his chest. "None."

He pulled her back down on top of him and kissed her deeply.

In those days, the sex had been hot. Their relationship had started with fire. But in the back of her mind, it bothered Lotus that Rob had been with Jagannath before the trail.

Spending time with Jagannath, she wasn't able to resist his charm. That disarming, boyish grin had captured her right away. The way he greeted people and looked at you like you were the only person in the room—he had a deep level of empathy and connection that she envied. Jagannath really cared about others in a way that she could not. *Doesn't he ever get jealous? Does he look at me and Rob and want what we have?*

The sound of a gong brought her out of her thoughts, back to the lemon and lavender, back to the scent of sweat, and back to the prick in her hip from lying on her side on the hard bamboo floor. She sat up groggily, and the class bowed to the instructor from their seated positions, repeating "Namaste" back to her.

After class, the thoughts of Rob and Jagannath still permeated Lotus as she and Nia walked to the coffee shop.

"Did you like it?" Nia asked.

"Yes. I want to ask the instructor a few things. Is it always so spiritually disconnected?" she asked a little hesitantly.

"I knew you'd say that. She usually tones it down until people come back to the class a few times. Don't worry—you'll get your *oms*. I'll even do it too."

She smiled in a way that made Lotus feel like she was seeing a genuine side to Nia. They hadn't been the fastest of friends, but because they both loved Penelope, they'd given each other a chance. Now that they were both pregnant, they'd started to see each other for more than their usual lunch dates and get-togethers with Penelope.

"Pen told me you're planning a home birth?" Nia asked.

Lotus nodded. "We have a great midwife. She's been in practice twenty years. She caught Blaze."

"You don't worry about needing to be at the hospital for any-thing?" Nia's tone was open and innocent, but Lotus hesitated.

Nia's husband was an obstetrician. Of course she was going to be indoctrinated that the hospital was the only place to have a baby.

"No. It's perfectly safe for a low-risk mother, which I am. If at any time I become a higher risk, I trust my midwife to transfer me. Birth is not inherently dangerous, despite what this culture has led us to believe."

Nia nodded thoughtfully. She was probably relishing the idea of going home to tell Edward what a dirty hippie Lotus was and how she was planning to "endanger her baby," as many ignorant people believed. Well, so be it. She knew what was best for herself and her baby. And her midwife did too.

"Did you hire a doula last time?" Nia asked.

Lotus nearly tripped. Nia had made no comment about the home-birth thing. *Is that what this is about—my experience with a doula?*

"Yes," she said slowly. "I did. Why? Are you thinking about hir-ing one?" She let out her *ha*. Sometimes she was wrong about people.

Nia gave her a shy smile. "Well. I haven't said anything to Edward yet. But I don't know. I mean, I just want whatever is best for me and the baby. I'm not saying I want to go natural necessarily. But Penelope was telling me that she's worked with a lot of really helpful doulas. It's still hard for me to talk to Penelope about it all, consid-ering her situation. But I don't want Edward to feel like he's less im-portant. And I want Penelope there, but I think she might be, I don't know, weird after her adoption and all. And Edward doesn't really do a lot of labor-type stuff in his everyday work. He's medical. And I know, in this case, he's the dad and not the doc, but he's going to have a hard time switching his doc brain off, and he's actually had some good experiences with doulas too."

"I think it's a great idea," Lotus said. "There's a Meet the Doulas night that you can go to. If you want, I'll go with you."

Nia wouldn't ask Penelope, who would otherwise be her go-to person. Penelope pretended to be fine. They both knew she wasn't, and as a result, Nia had lost some of the support she was used to.

"That would be amazing," Nia said. "Can I ask you, why do you make that exhale? The *ha* sound."

Anyone who spent enough time around her eventually noticed it. "Did I do it just now?"

"Earlier. When I asked about your doula and once when you first arrived at the studio."

"It's an energy-clearing technique. It helps me keep negative thoughts away." Lotus didn't elaborate or explain that she was trying to expel a currently plaguing negative or judgmental thought.

"Cool."

"If you're curious about the home birth, I have pictures and a video. You're welcome to view them." If they were going to be real friends, Lotus just didn't have the energy to hold back her real self.

Nia's eyes narrowed.

"TMI?" Lotus asked.

"No. Not at all. It's just... you're so generous, and that's so intimate. I didn't think we were there yet." She shrugged.

"I just meant, if you wanted to see some of what my doula did. Not just read about it on the internet but actually look at the pictures and video."

"That'd be really great," Nia said. "Why are you doing this for me?"

Lotus didn't know much about Nia's background. She was probably used to getting what she wanted, but Lotus had imagined that she didn't surround herself with open and generous people. Certainly not in the modeling business and probably not around the doctor's wives either.

Lotus shrugged. "I believe in community and sisterhood. I accept that you're Penelope's best friend, and I figured you could use some support, especially if you aren't going to birth like the rest of the doctors' wives."

"I sure could use some support," Nia said. "I sure could."

Chapter 26

"It says Yoga Baby. Aww." Nia held the onesie up to Lotus.

They stood among the eco-friendly layettes in the boutique in Decatur. Lotus had suggested the place, and after making it past the stroller dealership in the front of the oversized "boutique," they'd found a corner with some cute baby clothes. Nia didn't know the sex of her baby yet, and Lotus wasn't planning to find out for herself, so they dug through the gender-neutral clothes, picking whites and yellows that any baby could wear. The store smelled of baby powder, and there was a scented candle burning at the checkout counter that had Nursery Scented printed on the glass.

"So cute. I knew you'd like this place," Lotus said.

"Matching ones? Too cheesy?" Nia looked around the shop. It was midmorning on a Thursday, and she'd snatched Lotus up to go shopping while Blaze attended his Moms Morning Out co-op program.

"I think we're there," Lotus said, taking the onesies from Nia and adding them to Nia's growing pile of purchases. She smiled at Nia in that genuine way that had made Nia come to trust her.

While Nia would never say it to Penelope, it hurt that she couldn't share her pregnancy glee with her in an unrestrained way. Penelope's situation had created a strangeness around all three of their pregnancies. Nia wouldn't ask Penelope to go shopping with her. She wouldn't go on about her pregnancy symptoms, despite Penelope asking about it every time they got together. It wasn't an experience they were sharing. Penelope might be pregnant at the same time as Nia, but the outcome of the pregnancy was not going to be the same. While Nia shopped for baby clothes, Penelope shopped for adoptive parents.

But Lotus understood. Lotus was much further ahead in her pregnancy than Nia and more experienced since she'd been through it already, though she never acted self-righteous or like an expert.

"I found a diaper bag I might be able to live with," Nia said.

"Really? You didn't want me to make you one out of some left-over hemp I had from another project?"

"Very funny," Nia said, putting a yellow onesie with a giraffe on it in the shopping basket. "It's really pretty and looks more like a large purse than a diaper bag, but there are so many pockets! The straps are detachable. It's Gucci, and I think I'm in love."

"Can you live with the price tag?" Lotus asked as her gaze roved over Nia's Fendi handbag.

"You'd hate it. It has leather, and yes, I found it for less than two."

"Less than two... hundred?" Lotus asked.

Nia flinched and realized, in her excitement, that her privilege had bubbled out. Not that Lotus couldn't afford the Gucci diaper bag, but Lotus wouldn't *want* a Gucci diaper bag.

"Thousand," she said, swallowing. She shrugged. "Edward doesn't care. He wants me to be happy. Everything about this pregnancy and our baby makes me happy. I just *also* want a stylish and functional diaper bag. No offense, but carrying around a hemp tote is not exactly my style."

Lotus shrugged. "No judgment." She made that little sound with her throat that Nia was coming to recognize as a signpost of her judgment.

Nia turned to her. "I'm glad we're here together. I appreciate you. All I'm saying is that I don't want to lose myself. I feel like I'm becoming a different person. I'm going to be a *mom* soon. I'm going to have a whole person to look after who needs me completely." She thought of Lotus's son. She'd seen the way Lotus never sat down when they were together with Blaze. Lotus was constantly fetching him something, washing his hands, coaxing him up onto the wooden two-step stool, or asking him to *use his words*. It was exhausting just watching. But it was exactly what Nia had signed up for.

"I get it," Lotus said. "It's hard having a little one who's completely dependent on you for survival. If you need a Gucci bag to live through it, so be it."

The women laughed. Of course Nia didn't *need* a Gucci bag. She just wanted it. She wanted to still care about her shoes and her spin class and to still be *her* once the baby came.

Lotus pulled out her cell phone. "Sorry," she mumbled, scrolling through her messages.

It reminded Nia of Edward. Always on call. Checking the phone, waiting for the update that his patient needed him at the hospital. She imagined Lotus being on call in much the same way. The Moms Morning Out could call anytime to say Blaze fell off the playground equipment, or someone from the store could call to say they were all out of patchouli and needed to order more.

Nia admired Lotus. Keeping shit from falling apart was her full-time job. *Will I be able to handle everything with such grace when I become a mom?*

Lotus slipped the phone back into her cross-body patchwork purse.

"Everything okay?" Nia asked.

Lotus nodded. "Mostly."

"Want to talk about it?"

Lotus shrugged, her thin frame and bony shoulders twitching up and then down again. "Rob didn't come home last night. Which normally wouldn't bother me. But a friend of mine saw him at the X."

"Uh-oh," Nia said. Though she'd spent most of her partying years modeling, traveling, and hitting the nightclubs of New York City, the fact that she'd lived in Atlanta since she was six meant she knew of the clubs with reputations. People who went to those clubs were looking to score more than a one-night stand.

"You've heard of it?" Lotus asked.

"That place gets raided all the time. I mean, I know they raid lots of places, but it's known for the club drugs—ecstasy, Special K, and even heroin."

Lotus looked like she was going to be sick. She stood frozen in the boutique aisle surrounded by yellow and white sleepers, her brows drawn in, her mouth turned down, and a sour expression on her face.

Nia put a hand on her back. "You okay, Lotus?"

"I need to sit."

The eco-friendly baby boutique wanted moms and babies to shop there, so there was a massive empty nursing-mothers room with gliders, magazines, and a water fridge with a sign that read Free Water, Hydrate and displayed the universal symbol for breastfeeding.

Nia steered Lotus into the room and to a glider. Lotus sat and closed her eyes, taking some deep breaths and exhaling with a loud hiss. When it became apparent that Lotus was going to breathe for a minute, Nia sat in the glider across from her and, after careful inspection of the floor, set her purse down beside her.

Lotus opened her eyes. The tightness around the corners was still there, and her forehead was taut with worry. "Rob used to have a drug problem." She stated it plainly and calmly as if she was saying, "Rob used to work at Starbucks."

"Oh, Lotus. Do you think—"

Lotus nodded, a look of resignation on her face. "I've ignored all the signs. He's been smoking a lot more. Being distant. I assumed his anxiety was high because of adding a new baby to the family. I attributed the distance to the new girlfriend. New-relationship energy is a hell of a drug, which I totally get. But actual *drugs*?" She sighed heavily, propped her elbows on the armrests, and put her head into her hands, her hair falling beside her face like a curtain. "It's back, and now we have Blaze and this one." She gestured to her expanding waistline. "Fuck."

"What are you going to do?" Nia asked. But as soon as the question was out of her mouth, she regretted it. Lotus couldn't possibly know how she was going to solve the problem yet. "I mean, I know you don't know what to do yet, but what can I do? How can I help? You guys need some space? Do you and Blaze want to come and stay?" The offer surprised her, but it was out of her mouth before she could hold it back.

Lotus looked up at Nia, her eyes shining. She reached over to Nia and squeezed her hand. "You are so sweet, Nia. Thank you. I have to confirm things first. I don't want to accuse him without evidence. If he lies to me, I'll know what to do. But I've got to be sure first. All I have now is circumstantial evidence."

Nia nodded along. True, being at a drug-famous nightclub didn't mean he was using. Lotus would hopefully be able to find out, though, now that she suspected.

"But you can be sure I'm not leaving Blaze in his care for now. That should be easy enough since he's been shirking that responsibility lately anyway."

Nia couldn't imagine having to be on the other end of this problem. Sure, she'd done drugs—lots of them—during her party days before she'd had the last abortion and left the whole thing behind. But she'd never had a problem. A lot of the models did, though. Some of them survived on coke and lettuce.

The shining in Lotus's eyes finally burst free, and she cried.

"Lotus, I'm so sorry." Nia put a hand on Lotus's knee, which was clothed in a maxi skirt.

She sniffed. "I'm okay. This is just a trigger for me."

She cried like she wasn't okay, but Nia "sat in the discomfort," as Lotus had called it, letting her cry until it was out. She didn't ask any more questions, but there was a story lurking behind those tears, one that Lotus obviously wasn't ready to share. And behind Lotus's tears, Nia could see the pain, the regret, and most of all, the fear of what this problem meant for her family.

Chapter 27

The meeting with the attorney settled into Penelope's stomach and turned it. Jasper had to know about the baby. She couldn't go through with the adoption without him. She hadn't anticipated seeing him once he made it clear things were over. Despite the intervening time, she'd missed him. In truth, she would take him back if he wanted her. Maybe seeing him wasn't going to be as painful as she thought. Maybe seeing him would give them a chance again.

She squashed the glimmer of hope as soon as it rose. *No.* No sense in torturing herself. She knew where he stood. And she knew him well enough to know what he was going to say about this unplanned pregnancy.

She stared at the open blank message on her phone and blinked tears back, wondering what she was supposed to say. *I know you dumped me, but I'm pregnant with your baby. Don't worry—I just need a signature.*

She laughed. There was nothing she could say that would not make him suspicious that she still loved him and wanted to be with him—and that something was up. She couldn't tell him by text.

I need to talk to you. That was the best she could do.

She sent it. She couldn't tell him it was important. He probably thought she wanted him back. She didn't know what he thought, but it didn't matter as long as he agreed.

After twenty-four hours, when she'd received no response, she sent another text, this one intended to spur him: *I've thought about coming by, but I don't want to involve your wife. Will you meet me?*

The response text came in three minutes: *Involve my wife? What kind of game are you playing?*

She wanted to type, *I'm pregnant with your baby, you fucking idiot.* She even wrote it out and then deleted it. She wrote instead, *No games. I need to talk to you.*

After a little back-and-forth, he agreed, and they settled on a café not far from where she lived. He didn't want to meet her anywhere near his home.

At seven o'clock that evening, Penelope had been sitting in the corner booth for thirty minutes. She wasn't sure how to tell him, but she knew that walking in, sporting that bulge right in the middle of her body, was not the way to do it. So she waited, hiding her belly beneath the table.

In Jasper fashion, he arrived twenty minutes late. Inconsiderate of her time, as usual. She would forgive it if he would let her. He had all the power, and she had none. And now she needed something from him.

He sat in front of her, a look of forced patience on his face. "What's going on?"

"Just give me a chance to explain."

She would have to force the words out of her mouth. There was no way around it. Not unless she changed her mind about this adoption and disappeared with the baby. That would be the only way to avoid him. But he had made this mess with her. He was going to have to help clean it up. She'd have to count on the fact that she could keep it secret from his wife if they did it her way.

She cleared her throat. "This is not about us getting together or being together, okay, so let's just start there."

The tension gathered around his eyes dissipated slightly. Nice—so he was relieved to not have to fight her off. *Lovely.* But it was replaced with something new. Concern maybe.

"Are you in some kind of trouble?" He knew she didn't have any real family to rely on besides Lotus, and maybe he believed she would call him if she was in trouble.

"Sort of." She swallowed. She *had* to tell him. There was no way to avoid it. She had beat around every possibility. There was no easy way to do that.

She took a deep breath and let it out slowly. He leaned toward her. Yes, that was concern in his eyes. She didn't want that look to go away. He cared about her. He was not going to be pleased at the news.

"I'm pregnant."

"What?" Disbelief rang in his voice. "But we've been broken up for months. How can this—how is this—"

"I know."

"Are you sure it's—"

"Yes." She couldn't bear to hear him finish. "I'm almost halfway through the pregnancy now."

"Why didn't you...?"

He wasn't finishing any of his sentences. It didn't matter. He didn't need to.

"I wasn't planning on keeping the baby."

"Oh," he said. The relief in that one word told her so much. "But now you are?"

She swallowed and nodded. "I was too far along when I went for the abortion. I wasn't going to tell you because I was dealing with it. But then I couldn't get it."

"Oh crap. Okay, so now? Oh crap."

She'd expected this. She'd gone through all the possibilities in her mind before meeting with him. She knew his shock would result in a selfish response on his part. He was thinking about his life, his wife, and the shit hitting the fan.

"I'm sorry. It's just..."

That surprised her. *Sorry for getting me pregnant? Or sorry for reacting with his own selfish thoughts about how this will affect his life? What about* my *life?*

Maybe she wasn't that good a person, but she let him squirm for a minute. He ran his hands through his hair and then propped his elbows on the table and held his head. "I'm sorry for getting you into this. And for not taking it well. So, what are we going to do?"

She wanted to make it worse for him. But her heart softened. She knew what they had to do. "I think we should give the baby up for adoption."

Jasper couldn't hide his relief. This time he sighed loudly. He might as well have said, "Oh, thank God." At least he had the decency to look embarrassed.

"I think that would be best. I mean, you don't want this, right?" he said.

It hurt that he never considered what it might be like for her or asked, "Are you sure this is what you want to do?" But she hadn't dated him because he was the best person. He was beautiful and sexy and amazing in bed, and she'd wanted a fling. She had no right to be pissed that he'd turned out exactly as she'd expected. In a way, she deserved it.

"I don't need anything from you but signatures," Penelope said. A coldness had settled over her. She had cried. She had railed at the world. Now she was all business. "I'm going to meet with potential adoptive parents. I'll need you to go sign an affidavit now stating that you are aware of the options and ramifications and that you are interested in proceeding with the adoption. I'm going to work with an adoption attorney who matches families to birth mothers, and she will find a good family for the baby."

He nodded along with her explanation.

"Once the baby is born, we will sign again, and that will be that."

He reached across the table and put his hand over hers. It didn't electrify her as his touch used to, and that surprised her. Maybe she was over him. In any case, the feeling was different, maybe because of his reaction to the baby news or maybe because of her own process of dealing with this news for the past several weeks.

She squeezed his hand and then let it go, dropping hers beneath the table. His crystal-blue eyes met hers, and she softened a little. The unasked question hung between them. She had half a mind to let him squirm again, but she didn't.

"We can keep this between us. You don't have to tell your wife."

He nodded, doing a better job at hiding his relief.

She stood, and his eyes grew wide. She got a scarlet-letter feeling when he looked at her that way. But before she could say anything, he stood and wrapped her in a hug.

He mumbled into her hair, "I'm sorry I did this to you. You're so strong. I'm so sorry." His voice cracked, and she let herself melt into his embrace.

What if I'd found him before his precious wife did? What if he'd decided to love me?

She hugged him back, and he held her much longer than she'd expected. He finally let go and looked her in the eyes. "It's going to be okay."

"I know."

Chapter 28

Edward had left for clinic. Nia slipped into her morning routine. Crackers by the nightstand had been essential, but this week, the nausea abated. She got up from bed and headed for the bathroom, her first morning stop. On the toilet, she wiped groggily, and the tissue came back dark red, almost brown. *Carajo.*

She sent the text before she called: *You have to answer. It's an emergency.*

Edward picked up on the first ring. "What is it?"

"I'm spotting."

"Okay. Don't panic. That can be for a number of reasons. Want me to come pick you up? Come and do labs, and we can check your HCG. We can do an ultrasound, and that'll make you feel better."

Nia had been seeing Edward's partner, Rich. She would go into the office. Edward would be there in case something was wrong.

"I can drive," she said. "It's not that far."

A numbness settled over her. If she thought the worst, she'd spiral out of control.

She threw a T-shirt over her sleep tank, flipped her hair into a messy bun, and grabbed her keys. Nothing mattered more than checking on her baby—not what she wore or her lack of makeup or the fact that she hadn't even brushed her teeth.

The drive from their Buckhead high-rise to Edward's office was only a few minutes. But she had to get down to the parking first. And if there was any construction or traffic, it would slow her.

She let the numbness go, replacing it with a fervent prayer. *Please let my baby be okay.* She repeated it until she was pleading with God. It faded into the Hail Mary. Mary would help her. Mary cared about her unborn child. A tiny voice told her that wasn't true. It told her that she deserved whatever came.

She must have looked worse than she felt. When she pushed open the door to the lobby, Kayla hurried out from behind the receptionist's desk and guided her down the hallway as if she'd been perched there, waiting for the desperate woman to walk through the door.

"Dr. B and Edward are waiting for you. Come on," she said in a quiet, confident tone. Kayla was good at hiding. Nia searched her voice for worry or concern, but all she found was matter-of-factness.

Kayla led Nia to the big room, the one where Penelope had found out her baby was too big—where she had comforted Penelope, holding her hand, praying, hearing the news that she would not abort her baby.

Edward had been talking quietly to Rich when she came in. The ultrasound machine was up and running. He stepped away from Rich and folded her into a hug.

"We're going to check on the baby first. Then we'll do some labs and see what we can find out."

If her husband hadn't been a doctor, she wondered if she would have gotten the same treatment. Moments like that reminded Nia of her privilege and all that went with it. Immediate attention. Not having to wait two days for HCG blood test results.

She'd called Penelope on the way over and talked to the speaker in her steering wheel, begging Penelope to make it okay. "I'm spotting. I'm worried. How worried should I be? Tell me it's fine."

"It's going to be okay. No matter what. Going to get it checked is the right thing to do. Edward and Dr. B will take care of you."

Penelope had said "no matter what." That meant she knew that things could be going wrong. She was saying it would okay, even if the baby was not okay.

She kept emphasizing that Nia was doing the right thing. "Do you want me to come up?" she'd asked.

"No, not yet. Edward is there. I'll update you soon."

She looked into Edward's face as the gel spurted onto her abdomen and Kayla pressed the wand to find their baby. *Edward is here. I'm okay.* She repeated her prayer to Mary, begging for her baby to be okay. *Hail Mary full of grace, the Lord is with thee. Blessed are thou among women, and blessed is the fruit of thy womb, Jesus.*

The wand zeroed in on the shape of her baby. There. The profile outline of the baby's head was visible, even to Nia.

"Turn it up," Nia said. "I need to hear it."

Kayla moved the wand to the baby's chest, looking for the heartbeat.

"It is up," said Edward, the solemnity in his voice like a warning.

"Is everything okay? Tell me it's okay," Nia said.

Kayla and Dr. B exchanged a simultaneous look with Edward.

"No," Nia said, not waiting for the pronouncement. "No, it can't be. This baby is okay. I did everything right. I get to keep this baby. No." She couldn't stop the rush of words and emotions. While she knew what was happening, her worst fear coalescing into existence right before her, she continued to deny it. It wasn't true. She was overreacting.

But he would have to say it. She needed to hear it from him. "What's happening? Edward?"

In his quiet, solemn voice, he said, "There's no heartbeat."

Chapter 29

"What are your plans for today?" Lotus asked.

Part of her worried that Rob would be home and available and she wouldn't have an excuse to hire a sitter for Blaze. Part of her wanted him to be home so she could confront him. She'd been back and forth since she discovered he'd been to the X. If it was true, and she had no evidence, he could easily deny it. If it was false, there was no sense in creating a problem when there already seemed to be enough of a problem growing between them.

Rob sat at the eat-in kitchen table, spooning honey into his Darjeeling tea. He shrugged. The slow roll of his shoulders set her teeth on edge. His nonchalance was the prevalent symptom of his wake-and-bake morning.

"You need me for something? I was planning to try that qigong class. I guess it can wait."

"The CSA asked me to volunteer, but you should do your class. I can get Kendra to sit with Blaze. I'm sure she can do at least a half day before she heads to her afternoon class."

"You sure?" he asked.

She could hear the falseness in his voice. He knew it was decided. But he wanted to *seem* helpful.

"Yes. No problem. I'm sure Kendra will appreciate it too. She's still trying to save up for that car."

Lotus set Blaze down out of her lap and stood. The dishes weren't going to wash themselves. Blaze occupied himself with the wooden toys he'd already spread out on the floor. Now that he'd had morning milk, she could slip out from under him, freeing herself from the constant touching. She loved those moments together, but then she would get touch fatigued and need space, something that Blaze didn't understand. There was no reasoning with the tyranny of toddlerhood. *Please let him be content until nap time*, she silently begged no one.

She turned away, trying not to study Rob's face, avoiding looking into his bloodshot eyes. She'd been letting it go too long. She'd allowed the behavior, and now it was problematic. Lately, he didn't get up and get going in the morning without a smoke. If he was frequenting the X, he was already probably back to the hard stuff.

"You want to try to see a movie tonight?" he asked. He must have felt it, too, the gap growing between them into a chasm. He had no conception of how her day was going to go.

"I'm probably going to be too tired."

Between the store, Blaze, and the CSA, where she had to volunteer if she wanted to keep their discount and their membership, she was not going to be in any condition for a date that night. The snide comment at the last CSA pickup and the passive-aggressive reminder email from Katrina meant she couldn't miss again.

Rob pushed a loose strand of hair out of his face and tugged on the end of it. He did that sometimes when he was frustrated. She used to think it was endearing.

"What's your problem?" Just like that, it was out of her mouth and out in the open. "I'm the one who has to get a sitter, open the store, volunteer, manage a two-year-old, rush back to the store, and pray that Blaze doesn't melt down for the duration—all while lugging around my pregnant belly and hopefully finding time somewhere in there to get a bite to eat."

"My problem? I'm just trying to spend some time with my wife. And if your day is slammed, it's because you like it that way. Didn't I just offer to take care of Blaze and you said no? You said you'd call Kendra."

She bit her lower lip. He was right. She didn't want him to take Blaze. But she couldn't say it. *Rob, I think you're doing drugs again. Tell me the truth.* The words clung to her throat as if she'd swallowed the giant glob of peanut butter they gave Morgana with her medicine.

"Well, I wouldn't want to inconvenience you. Why am I the one volunteering at the CSA? You could step up and do that if you wanted to be helpful. Why is it me?"

"I'd rather just go down to the farmers' market on Saturday. The prices aren't that different. We can afford it."

Heat rose in her chest and neck. *"We" can afford it? I can afford it, is more like it.* She was the only one bringing an income into their home.

Lotus turned back to the dishes. She took a deep breath and exhaled slowly, putting her mug in the sink as the water filled. Lotus's hands turned pink beneath the bubbles. She left her hands in the water, letting the heat prickle her skin. When it was too hot to stand, she left them in longer, waiting for the prickling to fade as she adjusted to the water temperature.

Ellie, her employee, was only sixteen. She had never opened alone. Maybe Lotus should train her. Lotus had lucked into having her there in the morning because she was a homeschooler and didn't have to report to the high school every morning like other sixteen-year-olds. It wasn't an ideal solution, but she could probably make it work. Ellie would open, and Kendra would look after Blaze. She could probably be back by one o'clock.

"You going to do the shut-down thing now, where you stop talking to me?" Rob asked.

"What else is there to say?" Lotus pulled her pink hands from the dishwater and absentmindedly let the tan natural fibers of her dish sponge circle the rim of the coffee cup. She exhaled, bringing her mind to the deep yogic breathing she relied on so heavily.

She didn't need his help. And she wasn't Rob's boss or supervisor. He could choose what to do with his time, and she could choose what to do with hers. She *chose* to help at the CSA. If they all benefited, then so be it. She *chose* to run the Lotus Garden. It had been her dream. If it was hard work, then so be it. She *chose* to have Jagannath in her home. *Their* home. That was what friends did for each other. She would manage just like she always did.

But what will happen when the baby comes? At some point, she was going to have to trust Rob with the kids. She couldn't do it all alone. The work would shift more to Rob once the baby was born. She had to find out if he was using.

Her mind flashed to Stone. No one had known how serious his problem was. Not until he'd overdosed. It couldn't be like that. Not again.

Maybe Rob needed a little time to breathe and have some space before this big shift. Maybe he was just blowing off steam. They were both anticipating the change. She needed some time to figure it out because everything she told herself to make the situation feel better sounded like a hollow excuse. If she was going to find out if Rob was using or not, she needed a plan.

Chapter 30

Penelope looked through stacks of profiles like she was on a dating site searching for a match. Marianne—she insisted on being called by her first name despite conventional Southern manners—was competent and had at least vetted couples for her and sent her to some specific profiles. Once Penelope had made a long list, which ended up being ten couples, Marianne delivered a stack of folders for her to go through. After reviewing three of the files, Penelope gave up and piled them on her kitchen table, leaving them to collect dust. Two weeks later, two follow-ups from Marianne and the pressure to make a decision and return the files had pushed Penelope to give in and call Lotus, asking her to come sort through them with her.

"What about this one?" she asked Lotus.

Lotus slid the file across the dining room table, bringing the open folder in front of her. "The O'Dells. Okay, older couple. Ooh, the guy is a psychiatrist. He'll probably psychoanalyze everything."

Penelope's wry smile and side-eye were enough to make Lotus laugh.

"Okay, sorry. I thought you said those stream-of-consciousness thoughts were helping," Lotus said.

"They are. I'm just overwhelmed at having to choose someone. These are *parents* I'm choosing—people to raise this baby forever. People the baby will call Mom and Dad."

"I mean, the only way to decide who you like best is to rule out the ones you don't like. I thought you were trying to narrow it to three." Lotus flipped the page in the O'Dells' file, opening to a picture of the couple standing on the Great Wall.

"They travel. Won't it be cool if they keep that up?" Penelope said.

They looked like a happy couple and maybe a little like they belonged in a travel magazine. Penelope tried to picture a child standing there with them, an ephemeral being coalescing beside the mother, reaching up to hold her hand, or maybe sitting on the father's shoulders. Marianne said Penelope could meet with as many couples as she liked. She could interview them and choose the right ones for her baby. It was kind of nice having the power to give these people a person. And bizarre at the same time. She could have opted for a closed adoption. In that case, she wouldn't know anything about the potential parents. She would just sign over her parental rights, and that would be that. But no, she couldn't do it that way. She wanted to pick a couple who was ten times better than her parents. Ten times better than her.

"They might. At least, once they get through the toddler phase," Lotus said, her tone laced with doubt. Lotus took another sip of tea. The tightness around her eyes and the caffeinated beverage were staples in her life now.

Penelope shut the O'Dells' file and opened the next one in her stack.

"Did you see this one, the Drakes? They look super cool." Lotus pushed the file over to Penelope.

They looked like a down-to-earth hipster pair. Clearly, something Lotus would like. The Drakes owned a fair-trade coffee shop that the wife, Chloe, managed. The husband, Art, was a philosophy professor.

Each file came with one photo or several, and that drew Penelope in. She held up the photo of the Petersons, the O'Dells, the Ramirezes and the rest, one after another, and asked herself, *Could these people be my kid's parents?* The profiles showed their ages, education levels, careers, and whatever else the couple decided to include. She realized it was not very scientific to choose potential parents based on a three-by-five photo, but the pictures drew her in more than any of the information. Something inside her wanted to believe that she might just *know* when she saw the right ones.

Some of the couples had made a whole album, including pictures of them backpacking in Europe or on a boat or on some vacation. Penelope didn't know how she was supposed to sort and choose a quality parent based on vacation photos and demographic data. Then she reached the Drakes. Art was short and dorky looking with oversized glasses and a goofy grin. Chloe had wild curly hair and a smile that made Penelope want to hug her. Inside their folder was a handwritten note to Penelope. It wasn't addressed to her specifically but said *Dear Birth Mother* at the top of the page. Art's handwriting was a feminine, flowing script. The note had an introduction and some background information, but then it got to the part that talked about him becoming a father.

I can see myself as a father. I take seriously the pressure to be a father, to fill a most important role in a child's life. While being able to tell a dad joke and garner a laugh, I also know that the important things I say will be taken deeply to heart, sticking to the child and becoming part of his or her makeup, making an impression that will live in the child and be carried into their adulthood and the next generation. I am not the dad that wants to coach baseball, but I will be if that is an interest the child wants to explore. I want to teach a love for music and maybe play instruments together, but I'll go to football games if that is what he or she wants.

Ultimately, raising a child is about love. It doesn't matter if we have the same interests or process the world in the same manner. What matters is that we commit to being additional people to love, provide for, and nurture this child, offering wisdom, teaching kindness, and preparing someone to face the world. I don't envy the choice you have to make. But know that we will love and raise your child, honoring that you will love from afar.

Penelope wiped her eye, pushing the flooding emotions away. There was something about the brazen honesty and the acknowledgement of her role that moved her. But more than that, if Penelope was honest with herself, she wanted the adoptive dad-to-be just as good as or better than the mom.

Penelope considered what it would have been like if someone had hand selected parents for her. She surely wouldn't have been dealt the crappy people she'd ended up with. She imagined some deranged person with a sickly-sweet voice announcing, "And for you, my dear, we've selected an alcoholic mother and an absent father. There we go. Enjoy!" as they handed her over to her shitty parents.

This kid was lucky. Instead of getting a single working mother plus a cheating, uninterested father, it was getting two devoted parents who wanted nothing more than to embrace their new role. Yep, this kid had it good already.

She could imagine Art sitting down at the kitchen table, helping with homework. The Drakes probably had bookcases in every room. Penelope imagined Chloe ordering fair-trade coffee for their hipster shop and hiring local musicians to play. She could see the wild-haired woman squatting down to look her child in the face and kiss a boo-boo or patiently explain why she couldn't have three scoops of ice cream.

The Drakes were her first choice. They would be great parents—she was sure. Even if they were just good parents, they'd be far better than the alternative.

Chapter 31

There was something harsh about having the awareness of her dead baby before the miscarriage happened. The light spotting had been nothing compared to the days that followed. It was a cruel joke, knowing that it sat inside her, decaying, waiting to be ejected.

Edward switched his call days with Rich, gave his patients over, and took leave from the very minute they learned the truth. He drove them home, with Nia slumped in the passenger seat, crying, railing at the unfairness of it all.

"You can have the D&C if you want. Rich can take care of the miscarriage right away. You don't have to wait," he said as if the dilation of her cervix and the scraping out of her dead baby in a white clinic room would somehow relieve the problem.

No. No one was going to take away what she had. There was nothing Edward could offer her. She knew he would do anything to take away her pain, but she couldn't lie on that table and let him empty her womb. She'd done that. Twice. Except those times had scraped out a baby that was very much alive.

"No," she said softly. "I want to let it happen on its own."

Dr. B had said that her body would take care of it. They wouldn't have to do a D&C unless it didn't all come out.

Unless it doesn't all come out? What does that mean? She pictured her mother, standing in the kitchen fifteen years before, banging the bottom of a glass jar of thick spaghetti sauce. She could hear the pounding of her palm on the concave bottom of the almost-empty jar. But somehow, she never managed to get the last bit of sauce from that two-for-one spaghetti-sauce jar, the thick red liquid clinging to the bottom and edges, refusing to budge.

They curled into bed together, Nia resting her head on Edward's chest, listening to his rhythmic heartbeat. The soft beating held her in place like an anchor. "There's no heartbeat," he'd said. It echoed in her mind. She'd hated him in that moment. But he'd had to say it, confirming it out loud for her.

In the quiet moment, when she was grounded only by the sound of those beats, he said, "We can try again. Once the bloodwork comes back, we may have an indication of hormones or supplements or something."

"Not right now." She couldn't think of the next baby with a dead one lying in her womb.

The tears started anew. She cried until she fell asleep against Edward's chest.

A baby was crying. Nia went to it, moving through a long hallway. She had to get to the baby. It was crying for her. As she got closer to the sound, the hallway grew, a corridor stretching before her, disappearing into the distance. She knew that if she could get a little closer, she could reach the baby, pick it up, comfort it to stop the crying. Its screams echoed in her ears, and she knew it was her fault that no one could comfort the baby. *I need to get to the baby,* she said to herself over and over. *The baby needs me.* She picked her step up to a jog, barreling down the hall. She could make it. Suddenly the hallway turned, made a sharp left, and opened into a cathedral-like space. The high ceiling soared above her, and up ahead, there on the pulpit, was the crying baby. She moved slowly toward it. She couldn't run there, even though the baby needed her immediately. The pulpit was set like a stage at Christmas, with the holy birth, a barn, and hay. There in the hay, where baby Jesus should be, was her baby, alone, cold, and crying for her. She hustled to it, still trying to keep her pace churchlike, and scooped the infant up. The crying ceased, and she looked down to check on the baby, but the infant had turned to dust.

She woke from the dream with hot tears on her face. "She's dead. She's dead." Her heart pulsed rapidly. She inhaled, trying to breathe. *Why can't I breathe?* A tremor ripped through her. "I found her. I picked her up. I made her stop crying. Why? Why is she dead?"

"Shh, it's okay. You had a nightmare." Edward was on her, engulfing her. He wrapped his arms around her and held her tight. Safe. She was safe. But not her baby. It hadn't been a nightmare. Her baby was dead.

When she'd calmed herself enough to slow her breathing, she got up and went to the bathroom. Her face was ashen. She washed it and used the toilet. She expected to see blood. Worse than a period—the blood would carry her baby out. But it didn't come yet. She spotted ever so slightly.

Outside of the bathroom, she said to Edward, "Maybe he's wrong. Maybe they just couldn't find the heartbeat, but it's there. I'm not bleeding."

She could hear the false hope in her voice and knew it was wishful thinking. Denial.

Edward took her hand and looked into her eyes earnestly. "Your body won't miscarry until the HCG gets low enough. I don't think your body knows what's happened quite yet." The pain in his eyes and apprehension in his voice made Nia aware that he didn't want to tell her this truth, afraid it would be the source of more tears.

She nodded soberly.

"Can I get you anything? Are you hungry?"

"I have to tell my mom. My family."

"You don't have to tell them right now. There will be time."

"No. She'll shop. She'll call everyone from Caracas to Valencia to tell them. I bet she already has things picked out for the baby. I have to tell her."

He exhaled slowly. "Okay. Whatever you feel like you need to do."

Nia started calling. She called her mother and interrupted her while making dinner. She called her sister, who had to stop putting her kids to bed and leave the room to talk to her. She called Penelope, and when she didn't answer, she sent a text. Her phone rang five minutes later, with Penelope at work on the other end.

She wanted to call Lotus. After the lunch, shopping, and yoga class, she knew she could call her. Maybe they weren't close enough because they were so new, but somehow, they were now friends. They both had a pregnancy they wanted. They both loved Penelope. She debated making that call but did it in the end.

"Oh, Nia," Lotus said through tears. "My heart is absolutely broken for you."

Above her mother's laments in Spanish and her sister's feeble "You can try again" speech, there was Lotus, crying genuine tears for her and her baby.

"Nia, you listen to me. You don't let anyone tell you not to mourn your baby or to have another. It's total bullshit. This was your baby, and you get to mourn that loss. You take your time. Understand?"

After she hung up and finished her call list, Nia got back in bed. She didn't feel ill or tired, but it seemed like the right place to be. Edward came up from the kitchen with a plate of over-easy eggs.

"We both know your mom is probably bringing sancocho soon, but I thought you might like some eggs for now." He pulled out the lap tray. They only ever used it for special occasions like her birthday or their anniversary.

She ate slowly, not tasting the food but doing it anyway because Edward was watching her, and she hadn't eaten a thing all day. Edward removed the tray and returned to bed, carrying a small statue. Her guess was that it came from his mother.

"Is that from Okasan?" She used the honorific to refer to his mother the way he did. *Would our baby have learned both Spanish and Japanese?*

He nodded. His eyes were clouded with tears, and he didn't speak for a moment. She waited.

He handed the small gray statue to her. It looked like stone and was heavy in her hands, about a half foot tall. The figure had a bald head, and the ears stretched in the familiar way of Buddhist iconography. The face was round and serene with closed eyes and a smile, the third eye prominent between the brows. Hanging from the neck of the monk-like figure was a bright-red cloth bib.

"It's a Jizo statue," he said.

She had seen the statue before. The bib. The monk smiling like he knew something they did not. She had a memory of a garden in Japan, outside a monastery they'd visited on her first trip to Edward's birthplace. There had been hundreds of Jizo statues, all dressed in red bonnets or bibs, sewn or knit. There had been a young woman there, and Nia had stared at her curiously as she replaced a weathered bib with a fresh one.

She looked down at the stone monk. It must have been Okasan's. It had a weathered look. The tears came again, not just for her baby but for her mother-in-law's baby, Edward's brother.

"He's the guardian of children. The protector of babies. Our baby." He cut off.

She pulled him in and held him. "Edward," she whispered. "Thank you."

Chapter 32

The warm smell of sandalwood filled the shop. Lotus stood behind the jewelry counter, a long continuous row of glass cases housing everything from tulsi beads to turquoise to silver zodiac pieces. Inventory spreadsheets covered the long side counter, preventing anyone from gazing into the top of the case. It was not an ideal place to do the work if a customer wanted to see what was inside without pressing their face to the glass like a toddler looking at a snake in the zoo. But she couldn't go back to the office when she was the only one there.

The morning had been worse than she'd expected. Blaze now slept peacefully in the back office in the playpen she'd bought just for occasions like this. She wasn't a fan of the "baby jail" pens and for the longest time had refused to buy one. That day, she was relieved he was safe and enclosed and not awake, drawing on the walls or removing all the printer paper. Exhaustion had taken him after he'd had a meltdown because one of his socks had gotten wet. Trying to reason with him was like talking to a stubborn goat in the wrong language.

Lotus rolled her shoulders to release the tension. The bell of the front door chimed, and she looked up, expecting Rob, who was supposed to come and take over the inventory. Instead, Jagannath strode through the front door, wearing a tie-dyed tank top and pale, loose linen pants.

"Where's Rob?" she asked. Her suspicion spiked, and she could hear the pitch of her voice peak through her gritted teeth.

"He has a migraine. I'm here, though. I'm here to help." He flashed his disarming smile at her.

Lotus forced herself to smile back. She could feel the tightness around her eyes. But it wasn't Jagannath's fault Rob wasn't there. She'd wanted to talk to Nia about the issues with Rob again after their shopping trip, but then Nia had miscarried, and despite their growing closeness, this was not the time to burden Nia with her own problems. Flashes of Stone crept into her mind. She saw her brother on the bed, the needle still in his vein. The image was etched so firmly into her memory that she could close her eyes and bring it up. He hadn't been passed out that time. He'd been gone.

"He sends his apologies. And me. I can handle it—don't worry. You want to go take a break or something?"

"I'm fine," she said, shaking off thoughts of Stone.

Lotus worked her jaw to release the tension. Between juggling Blaze's meltdowns, worrying about Rob, and taking care of the store—all while tired and carrying around her protruding belly—there wasn't much left in her reserves.

Jagannath's hands came down on her shoulders, milking the tight muscles. Lotus froze beneath him. But the massage felt so good that she didn't stop him.

"I'm sorry. I should have asked." Jagannath pulled his hands away. "May I?"

Lotus nodded and let him continue. Jagannath was one of those people who didn't define himself in terms of his job or his skills. He defined himself in terms of his passions. He didn't practice as a massage therapist, at least that she knew of, but he'd gone to school for it many years back. She sighed beneath his hands as she felt the tension and anger at Rob leave her body.

Jagannath pulled away with a gentle stroke and sat up on a stool in front of the inventory. "I'm sorry you were disappointed to see me instead of Rob."

"It's not about you, Jagannath. I'm overwhelmed right now, and I needed a partner today." The stark honesty surprised her. Maybe it was the massage or her exhaustion from Blaze's meltdown, but she didn't care if she was revealing too much.

"Have you said that to Rob?" he asked.

Lotus looked down and shook her head.

"He has to know your needs if he's to meet them." Jagannath sounded like a therapist.

She knew she should share more with Rob. She had it handled most of the time. She was used to juggling everything. But lately, she couldn't shake the feeling of always being overwhelmed.

She nodded. "I know. I sometimes have a hard time asking for help when I need it. But I'm not getting much from him, and I feel let down. Why do I always have to ask? Why isn't he capable of seeing all the balls in the air and trying to catch one of them?"

"I understand." Jagannath glanced toward the row of T-shirts on the far wall but not before Lotus caught the far-off look in his eyes. "I understand completely."

She'd heard Rob's explanation of their breakup. Jagannath had broken his heart. Rob had been in love with him and thought Jagannath reciprocated. But out of the blue, Jagannath said he had to move on. He blamed Jagannath for being a loner, having wanderlust, and not giving a damn about his feelings.

"I made the same mistake," Jagannath continued. "I took too long to express my needs. In the end, they couldn't be met."

"He couldn't figure out what you needed?" She didn't say Rob's name, but they both knew that was who she meant.

"Maybe I should've been clearer," Jagannath said. "By the time I decided to, there was so much resentment, so much hurt built up, I couldn't move past it. I had to move on."

"It broke him, you know." Maybe he didn't know.

"I know. It broke me as well. I did love him. In the end, that wasn't enough. Relationships are strengthened or broken by what happens in the hard times. Anyone can make it work when everything is happy and easy, but the real test is when your relationship is challenged and you still get through it. We couldn't."

Lotus nodded. Rob had always made it sound like the breakup was Jagannath's fault for discarding him when the honeymoon phase was over.

"Selfishness will break a partnership. You have to be willing to go the extra mile for your partner's needs. That's the bottom line." Jagannath shook his head and ran his hands over his bald scalp. He cupped the tuft of hair at the back and pulled his fingers through the long strands.

He still sounded like a therapist, even if he was right. The permanent twinge in her stomach flipped over. "But what about when you suspect something is going on with your partner?" It was out of her mouth before she could think it through. But she hadn't been able to talk to anyone about it. She needed to figure it out.

He pursed his lips in thought and waited before answering. "I think you have to be willing to have those hard conversations. Admit your suspicion and your fears."

She continued to be surprised by him. He hadn't asked what, specifically, she was talking about but had dug below her suspicion and found the fear down there. Before she could stop it, tears spilled out.

"Hey. I'm sorry. I didn't mean to trigger something for you." He stood from his stool and wrapped her in a firm hug. Not like the wimpy, polite hugs that she would give to an aunt but a strong, firm hold as if he was trying to envelop her and shield her from the outside world. It was another one of those strange things about him—he wasn't afraid to touch people, to connect.

She let go. Her tears melted into anger. She stepped back, wiping her eyes. Before she knew it, she was telling him about her suspicions that Rob was using. The club. The morning smoking. The disappearing act. Shirking his responsibilities. To her, it all added up to a much bigger problem.

"I didn't intend to share all that. I just—I don't know what to do."

Jagannath put the Back in Ten Minutes sign on the door and locked it. She sank to the floor behind the counter, with her back to the jewelry case, and he sat down beside her. He listened. She talked.

"Drugs are a big problem for me. I mean, growing up like I did, there's this sort of nonchalance around the whole thing. My parents grew marijuana plants like they were tomatoes or rosemary. It wasn't really a big deal back then. Until my best friend, Sunshine, was taken away. Her parents were charged with intent to sell. I thought it was just the weed back then, and it wasn't until I was a teenager that I found out there was way worse shit going on over there than I knew about. But everyone just covered it up. They covered up her mom's problem, and they covered up the drugs, but then they were busted. All the growing stopped after that. My family got lucky." *Until Stone started using.* But she didn't say that. She couldn't talk about him.

Jagannath's intent eyes were focused on her, taking in everything she said. He did a thing Lotus wasn't used to—he listened and held space and showed empathy. He was starting to be the most helpful person in her life, and she felt a little shitty about being judgy about him and his goofy bald-head-ponytail thing. A half hour later, they still sat in the floor. She felt better but spent.

"I think you're right," Jagannath said. "You aren't going to feel better if you confront him and get nothing but lies. If he *is* using, he'll certainly lie about it. It's classic addict behavior. We'll figure it out. But I agree—you have to wait until you have more information."

That was Lotus's gut feeling about it. Once he knew she suspected, he'd just do a better job hiding it. That was what had gotten Stone in trouble.

"Let me see what I can find out. Do you trust me?" He turned to her, his dark eyes penetrating hers.

She nodded. *What other choice do I have?* Jagannath was right—he could get close to Rob and see what was going on. Then she'd know the truth.

He stood and helped her from the floor. "It's going to be okay. No matter what. You take care of yourself and this baby and let me worry about Rob for now."

She nodded again. "I'd better get started on this inventory if I'm going to make it home by bedtime."

Lotus washed her face and flipped the sign on the door. She stayed in the front of the store while Jagannath went to the back and started counting. She chided herself for misjudging Jagannath. He was not what she'd expected at all, and the way things were going, Jagannath's presence in their lives felt like divine intervention.

Chapter 33

At midnight, Penelope was next in the rotation for a new patient assignment. She'd shoved a protein bar into her mouth between checking on her other two patients. The patient assignment was a crapshoot. She could end up with a really sick patient who needed a lot more than a labor nurse should be providing. Or she could be dealing with a fetal demise, a labor and delivery that would not result in a live baby. Or it could be a difficult family situation that would inevitably turn to drama—and maybe a call to security.

That night, the next patient in line for her was an adoption. It was like the universe was trying to bitch slap her. Sure, she'd worked with adoptive families before. But that night, after meeting and choosing the Drakes, it felt like a punch in the gut. She would have to comfort a birth mother, accommodate an adoptive mother, and ensure that everything went smoothly. She loved the patient-care aspect of nursing, which was more than taking blood pressure, adjusting fetal monitors, and scribbling notes in charts. But not this. Not that day.

The patient, Bridget, went through admissions alone, and once triage had her placed in a room, Penelope went in to find out what the birth mother wanted. The situation required all the standard admission procedures and then some. Introductions and the basics were followed by the adoption-specific items.

"I just want you to feel comfortable and safe here. Do you have a support person who will be joining you?"

The young woman shook her head gently.

"After the birth, you have the option of holding your baby. Some women want to, and some choose not to. It's entirely up to you. If you want the adoptive parents to bond with the baby in another room, I can arrange that for you. Or they're welcome to be in the same room as you, and you can be included in everything."

"I don't know. Whatever she wants is fine."

So it's like that. The adoptive mother is calling the shots. "Will the family be joining for the delivery or coming at a later time?"

With that, the door opened, and a woman strode in with a look of confidence like she owned the hospital. She had dark, determined eyes, and her hair was pulled back away from her face. Although it was midnight, she still looked like she'd filled in her eyebrows and had time to apply a lip color.

She approached the bedside and pulled the birth mother into an embrace. Then she backed up and looked over her like she was inspecting a new pure-bred puppy. "How are you, Bridget? Are they getting you everything you need? Do you want your epidural now? Did you decide on getting the epidural?"

She turned to face Penelope, and the questions continued to fly. Penelope hadn't even introduced herself, but it was clear what this woman thought of the power dynamic. She was used to being in charge.

"I'm just getting her admitted. Why don't you go to the family room while I finish, and then I'll come get you? HIPAA and all." Penelope gave her best *I'm in charge* condescending smile and shooed her out, but not before the woman's eyes darkened even further. "Family room" was a fancy way of saying "waiting room." Someone on the board must have thought it sounded more patient centered. By the looks of her exit, the adoptive mom was aware that she was being dismissed.

As soon as she was gone from the room, Penelope turned and found Bridget crying.

"I'm sorry. Did you want her to stay?" *First patient of the evening, and I'm already screwing things up.* She should have asked Kathy to take this patient for her. Not that the crying bothered her. Patients cried all the time in Labor and Delivery. It was part of the territory.

But Penelope couldn't help but feel like she was the wrong nurse for Bridget.

The woman shook her head. "No. I just—I'm giving Caroline my baby. It's good. I know. I trust her, and this is what's best. She's smart. She's a CFO, you know, and she makes more money than anyone I've ever known. This baby will have anything he needs. Everything. It's just—this is it." Agony turned the young woman's face into a mess, and Penelope imagined that it looked the way her insides must feel. Twisted, sick, and torn.

Penelope sat on the edge of the hospital bed. "You know, you have three days. I just want to remind you. You can't sign the final paperwork until this baby is seventy-two hours old. I know it's hard. And I can imagine you're going to have a roller coaster of emotions over the next few days. You know what brought you here. I'm here to support you. I can get an advocate in here for you in a heartbeat. Or your adoption attorney or someone appointed from the hospital or the state. You tell me what you need, and we can get through it."

Tears shone in her eyes. "Thank you. I needed to hear that. I know I'm doing what's best. They said it would be hard. But he's not even here yet. Seeing her—it's just hard."

"She doesn't have to be here."

"I know. I decided ahead of time that was what I wanted. She's been so kind to me. Really."

"Okay. She can be here. She can stay with you. But just so you understand, you have a right to choose at any time. Even if that's not a choice you made before or even if it simply changes. You understand?"

She wiped her eyes. "I do."

Penelope went out and got the adoptive mom at Bridget's request. "I'm Penelope, and I'm going to be Bridget's nurse. We talked over her plans, and she'd like you to be present. I know you all discussed that ahead of time. It's important to understand that may change once she's further along in her labor."

The woman nodded and clutched her oversized Louis Vuitton bag to her side. Penelope recognized it because it looked just like one Nia owned. "I'm Caroline. My husband is traveling, but he's on the first flight home. I want to make this a good experience for Bridget. She doesn't really have anyone, you know?" She fingered the Tiffany necklace resting between her collar bones.

She said the right words, but there was something off about Caroline. Penelope didn't hold it against her that she had money. Her best friend bought stupidly expensive purses—*Oh wait, "bags," not purses*—and if she really was a CFO, she probably still had on her makeup because she was up working late hours.

Clearly, this woman bought whatever she wanted. But to Penelope, it looked like that included a baby as well. Strictly speaking, it was against the law for adoptive mothers to bribe birth mothers in any way. However, they were allowed to give gifts and provide for anything that made the birth mother more comfortable during the pregnancy. Who knew what it took for Bridget to be comfortable. All Penelope knew was that the power dynamic didn't make *her* comfortable.

Penelope left them alone but couldn't get the thought out of her mind. *Does Bridget feel like she's been bought? Does she even have the experience to recognize it?* Something about the whole thing rubbed Penelope the wrong way.

She excused herself and went to the lounge to get some ice then stood for a moment with her head in the freezer. She would never give her baby to a woman like that. Of course, she wasn't a teenager. *Why doesn't Bridget have her own mother here? What kind of mother lets her child give her baby up alone? Where is her family or the birth father—or at least a friend?* The thought that maybe the girl didn't have a friend released a heavy sadness that settled in Penelope's chest.

She pulled her head out of the freezer and went back to checking on her patients. It was going to be a long night.

Chapter 34

It wasn't fair that Edward had to go and catch babies as if he hadn't just lost their own. And it wasn't fair that Nia was left alone with her grief while he did. Her focus on becoming a mother had become a full-time job, and Nia was starting to feel like she was consumed by it.

Edward's phone had pinged at the dinner table with news from the answering service, and he picked up his cell phone and called his patient on the spot. After a moment of listening, Edward said, "Okay, that all sounds like early labor. Remember, I want you to go to the hospital when they're about four minutes apart, or sooner if your water breaks. Sounds like you're establishing a good labor pattern." He paused, twirling the fork in his fingers and not putting another bite on it. "Yes, that all sounds normal. Your baby should be moving during this time." After a few more guidelines and words of encouragement, he hung up and met Nia's gaze.

"Do you think it's going to be quick? Is it a first baby?" She tried to keep the distress out of her voice, but there was no way to hide her true feelings from Edward.

He reached across the table and grabbed her hand. "Do you want me to take you to your mom's?"

Nia winced. "No. I don't need a babysitter. I need you."

"I know. I don't have to go just yet, and I'll be home as soon as she delivers, as long as no one else shows up. But I can't ask Rich to do it all. That's not fair."

She wanted to pout. She wanted to scream. She wanted to throw a handful of the mashed garlic yuca in his face.

The feeling passed. But she felt alone, and worse than that, she felt lonely. "Will you wake me when you get back?" she asked.

She usually slept fine without him—years of his call schedule had made the all-nighters and unpredictable hours somewhat routine. But the recent nightmares had her on edge. When he crept into bed and put his arms around her, that was when she felt the safest.

"Promise," he said.

After dinner, Nia carried her plate into the kitchen, and Edward took it out of her hands. "I'll do them."

Nia settled into her favorite chair. *Why does Edward have to be so perfect all the time?* Even though she didn't want him to leave for work, she knew he was doing that for her and for their family. She flipped open her laptop. She didn't want to feel like a helpless mess every time he got a labor call. She was going to have to find a way to cope better.

The TTC message board was open on her browser. Feeling cynical, she couldn't bear to scroll through the messages. She wasn't in the mood to comfort the other women with losses. She couldn't bear to hear anyone else's pregnancy announcement. Life was getting back to normal all around her. But she wasn't ready for "normal." She still needed her grief.

She typed out a quick message to the board: *DH is working overnight tonight. Not sure how I'm going to handle these fierce nightmares without him.*

It would help to hear from others, though only the moms who'd had a loss *and* had a DH—dear husband—with a busy work schedule would understand. She didn't know what she was looking for. Reassurance maybe. But she didn't want to sound desperate for attention.

She added to the message: *How long did you wait after your miscarriage to DTD or try again?* That would get some responses. The message board was the perfect place to anonymously talk about details like when women got back to sex—*doing the deed,* as the lingo went—after a loss. She published the post.

It would take time for women to respond to the message, so she turned to checking her email, her second favorite distraction. She composed a short note: *Duncan, I'd love to hear about it if you hear of any casting calls that might be a good fit for me. - Nia*

Then she sat back, watching the cursor blink. *Is that what I want—a job?* Duncan always brought up potential jobs when they spoke. While he was technically still her agent, it had been quite a while since he'd put her up for anything. But over the years, they'd become friends, and even if they only spoke to play catch-up, there was always the potential for an opportunity.

She moved her mouse. The cursor blinked. She hit Send.

At least she was doing something. Maybe it would amount to nothing in the end, but she had to do something, anything. The evening played on like any normal evening, with the looming knowledge that Edward would leave at some point. But eventually, they both found themselves tucked into bed with the light out and no further calls from the laboring patient or the nursing staff.

Nia woke to find the space beside her empty and cold. She picked up her phone and clicked it to light the screen—4:24 a.m. She hadn't heard him leave in the night, her exhaustion had pulled her into a deep sleep. Nia typed a message to check on things and then deleted it. He would come home after the delivery.

After tossing for a while, she threw the duvet back and got out of bed. A glass of wine would make her sleepy enough to forget. The row of bottles in the wine rack had been undisturbed since Nia found out she was pregnant. She pulled a bottle of red from their Napa Valley trip and barely glanced at the 2008 vintage before popping it with the electric opener. Only after tasting it, she realized she might have opened the bottle Edward was saving. The smooth, full-bodied wine had hints of vanilla, eucalyptus, and blackberry.

With her glass in hand, she went to bed and back to her browser. The ladies on her message board were the only ones who *really* understood. She dove into her normal corner of the internet, clicking her message to find a few replies.

Mum2FurBabyz: *So sorry you are struggling at night. Sleep during the day? Or consider a sleeping pill? We started DTD six weeks after the m/c. HTH*

FrealDeal216: *I was pregs in the next cycle after the m/c. I think we DTD 2w later? Also, have you tried melatonin? That might help at night. <baby dust>*

The suggestions and consolations did nothing to dissuade her self-pity. She downed the rest of her wine and went into the baby's room. They lived in a four-bedroom condo, and the second office had already been dismantled, but there was no furniture in the baby's room yet. Nia had just picked the paint out. Cans of Sheer Mist gray paint were stacked on a drop cloth in the corner. She hadn't committed to the rest of the design, waiting for the ultrasound to determine the sex of the baby. But if it was a girl, she'd wanted to do a Japanese cherry-blossom tree above the crib, against the gray background, with a sprinkle of the white and pink blossoms painted as if they were blowing off the tree and across the room. In her dreams, the baby was a girl.

In the top of the closet was a bag from the eco-boutique in Decatur. Nia pulled the Yoga Baby onesie free from the recycled-paper shopping bag. Lotus's little one would have a matching onesie to the one her baby was supposed to wear. She shoved the onesie back in her bag. She would have a baby. She didn't care how long it took or what she had to do. Getting rid of the baby clothes—or the beanie Penelope had knit for her—would be like admitting defeat. And Nia might be a lot of things, but she wasn't a quitter.

Chapter 35

Jagannath and Rob had gone out at eleven. Blaze was tucked away in his room—not that he would stay in his own room for a whole night, but he was there for the moment.

She'd sent a text message to Jagannath a half hour earlier: *Did he want to go to the X?*

And after midnight, her phone was buzzing the answer: *Yes. I'm keeping an eye on things. Don't worry.*

She exhaled, closing her eyes.

Thank you, she sent. *I couldn't do this without you.*

The two of them had taken to texting each other regularly, reporting on the state of the situation with Rob. It was like they were coconspirators in a private investigation. *Into my own husband's life.*

She pushed the thought away. Twinges of guilt crept in. Maybe she would be better off just confronting him. Part of her wanted to do that. She wanted it all on the table and over with. But fear took over. She'd confronted Stone, and now he was dead.

"Are you using? Tell me the truth." Lotus had sat across from Stone in the coffee shop in New Orleans. Her chicory coffee sat untouched in front of her. He'd already finished a cup and started on another.

The dark circles around his eyes made him look like he had two mostly healed black eyes. But it was more than that. He had a jittery energy around him, like a caged animal looking for an escape. He disappeared for hours on end. He always had someone to meet or somewhere to be. He took too long in the bathroom. Lotus had finally added up the odd behaviors to an answer she wasn't prepared to face. He was using.

"Of course not," he said, unflinching.

It was so convincing. He launched into a story about a vitamin deficiency. He told her he didn't want her to worry but that he'd seen his doctor, and they were doing some tests. And just like that, she'd been redirected. *What do I know about drug abuse? What do I know about the telltale signs of a user?*

Determined not to repeat that situation, she'd do anything necessary to get to the bottom of this thing with Rob. Even if that meant sending Jagannath to spy on him. Or searching through his stuff. She didn't want to catch him red-handed. But if she confronted him, she'd have to rely on him to tell the truth, and that wasn't a risk she was willing to take again. She couldn't help but think that if she hadn't been so naïve about Stone, he might still be alive.

If Rob was making this choice for his life, she couldn't let him use in the house with their kids. She wasn't going to have a situation like Sunshine's happen to them. She would not risk her children being taken away from her or, Goddess forbid, having something bad happen when he was high around the kids.

Her mind flashed to the commune. Growing up in a place that had loose boundaries and loose interpretations of the law had been the problem that led Stone to heroin. To his death. She couldn't stand by and watch it take Rob. The pot had been different. She'd grown up watching a joint pass from hand to hand and seeing the plants in their garden. Until it threatened their lives, she'd looked the other way. But if baking on pot meant hanging out with drug dealers and going to places like the X, then she was done with that too.

Her phone buzzed. *Seems kind of creepy that I'm following him into the bathroom. If he hits up a stall, you're out of luck.*

The text wasn't funny, but she laughed. There wasn't much else she could do. Lotus pictured Jagannath standing in the foggy club mirror under the harsh bathroom lights, smoothing his palm across his bald head, running his fingers through the tuft of hair on the back. *Why doesn't he just shave it all?* She could see finding him attractive if he would just choose a hairstyle.

You're a good detective, she sent back. *Way to take one for the team.*

If she didn't joke, she might just cry. She held the phone, hoping to get another text. There was a sick excitement about digging to the bottom of this problem. She dreaded the confirmation that Rob was using but dreaded worse what she was going to do if she didn't get a definitive answer, one way or another, soon.

Chapter 36

Lately, Penelope enjoyed the nights without deliveries even more than the nights with them. She was lackadaisical about the Pitocin drip. She didn't encourage breaking the amniotic sac. She let moms "labor down," even if they were complete more than an hour before shift change. More often than not, her mood dictated what she told them. She didn't want to be there for the deliveries anymore. She didn't want to put squishy babies into their happy, exhausted mothers' arms and congratulate dads. She considered transferring out to another unit. But after nine years in Labor and Delivery, it was her home.

At five in the morning, Bridget's room buzzed the nurses' station. Penelope had come to find that the adoptive parent, Caroline, was most often the one pressing that button. Her husband's flight had arrived, and he'd come straight to the hospital but had barely been off his phone since walking in the door. But whether it was Caroline or the teen mom calling for a nurse, the fact remained that Bridget needed Penelope.

Just a few short months before, she'd thought of herself as a good nurse. She would go the extra mile to advocate for her patient, stay past shift change if she was pushing with a mom, and do the right thing no matter how inconvenient it might be. That was the kind of nurse Bridget needed. Penelope wasn't sure she was that nurse anymore.

She entered the room, determined to be professional. Bridget's eyes were wide with fear. "Something's happening."

"Okay. That's okay. Things are going to change. That's how it's supposed to be. That's normal. Do you want me to check your cervix?" The rapid changes in Bridget's body probably felt anything but normal. Though the girl was eighteen and legally an adult, she

169

was just a child. Labor was not meant to be handled by children. At least, not in Penelope's generation or even the one before her.

Fear in the eyes of a laboring mother was not out of place. But this kid should be worrying about what dress to wear to prom and what kind of makeup to apply for her day at the mall. She should be trying to figure out where to go to college and navigating gossipy girls. Instead, she was wearing a hospital gown, putting her body through a grueling experience, and giving birth to a baby she was about to hand over to Caroline to raise. There was more than fear in her eyes.

"Can everyone go for a minute while I check her?" Penelope asked.

Though Bridget might let them stay when the baby was being born, everyone didn't need the show of a cervical check. Modesty generally went out the window during labor, but there wasn't much else Penelope felt she could preserve for Bridget.

"You okay?" she asked when the two of them were alone in the labor room.

Bridget shrugged. "This sucks. I know it's the right thing to do, but it sucks."

"Where's your mother?" she asked quietly.

Maybe she was crossing the line by getting personal with her patient, and maybe it was the fact of her own baby that forced the question from her. She'd never let her personal life interfere before. She certainly didn't want to start now. But she had to know why Bridget had come alone.

"She didn't support me. She's a real piece of work. She wanted to raise the baby herself when I didn't want it. To make up for all the mistakes she made with me. She was seventeen when she got knocked up with me. Well, I don't want that. I don't want her life, and I certainly don't want to watch her raise my baby. She'll just fuck it up."

"She never came around once you made your decision about adoption?"

"I never gave her the chance. It was too late."

Bridget's face collapsed, and the tears came again. Anger was there with the fear before her face crumpled. Penelope passed her a tissue and sat in silence next to her. She imagined that Bridget's family wasn't unlike her own. Trashy mother. Terrible choices. Rinse and repeat. She'd felt very much like Bridget, not wanting to make the same mistakes her mother had. *Is that what life is—constantly trying not to be your parents?*

"This is the best thing for my baby. I got into Penn State. I can't give that up. Maybe I'm selfish. But Caroline can give this baby a chance. He won't have to live off government assistance while I work two jobs and settle for someone else's life. I said it. That's why no one else is here. Because I'm selfish, and I'm fine with it."

She nodded. Penn State. *This girl is much smarter than me.* Bridget was giving up her baby despite wanting it, because she had the maturity to see what would happen. Penelope swallowed hard, her own bulging belly a reminder of her position.

A contraction interfered then, and Bridget's face screwed up in pain. "I'm definitely feeling it through the epidural. What's happening?" The words came out through gritted teeth.

"I'll check you when the contraction ends. Breathe through it like you did with the early-labor ones."

She could adjust the epidural or get a bolus. But if Bridget was complete, or near, as she suspected, she might want to be able to feel to push. That would be quicker and better for Bridget in the long run.

She gloved up and performed the exam, feeling the baby's head and searching with her fingers around the edges to feel the remaining lip of cervix. "You're almost complete. Something's happening all right—you're getting close."

Bridget nodded. "Okay. What about the epidural?"

"Remember how I said labor would be full of choices? Here's another one. If we increase the epidural now, you'll be less likely to feel anything to push, which means it might be harder to push the baby out and probably take longer. If we leave it alone, you'll feel the contractions more now, but that'll be really helpful when it's time to push. The other benefit is that the better you can feel to push, the less likely that you'll tear during the delivery—which is better for you in the long run. I'll do whatever you want to do. There's no wrong answer here."

Bridget shrugged. "I don't know what to do. God, why do I have to feel the baby coming out? That sounds horrible."

"You don't have to. It's up to you."

"I don't want to get all torn up. That really happens?"

"Sometimes it does," Penelope said. "And letting the epidural wear off doesn't guarantee you won't tear. You still might, although I'm pretty good at preventing tears with pushing."

Bridget looked away, out the hospital window into the darkness beyond. "She's helping me go to college, you know. I know she's only supposed to help with baby-related stuff, but she's done more than that. I probably shouldn't be telling you that, huh?"

Penelope compressed her lips into a flat line. "Well, the conflict is that you aren't supposed to feel indebted to her. If you were to change your mind about the adoption—and you know, you have three days after the birth before you can sign all the paperwork—you might feel guilty for taking money unrelated to pregnancy-related expenses."

"I didn't take it yet. But I probably will."

Penelope nodded, wondering if she was obligated to report that to the patient advocate or social worker.

"I think I'll increase the epidural. I don't care if it takes longer. Can you still help me try not to tear?"

"Of course." Penelope opened the door and invited Caroline back into the room.

Caroline squeezed Bridget's hand at the news the baby was close. She exchanged a worried glance with her husband. Excitement and anticipation buzzed in the room. It happened often when a baby was about to be born. Bridget could have a while still. Penelope often predicted the labor patterns, but this one had gone faster than she'd expected. If it kept on, Bridget would have her baby before Penelope went home in the morning.

She let herself out of the room and kept a close eye on the monitor at the nurses' station. As soon as the contractions changed, she would know it was time for pushing. Then she was distracted by another patient. Postbirth bleeding with the mom in room six had slowed, and her uterus felt firm. She was ready to transfer into the postpartum unit.

A page came over the intercom and called Penelope to room five. She left the mom with the newborn and popped out of the room and into the one next door. Endless running. It was one of those busy nights she usually longed for. But that night, her ankles were swollen, every patient seemed demanding, and Bridget's problems alone were big enough to be the only thing needing Penelope's attention.

By five thirty, she was back with Bridget. Fear had laced the girl's eyes before, but now they were filled with terror.

"What's wrong? Something's wrong," Caroline said. "Didn't you increase her epidural?"

The fetal monitor beeped loudly, and Bridget groaned. Caroline whispered furiously at her husband, and he hung up his phone.

"Bridget, take some slow, deep breaths. I'm going to check you again and see what's happening." Penelope turned the monitor down before gloving her left hand. She put her other hand on Bridget's abdomen. "Okay, you're feeling all that pressure now because you're complete. It's time to push your baby out. Nothing is wrong. What you're feeling is normal. You can still feel pressure even with the epidural."

The terror remained in her eyes. "I only feel it on one side."

Penelope nodded. "Sometimes that happens. I'm going to direct you when you have contractions and help you push."

This was it. Pushing, having the baby, and then... Bridget's baby was going to Caroline.

Bridget listened to Penelope's directions and gave a good push. Caroline and her husband stood at either side of Bridget, anxiously awaiting their baby. They pushed together for the better part of an hour before Penelope called Dr. Ashburn. He gloved up and joined them for the last three pushes. Bridget's pale face had become pink and splotchy from the effort. In the last push, Bridget cried out as the baby left her body.

Ashburn cut the cord and passed the baby to Penelope. She swept him into a thin, clean towel and set him in the warmer. The heat lamp above him regulated his temperature while she cleaned him, gently wiping the birth fluids from his skin. His hands and feet were blue, as expected, but he screamed and pinked up quickly everywhere else. She rubbed his chest to get him to scream again. Caroline had joined her at the warmer, wiping her eyes and stepping anxiously from foot to foot.

Penelope attempted to make eye contact with Bridget to confirm her prebirth decisions, but Bridget kept her eyes trained on Dr. Ashburn. After covering the newborn's bald head with a beanie, she placed him in Caroline's arms. Caroline's cheeks glistened as she cuddled the child. Her husband pulled out an enormous camera that made him look like a tourist and snapped photo after photo of Caroline holding the baby.

Penelope turned her attention back to Dr. Ashburn, who was performing a vigorous uterine massage. Bridget's eyes squeezed tightly against the pain.

"I'll take over, Dr. A," Penelope said. It was the best she could do to make him stop and let her do it her way. Sure, the uterus had to tighten to stop the bleeding, but he didn't have to make Bridget miserable.

Dr. Ashburn shrugged, finished with the placenta, congratulated everyone awkwardly, and left the room. Penelope cleaned up behind him and tried to ignore the uncomfortable air that had settled in the room. When she stepped close to Bridget to check her blood-pressure readings, Bridget whispered, "Just get them out."

Bridget caught her eye with a decisive look. Penelope wheeled the baby out in the bassinet and escorted the couple to a bonding room. When she came back, she sat in that same spot on the side of the bed.

"Do you want to talk about it?"

Bridget's tears started. "What's to say?"

"Bridget, you can see the baby if you want to. Or I can keep them out of here. Tell me what I can do to make this easier for you."

Bridget wiped her eyes with the back of her hand. She looked like a child crying over a broken toy. She was a child. Then her eyes cleared, and she sat up straighter. "No. There's nothing you can do. It's done." The look on her face was probably meant to reassure Penelope, but she saw through it. "You can go. I'll call if I need anything."

Penelope nodded, stood up, and took her charting back out to the nurses' station. The look in Bridget's eyes stayed with Penelope. She wore determination like a mask, but beneath it, there was something else. Bridget might be determined to ignore this blip on her life's mapped course and to move past it. But she looked frayed. She could dry her tears, nod assuredly to Penelope, and sit up straight. But that shadow at the edges would always be there, haunting her.

Chapter 37

It wasn't a New York runway, but the casting call for Nine in the Mirror was exactly what Nia needed. She'd saved the voicemail from Duncan, her agent, and played it aloud for the third time in the car.

"Listen, honey, I know you've moved on to this mommy thing, but I have the perfect gig for you. They'd die to have you. I just know you'll get it. Go to the casting call at Nine in the Mirror on Wednesday. I'm sending you all the deets in email. Kisses."

Nia smiled at the sound of Duncan's voice. He could be a cold, ruthless bitch, but he was hilarious, and he knew fashion. Even after her email, she was surprised to be on his call list for a job. It had been a while since she'd said yes to any casting calls. Eventually, after she'd said no enough times, her name stopped coming up. Duncan had shown the proper amount of enthusiasm and support for her pregnancy announcement, though he'd still called her a "breeder" twice during their last lunch. She smiled ruefully.

When she told him later about the miscarriage, he was so sincere that she thought he might cry. "Oh, honey, I am so sorry." He didn't get it—not really. But he understood loss. He understood she was hurting.

She hadn't expected him to get back to her so soon, but it was like he had been waiting for her to reach out. She needed to take her mind off her miscarriage. *But Nine in the Mirror? Can I do it?* Yes, they'd captured some of the best designers for their line, and their chic name said it all—nine months of pregnancy. Nia liked their clothes quite a bit. She'd even bought an outfit in early pregnancy. Her size hadn't changed yet, but the comfort of their early-pregnancy line was supposed to carry over to postpartum. But more importantly, they *wanted* her. Maybe they'd even asked for her. Duncan wouldn't send her unless he knew she could get it.

"But what about the miscarriage? I thought Nine's whole premise revolved around only using real mothers as models."

"You'd be too early to show anyway," Duncan said. "I put you up for the early-pregnancy-postpartum crossover line."

Nia could feel a flush coming up her chest. "So, am I supposed to... pretend I'm pregnant?"

"Honey, no one's going to ask. You're there for the early-and-after line, so it doesn't matter. Don't you want this one?"

When they hung up, Nia thought about his question. Even though she wanted to push aside anything that reminded her of her pregnancy, she did want this gig. *What else do I have?* She didn't have a job. They were certainly near the bottom of the adoption list. Her best friend was more and more unavailable, working extra shifts. And Lotus had decided not to leave Blaze alone with Rob, so she was more overwhelmed than ever. Edward busied himself with his practice. Besides her spin class, Nia didn't have much, and she could feel herself spiraling. She had the moms on the TTC board. But they were all so far away. In some ways, they weren't real. And this was her first miscarriage. Some of those moms had had five or more. *How much can I really complain to them?*

That was how she ended up at the audition.

Nia parked her Audi S8 in the lot and made her way upstairs. Nine in the Mirror was based in London, but Duncan's email said they wanted American models for the autumn rollout. She checked in at the desk and was taken to makeup right away. Nia had forgotten how stressful shoots were, especially audition shoots. The constant weighing and measuring of the girls beside her or in the opposite mirrors kept thoughts of her every flaw whirring in her brain. Maybe they wouldn't choose her because she was Hispanic. Maybe they wanted an "American" looking model—taller, blond, blue-eyed.

It had been a long time since she'd gone to an audition and not been selected. *Am I washed up now? Too old?*

She hadn't told Penelope or Lotus about the audition. She hadn't told Edward, either, maybe because she wasn't sure she'd get it or maybe because it wasn't the best idea. *Too late now.*

The bright lights of the dressing-room mirror shone in her face as the makeup artist brushed her skin with the soft bristles. After hair and makeup, they dressed her in a black Alexander Wang A-line skirt that retailed for 475 pounds. It had a comfortable waistline that was supposed to be slimming. The stylist added a jacket. Wang's New York-based line was familiar, though she had never modeled it before. She liked the modern, sporty look and was happy with the way her outfit came together.

Nia was headed toward the photographers when the sound of her name made her turn around.

"Nia! How are you?" Kate. Tall, gaunt cheeked, as thin as a reed, and gorgeous as ever. "I didn't know you were expecting!" Kate swung her belly out in front of her, thin everywhere except her middle. "Congratulations!" She kissed Nia on the cheek. "You look amazing."

It was a thing they said to each other. Even if Nia didn't look amazing, Kate's enthusiasm might convince her that she did. "Wow, Kate, you too. Congrats."

Kate beamed. "I'm thirty-two weeks already. How far are you?"

"I'm here for the first trimester-postbaby crossover line." *How far along? Am I supposed to answer that?*

"I'm having a girl. You?" Kate pressed on as if the baby inside her had consumed her and everything they had in common was their babies.

Luckily, Kate was too self-centered to notice that Nia had dodged the question. Nia smiled, plastering on the social facade she'd perfected. "Too early to say." It was the best she could do. Completely dodging two in a row would surely give her away.

Women streamed down the hallway. Some with tiny bumps, others leading with their belly, centered on long, thin frames. Everywhere around her, mothers hovered, moved past, and mocked her because they all had babies. Everyone but her.

"I didn't realize you were still working. I thought you'd given it all up."

Nia shrugged. "I don't take very many jobs these days, but I never close doors. This one felt like a good fit for me."

Kate gestured to her outfit. "Plus, aren't these cute? I see why they started the line." In her pale-blue maternity dress with flutter sleeves, Kate had an elegant, ladylike aesthetic.

"Who are you wearing?" Nia asked.

Kate smirked. "Valentino." She was the same as ever.

Great. Valentino. They had put Nia in a five-hundred-dollar skirt and Kate in a five-thousand-dollar dress.

"I'd better get to the photographers," Nia said, trying to excuse herself from Kate.

Why did I even come? For an ego boost? To prove to myself that I have something in my life besides Edward and a miscarriage? She should have told Duncan no.

It wasn't just Kate. It wasn't that Nia hadn't been in front of the lens in a while or touched base with her former life and all that it represented for her. The problem was the swarm of pregnant women. All of them had something in common with each other that Nia did not—they were all going to be mothers soon. Nia felt the lie on her face, crawling on her skin, her flat stomach a reminder that she was missing everything they had. She realized too late that her breath was coming fast, and the edges of her vision had darkened. She had one hand on the wall just before it went black.

Chapter 38

Lotus turned the corner onto Euclid, Jagannath by her side as they walked the half mile to the Lotus Garden. "And you didn't see him actually do anything?"

"I mean, it was bad enough having to follow him into the restroom that one time."

"Maybe I don't need confirmation before I confront him. Maybe I should just ask."

Jagannath shrugged. "I'm surprised you haven't already, but I'm not sure you're going to get what you want that way."

"If he lies to me, I've got no way to bust him. Then I'm faced with making a decision based on a gut feeling or allowing this to continue and alerting him that I'm suspicious."

"It's a no-win situation." Jagannath stopped on the sidewalk, and Lotus abruptly stopped next to him. He reached out and grabbed her hand. "I'm sincerely sorry you are dealing with this." He shook his head. "It's not fair to you or the baby. I wish I could do something."

A flutter of excitement surprised Lotus. She was devastated and starting to feel like her marriage was ending. And in the midst of it, there was Jagannath. Supportive. Empathetic. Available. By the rules of their marriage, she was free to date whomever she wanted, but she hadn't imagined it happening quite like this.

She swallowed. "I appreciate it. It means a lot to me that you're here now. I feel like you've come into our lives right now for a reason."

He squeezed her hand. "I do too."

They dropped hands and started back on their walk. Lotus looked straight ahead. Maybe it would help if he knew the whole story. Without making eye contact, she could probably tell it.

"My brother died of a drug overdose."

"Oh, Lotus," he said.

She nodded, forcing herself to continue. "He was nineteen. I'm only eighteen months older. I was the one who found him."

She choked on the last sentence and tried to swallow. She tried to breathe. It wasn't something she talked about. Not to anyone. She strained to tell the rest.

"Our grandfather had taken us on a trip. I was just barely old enough to drink, so I was partaking and sharing with Stone. He'd already been using for a couple of years by then, so he didn't care much for the alcohol because he was high most of the time. My grandpa let us go out to a party. I mean, New Orleans—we were nineteen and barely twenty-one. But we were adults. We got separated, and I ended up... well, it doesn't matter. I ended up making the kind of choices we all regret at that age. He was already back in the hotel room by the time I got home at four in the morning. Grandpa was asleep in the room next door. But Stone was there. Lying back on the bed, the needle still in his vein."

She let the tears go. It never got easier. There were days her grief was muted, and there were days it pained her just as much as the day she'd found him.

"I just thought he was passed out at first. But no. That was it."

Jagannath placed a hand on her back and held it there gently. "Lotus. I am so sorry you had to go through that. And I'm even more sorry that you're dealing with Rob right now too."

"I won't do it again. I can't. And everyone blamed my grandfather. Dad stopped talking to him completely. All his children did. They blamed him for taking us there. For not monitoring us more closely. It wasn't his fault."

"I know," Jagannath said. "And it wasn't your fault either."

She let the hot tears streak her face then stopped again on the sidewalk and faced Jagannath. "Thank you for listening." She put her arms around him and sank into his chest.

He wrapped her into a firm embrace and held her there. "We're going to figure this out. I'm not going to let that happen to you again." He said it with such conviction that she almost believed him.

But what control does anyone exert over another person's life and its direction? The scene of Stone lying dead on that hotel mattress would forever be burned into her mind. Sometimes, she'd watch old videos or get out his pictures to try to replace that image with an older, clean version of Stone. She thought of the one of him at fifteen when he'd tried the '80s-punk fashion look. Or the one from his ten-year birthday with the cake all over his face. She couldn't think of that picture without smiling. But she hated that her memories had been replaced with photographs and videos. She didn't want him to fade.

"I won't let it happen. Not to Blaze and not to this one either." She put a hand on her abdomen. "I can't."

"I know," Jagannath said.

The ten-minute walk to the store had turned into more than a half hour with their stopping and her crying. But by the time they arrived, her step felt lighter. Jagannath had taken some of the burden from her. She needed someone to understand. She needed someone to help her fix this.

Chapter 39

Nia looked up as Penelope approached the table. She wasn't wearing the outfit she'd adopted as her pregnancy uniform—a baggy old T-shirt two sizes too big and too tight in the middle of Penelope's expanding waistline. Instead, she wore a maternity top that hugged beneath her breasts and showed off her pregnant belly. Nia hadn't thought she owned any maternity clothes. Penelope's blond hair was pulled into a messy bun, and she didn't have any makeup on. Dark circles beneath her eyes told Nia she had just come off a string of night shifts.

"Rough week?" Nia asked.

Penelope nodded. She sat, unfolded her napkin, and took a sip of water.

"Anything you want to talk about?" Lotus asked. She had her long dark hair pulled back into a loose, thick ponytail and her signature thick fabric headband around her temples. Lotus wore eye makeup, but it was subtle and natural looking.

"Not really," Penelope said. "What's new with you guys?"

"Lotus was just filling me in about her new best friend." Nia smiled, shooting a look at Lotus.

Penelope raised an eyebrow.

Lotus pressed her lips together as if she were offended, but her eyes said she was amused.

"New best friend? Do tell," Penelope said.

"I was just telling Nia how helpful Jagannath has been. With Blaze, with the store." Lotus ran a hand through her hair, fingering it. "With me."

Nia was glad Lotus had someone helpful to rely on besides Rob, who was proving to be a real pain in the ass. She glanced at Penelope to see her reaction, but there was a far-off look in Penelope's eyes.

Nia met Lotus's gaze. She wasn't sure if Lotus had shared her suspicions about the drugs with Penelope.

"It's weird. I've started to form a friendship with Jagannath. He told me about their breakup. More and more, I don't think he's the villain Rob had made him out to be. Then the other night, he went with Rob to the X because I've been wondering if Rob's been using again."

"Oh fuck," Penelope said.

Nia looked between the two women, and something told her there was more to the story.

"I can't believe I'm going to share this story twice in the same week. I never talk about it." Lotus sighed, a look of resignation on her face. She launched into a story about her brother, who'd gotten involved with drugs and overdosed. Nia was horrified.

Penelope reached across the table and held Lotus's hand. "Yet another reason not to talk to my fucked-up mother. We got a much different version of the story at the time it happened. I had no idea, Lotus."

"Everyone was pissed at me for sticking up for Grandpa. And even more pissed when he left me everything."

"I was never close to Frank. It didn't bother me," Penelope said.

Nia barely had the family tree figured out. But the scandal was a familiar story. Penelope had given her some background on it before she met Lotus for the first time.

"So, you still don't know if he's using?" Nia asked. "Jagannath didn't find anything out at the club?"

Lotus shook her head. "Not yet. I'm trying to bide my time. If he's using... I don't know. It might be over. I just can't. I can't do this again. Not to myself. Not to our kids." Her face clouded over then cleared when Nia met her eyes.

"I'm sorry you're dealing with this. It must be so stressful," Nia said, knowing she wasn't the best at showing empathy. It wasn't modeled for her very often. But she tried.

"You're going to have to catch him using," Penelope said quietly. "I know that sounds awful, but it's the only way to know for sure."

"I know," Lotus said. "I've been considering that. I'm also thinking about just asking him to move out. I don't know."

"But you might need confirmation if you have to advocate for the kids. And visitation. I get it. I'd want to cut him loose too," Penelope said.

"I know. I just feel like I have to be sure."

"You let people walk on you, Lotus, and you can't let this one go. Rob has been taking advantage of you for years. When is enough going to be enough?"

"Penelope—" Nia said.

Lotus held up a hand. "No, she's right. Enough is enough." There was a look of determination on her face as if a decision had been made.

Nia wasn't convinced, but she sensed the conversation was over, so she changed the subject. "I passed out at a photo shoot."

Penelope and Lotus talked over each other, asking questions and reacting to Nia's news.

"It was nothing. I hadn't eaten," Nia said, embarrassed. "I just got a little overwhelmed and lightheaded." *And I couldn't bear the thought of being a total fake in a room full of pregnant women.* But she couldn't say that in front of her two pregnant friends. She offered them a reassuring smile. "I'm fine."

"Since when are you working again?" Penelope asked.

Nia folded her arms. "I can work if I want to. What's the big deal?"

Penelope raised an eyebrow. "I just didn't think that's what you wanted."

Nia looked down at her food. The broccoli had gone cold, and more than half her plate remained untouched. "Well, I can't have what I want right now."

"Oh, Nia," Lotus said. "It'll happen."

Penelope barreled on. "I'm sorry you're not pregnant. I really am. But I worry about you. You got out of the biz because you *hated* it, so I just hate to see you struggling with it again. Why do you need this right now?" She was so much blunter than normal. It was like Penelope's brain had been infected by the placenta. Nia was used to her being fairly direct, but this was a little much.

Nia nodded slowly. "Thanks for your opinion. I'm not going back anyway. It was for a maternity line. And I can't handle being around all those pregnant women right now. Sometimes I wonder how I can be around either of you. Maybe it's a mistake to be around other people. Maybe I should just take some time to myself."

Penelope's mouth dropped open, and Lotus's eyebrows knit.

"I'm sorry you lost your baby," Penelope said. "And I'm sorry you feel like that. But that doesn't mean we're going to go away. I'm your best friend. And from the sound of it, Lotus is sticking close by too. You don't get to shut us out because you're hurt and angry. That's not what friends do."

"Oh, but you get to?" Nia asked.

Ever since Penelope had walked in the door, she'd been off. She was shutting them out. Lotus had revealed her worst nightmare and talked about reliving her brother's death and watching her husband tread the same path. Her marriage was disintegrating, and every detail was out there for the three of them to talk through together. And Nia had chosen to tell them about the modeling flop because they were her best friends. But Penelope hadn't shared anything about her life. Not one word about Penelope had been passed among them.

Penelope looked at her defiantly, saying nothing. Nia met her stare for stare.

"What is it? What are you hiding?" Nia asked. They'd been friends long enough. Once you'd known someone that long, the tells were obvious.

"I didn't want to say anything until I was sure." Penelope fiddled with her napkin.

Nia looked at her. She wasn't going to drop it. "And...?"

"And... I've decided to keep the baby."

Chapter 40

Penelope paused at the stop sign, not long enough to lose her nerve, only long enough to check both ways before turning onto Jasper's street. Both cars loomed in the driveway. They were home. It was time. She parked in the street and got out.

Don't think. Don't think. Don't think. She knew she could talk herself into, or out of, anything. But not this. This thing she had to face head-on.

She hurried up the drive, onto the walkway, and to the front door and knocked without taking a breath. As soon as the sound of her rapping on the door reverberated, she took a deep breath. *Exhale. You have to do this.*

She came to the door. Jessica. Good. Penelope had to talk to both of them. If it were only Jasper, she might have to make a scene. Better for Penelope that she didn't have to force him to involve the wife.

She was much shorter than Penelope and beautiful. Her hair was cropped in a pixie cut, but she had the face to pull it off. She smiled. "May I help you?"

Penelope swallowed and had to look for her voice.

"I... uh... I'm a friend of Jasper's, and I need to talk to you. Both."

Jessica's eyes narrowed, but she didn't appear to guess the totality of the situation yet.

Penelope resisted the urge to look down at her feet or her belly. *Fuck.* This was going to be harder than she thought. Not thinking about it had only worked to get her to the door. *Now what?*

Jessica had already stepped back, opened the door wider, and invited her in. Penelope tried not to think about the bulge that protruded out in front of her, calling attention to the reason she was there. Then again, maybe she wouldn't have to say very much. Maybe she could just point to her belly and let Jasper do the explaining. No. She couldn't trust Jasper—that part was certain.

Jessica invited Penelope to sit and offered her a drink, with her Southern manners, then went to get Jasper. Penelope sat erect on the couch for ten seconds then stood and paced. Maybe she should have talked to Jasper first. Maybe she was going about it all wrong. It was too late now.

The expression on Jasper's face when he entered the formal living room almost made Penelope laugh. She imagined that was the look on her face the first time she saw those two little lines that changed everything. Jasper's equivalent horror flipped her stomach. She wasn't there for revenge. She wasn't there to hurt Jasper. She was only there to do the right thing. And now here they were, in his home, in front of his wife, after Penelope had promised not to involve her.

"What are you doing here?" His tone was quiet and resigned.

He knew exactly what she was doing there. There was only one reason for her to be there, so it had to have been shock that pulled that question from his lips. She wanted to point to her enlarging belly and ask why he was so fucking stupid... but no, she was more sensitive than that. She pitied Jessica in a way. Penelope swallowed back the sick rising in her stomach. She was about to ruin people's lives.

Jessica walked up behind him with a glass of water in her hand and held it out toward Penelope, whose throat was a desert.

"Thank you," she mumbled.

Knees shaking, Penelope decided it might be better to sit and lowered herself back down to the couch with all the grace of a baby elephant. Her ever-changing body didn't boost her confidence, but she pressed on. "Jessica, I know we haven't met. But I'm afraid this involves you too. And I am sorry for what I am about to drop in your lap."

Jessica's eyes grew wider. She wasn't stupid. A *friend* of Jasper's whom she didn't know, showing up at their house, eliciting a horrified response from Jasper... she had to have guessed what that meant.

"What's going on? Jasper?" Jessica turned toward her husband, a look of horror growing on her face.

He looked at his wife with an apologetic and disarming expression. That was the face that had melted Penelope the first time. Jessica turned back to Penelope with what could only be anger.

"Jasper and I had an affair. It's over now. It's been over for months. After it ended, I found out about this." She pointed to her bump.

"Again?" Jessica said in a low, deep tone.

Jasper ignored the question. "I didn't know. She didn't tell me. At first."

"It's true. He only just found out." Penelope turned to Jasper. "What does she mean by 'again'?"

"And the baby is going up for adoption," Jasper added, focusing on Jessica and ignoring Penelope.

Jessica's eyes were tight and her lips pressed together. She looked like she was feeling a tangle of emotions. Penelope had felt them all too. Denial. Anger. Regret. Despair.

"I'm sorry, Jessica. I know that might not mean much coming from me. But that's why I'm here. To tell you the truth, this affects you too." She looked at Jessica and back at Jasper. "I'm keeping the baby."

"What? Why? I thought it was all worked out. I thought you already chose the new family." His deep voice had risen an octave.

It hurt that Jasper just wanted his little problem to go away—he would have been off the hook if the adoption had gone through. And it hurt even more that she would have to see him, deal with him, and let Jessica be the baby's stepmother.

Before Penelope could answer, Jessica turned on Jasper. "What? You don't even want your child? You just want to put this baby up for adoption and never see him—or her?"

"It's a girl." Penelope swallowed and blushed. She hadn't told Jasper it was a girl.

"It's a girl," Jessica repeated. "And that's your baby and your responsibility. I can't even look at you right now." Jessica turned to Penelope, the emotion still on her face but her voice was calm. She reached out and grabbed Penelope's hand and squeezed it. "I'm sorry too. I'm sorry you ever got involved with him, and I'm sorry you're having a baby with him."

Penelope could hardly register what had just happened. Jessica was *sorry* that Penelope was going through this and had to deal with it.

Jessica turned back to Jasper. "You promised after the last one that this was not going to happen again. After all the therapy? After everything? And now you got someone pregnant." She stood. "I'm done. I want you out." She folded her arms. "It's over."

"Baby, please." Jasper stood and started begging Jessica to listen to him. To forgive him. To try to understand.

Penelope felt like an intruder listening in on a private conversation. Jasper claimed a sex addiction, and Jessica remained firm that he had been given enough chances. It was jarring to hear a conversation about her that she wasn't really a part of.

Penelope suddenly wanted to leave but didn't think she could get up and go in the middle of it all. She hadn't meant anything to Jasper. She had been part of his addiction. It made so much sense now—if it was even true. This was her life. Penelope was the other woman. She was having a baby with a serial cheater. Sitting on the couch of a woman who felt sorry for her, it dawned on Penelope that Jessica was the lucky one here. At least Jessica could escape the situation. Penelope would have to deal with Jasper for the rest of her life.

Chapter 41

Nia placed the vegetables delicately on the round crystal platter, following the pattern in the picture, with flower-shaped radishes interspersed among the vegetables. It was over the top—she knew that. But she didn't care. She couldn't have her whole family over without preparing something, even if her mother and sister asked her five times each not to go out of her way for them. She and Edward rarely hosted. Between the expensive decor from Japan lining her china hutch and their rowdy nieces and nephews, her and Edward's condo was often passed over in favor of one of the more child-friendly houses. *For the yard. The kids need the yard,* her mom or sister would say.

But this time, everyone had insisted. *We want to come to you. You need to rest. We will do all the work.* It was like she was a piece of kintsugi pottery, delicate and broken. And her family was the gold, coming to fill in the cracks to repair her.

"You sure you're ready for everyone? I know you've been anxious about having them all staring at you, asking questions," Edward said.

"They've all done it individually. Might as well face them as a group." She put the flowers in the vase in the center of the dining room table. "And maybe it will just be ignored if everyone is here."

It, they both knew, was the miscarriage. *It* was her lack of pregnancy, their lack of a baby.

Edward's forehead smoothed as his eyebrows dropped. "Really? You think they're just going to let up? Not really their style, you know."

She turned toward Edward and wrapped her arms around his waist. "I don't need their approval. I don't care what they think. I just need you."

"You cared when you dropped that pamphlet out of your purse. I had to practically shove your mother to get her away from you. I'm sorry they don't approve of the adoption plans."

Ouch. There were so few moments when Edward challenged Nia. It stung a bit. "Well, it's time we tell them that is the plan, because Marianne could call at any time and let us know that our child is ready. We've done everything right. Maybe it was good we lost the baby."

She choked on the word *good*, and a wave of emotion crept up and over her. Her throat tightened.

"I know you don't mean that. If you need to see what happened in that light, I accept it. No one should have to experience what you went through, though."

Nia swallowed and looked up into the dark pools of Edward's eyes. He didn't see their loss as a clinical mishap, like she'd suspected he might. "You're too good, you know that?"

He smiled, his soft eyes gazing down on her. "No, I'm not."

Within the hour, Nia's family spilled into the condo, bringing noise and chatter. One day, Nia wanted it to be like that with her own kids. She wanted a houseful, even if they had to adopt every single one of them. She didn't mind when Ricardo and Andres used the celery sticks as makeshift swords and chased each other around the dining room table until Miguel intervened. She smiled at her sister and sister-in-law when their girls, Maria and Isabel, came out of her bedroom holding her diamond drop earrings, one over each of their tiny lobes, and asking everyone if they looked like princesses. Ana Sofia giggled and said they most definitely looked like princesses.

Miguel's wife flushed and said Isabel's name like a curse. "No, give that back."

"It's fine. They're having fun," Nia said. Then she realized it might have looked like she didn't treasure the expensive earrings. Another thing to create a divide between the women.

But she didn't care. It *was* fine. At least they were there, playing, giggling, and trying on the earrings. The silence of the days following her miscarriage and the stupid decision to model again were all washed away by the noise and laughter.

The dinner felt eerily familiar, like the one during which they'd had to announce her pregnancy. But that announcement had been met with praise and congratulations—and was anticlimactic, since her mother had already known. Nia knew how her mother felt about them having a baby that was *not their blood*, but that wouldn't change her mind. She and Edward had started the journey before she had known she was pregnant. Even after she'd become pregnant, they'd never put the brakes on the adoption. This time, the call was going to come, and they would have a baby. It wouldn't be Hispanic like her mother wanted. It wouldn't be partially Japanese, like Edward. But it would be *their* baby.

Mamá had brought another lidded bowl of sancocho with her on this visit. But she didn't serve it for dinner. Instead, she placed it in the freezer, took over Nia's kitchen, lightly fried salmon fillets, and served them alongside a green salad. She said the fat in the salmon would help Nia heal. Nia poked at the thick fillet, waiting for the right moment to drop their news. The room grew quiet as everyone focused on eating.

"We're adopting a baby," Edward blurted into the silence.

Nia could feel her eyes bulging. She looked over at him, incredulous, and he shrugged.

"Is this because you lost your baby? You can try for another," her mother said.

"No, Mamá, it's not because of that," Nia said, surprising herself with her quick response. "We started on adoption before we ever tried the IVF."

"But you want to take someone else's baby?" her mother asked, the skepticism and judgment heavy in her voice.

Nia could feel her emotions, already at the surface, threatening to bubble over.

"Enough, Mamá," Miguel said in a tone of dangerous solemnity. Nia turned to her brother, surprised.

"No more. Any baby that Nia brings into her home and raises will be a Menendez." He glanced at Edward. "And a Simmons too."

"I just—"

"No, Mamá. No more. We support them, and that is the end of it. I don't want to hear about this baby not being *our blood* anymore." His tone had a finality that ended the conversation.

Mamá's mouth hung open, the sag around her chin exaggerated by her expression. Nia held her breath, waiting for Mamá to admonish them all. Slowly, she closed her mouth and let the silence hang in the air. Tears welled in Nia's eyes. Edward reached under the table and squeezed her hand.

After the uncomfortable dinner, made only slightly better by Hunter's anecdotes of their trip to Cancun, Mamá retreated to the open air of the balcony by herself. She stood, arms crossed, facing the city-in-miniature view off the balcony.

"Thank you," Nia said to Miguel in a breathless whisper. Although he'd stepped up in a lot of ways since Papa died, he'd never defended her so ferociously and wholeheartedly.

"No problemo, sis. The authority of the patriarchy has to earn me some power, right?"

She smacked him playfully on the arm. "Very funny." It felt good to smile. "I don't understand her. She sees Ricardo as the most important grandchild anyway. Because he has your name and he's the eldest boy. So why all the fuss over adoption?"

"Ignore it. She's just old-school. Family is blood, blah, blah, blah. She'll get over it when she meets your baby," Miguel said.

"How can you be so sure? What if she treats him, or her, differently because of it?"

Miguel's apologetic eyes and reassuring smile didn't do much to comfort her. He knew as well as she did that their mother might *not* come around. There was a stigma on children who weren't part of the line of proud, strapping Menendez boys. There was something *less* about being a girl. It had seeped into her as a child. She knew she'd had fewer advantages than her brother.

"I'll be here. I'll be around. She accepts my authority now in place of Papa. We'll make it right." It was the best he could offer, and they both knew it.

Chapter 42

Keeping the baby meant Penelope had a limited amount of time to prepare for it—physically and mentally. It also meant fighting down the doubts that sprang into her mind to tell her she was ill-equipped for this job. Even if the last time she'd spoken to her mother hadn't been disastrous, she still would have called Grandma Hattie first to give her the news if she'd been alive. Her heart ached with the loss of her grandmother, the only death she'd ever really known besides her cousin Stone, whom she wasn't close to.

She remembered the weekend she'd returned to Watkinsville for Grandma Hattie's funeral like it was yesterday. The memory was seared into her soul. She'd parked in the long driveway that led up to Aunt Rose's house and killed the engine. She clutched and released the steering wheel, concentrating on slowing the beat of her heart and calming her stuttering breath.

It's only one weekend. I'll get to see my cousins. It's not going to be that bad.

One of those sentences was a lie.

Aunt Rose opened the door, a wide grin spreading on her dimpled face. She looked surprised. Not because Penelope was at the door but because ever since her facelift, her eyebrows rose in a constant expression of astonishment. Their exaggerated shape reminded Penelope of the McDonald's arches.

"Penelope, you made it," Aunt Rose said quietly.

A twist in Penelope's stomach confirmed that she had, indeed, made it *home*. Though it didn't take much effort *not* to think of this as home anymore. They hugged, wrapping their arms around each other, and Penelope gave her a genuine squeeze. She adored Aunt Rose, which made her feel shitty for fixating on her bizarre eyebrows.

"Who's here so far?" Penelope asked, bracing for the answer.

"Not your mother." Leave it to Rose to cut right to the quick. "Just Roger and the *California cousins*, as y'all like to say. What time does your brother get in?"

"I texted him, but I haven't talked to him. Sounds like he isn't coming until tomorrow." She struggled to keep her tone light, to hide her irritation at Elliot. It was hard enough to deal with the family, especially Mom, and he was probably avoiding it as much as possible by being on the last flight in and the first flight out.

"Come, get settled. I put you upstairs next to Lotus and Rob. Have you met Rob?"

Penelope shook her head. She'd had coffee a couple of times with Lotus since she'd settled in the city but hadn't been to her house yet or met the guy.

Aunt Rose took Penelope's hand and dragged her through the modern farmhouse. Her home invoked a mixture of fond memories and horrifying moments. They passed the formal living room, and Penelope looked at the empty corner where a Christmas tree had stood in 1993. They went up the stairs, and as she reached the landing, she remembered lying there on beanbags, reading comics with her cousins, one holiday. Aunt Rose led her to her room for the weekend, and Penelope stared out the back window at the acreage of backyard that extended all the way past the horse barn and pecan trees. Her gaze rested on the woods where she'd fled that year Mom blacked out and called her a bitch in front of the whole family.

She set her duffle bag on the quilted blanket and turned to Aunt Rose. "Thank you."

"I'm just glad you came. There was a moment when I thought you might not."

"I don't care how awful Mom is and what has transpired between us. I wouldn't miss Gram's funeral for the world."

What Penelope couldn't understand was why they were having the funeral and internment in Watkinsville and not in Palm Coast.

Hattie had not been a traditionalist. Often, she would tell stories about "women my age" and launch into something to remind everyone that she was not like those women. "Women my age got married in a time when divorce just didn't happen. They stayed, no matter how unhappy they were. Well, not me." Or "Women my age didn't go to college in droves like you all do. Only progressive women made that choice."

Yet for her final resting place, she'd chosen to lie next to her ex-husband, Frank, a man she'd pretended to despise, whom she was ecstatic to have outlived even if only by a couple of years. Rumor had it that she'd simply forgotten to change the documentation that outlined her wishes for the afterlife. Penelope didn't think that sounded very likely and, deep down, believed Gram had wanted to be buried with Grandpa on the family plot.

She made her way into the kitchen and saw her cousin Lotus. Her pixie cut had grown shaggy since she'd seen her last, but Lotus looked happy, or as happy as she could, considering the circumstances of their reunion. They touched fingers but didn't hug. They reconnected while walking toward the wood line at the back of the property.

It didn't take long before Lotus had plunged neck-deep into the murky end of the conversation. "Things still weird between you and Aunt Ruthie?"

Penelope glanced at her cousin. She should have known Lotus wouldn't beat around the bush. "Nope. Not for me."

Lotus gave a tinkling laugh that came off as a bit nervous.

"How about you?" Penelope asked. "You probably haven't seen some of these people since Grandpa's funeral. Anyone giving you shit about the inheritance?"

She shrugged and looked down for a bit as they walked, the evening light filtering in through the trees above. There were plenty of places on the property to hide from the family dysfunction.

"It's not your fault Frank left everything to you," Penelope said.

"You seriously still calling him Frank?"

Penelope shrugged. "I didn't know him like you did. My mom was too scared he'd see through her bullshit."

"You're right. I had to decide to ignore everyone's opinion on the will to move out here and live in the house."

"I'm glad you did. We probably wouldn't even talk if you hadn't made the move to Atlanta." Having Lotus close by made Penelope feel like she had a family again. She'd become more and more estranged from them since Elliot had moved to Denver. "So, this Rob thing is getting serious?"

Lotus nodded. "I think so. We might even get married."

"Wow. I thought you said he didn't believe in that sort of thing."

"We have to have something stable if we're going to add kids to the mix. It's on the table—that's all." Lotus shrugged like she didn't care one way or the other, but it was pretty clear that she did.

They reached the end of the trail at Porter's Creek, which touched the back of Aunt Rose's property line and reached all the way to the Oconee River. "Remember when we used to tube down the Oconee? And jump off the trestle bridge? God, I used to love the big yellow house with the weeping willow."

"You miss her?" Lotus asked.

Penelope nodded, feeling the emotion her question stirred. "Terribly."

***

The family alternated between calling it a wake and a viewing. But the casket stood open, and Grandma Hattie wasn't Catholic, so Penelope settled on *a viewing*. Gram would have loved the look of horror on some people's faces at seeing her dead body. Her skin had a plastic sheen, but her makeup was perfect, just like during her life. The mortician must have had a good picture to copy her makeup so accurately. Except Penelope was sure there was no lipstick stain on Hattie's teeth that day. She was dressed in a blush Chanel pantsuit reminiscent of her daily wear, though Penelope didn't recognize the outfit. Knowing her, it was possible she'd bought it in advance and saved it for the funeral.

It was hard to look at her. Gram's eyelids were permanently closed and precision lined with liquid eyeliner. Her lips were pressed together, hiding her infamous snaggle tooth. Uncle Roger stood by the foot of the casket, six foot five and crying quietly into his big hands. Lotus lingered near him, her gaze darting like she was looking for an escape.

"Can I talk to you?" Penelope asked.

Lotus gave a grateful nod, patted her dad on the back, and walked away with Penelope. "What's up?"

"Nothing. You just looked like you needed my help."

Lotus shivered, and her shoulders shook visibly. "I just hate the open casket. I mean, she's not *there*. It's not her. She's not in her body anymore." She stopped talking and searched Penelope's face.

Penelope might not have held the same beliefs as Lotus, but she didn't disagree with her, so she let it go. There was no harm in Lotus's speculation on the body-soul-whatever that she believed in. "You don't have to stand in there if you don't want."

"I didn't feel like I could walk away from Dad." Lotus looked down at her sandaled feet kissed by her wide brown skirt. "I'm all he has now."

Penelope reached over and rubbed her back, not sure if it was the right thing to do, but could only think of what Lotus had not mentioned—her brother. *How many funerals does a twentysomething typically attend?* There had been too many in the last handful of years, that was for sure, between Stone, Grandpa Frank, and now Gram.

Penelope's brother, Elliot, strolled over, wearing a custom-tailored suit. A black button-up shirt with no tie hid partially under the jacket, which had a subtle sheen that made it look silver instead of gray. Her years apart from him had changed him into a man Penelope barely recognized. He was not the boy who'd put glue in his hair to get it to stand on end in his mimicry of Sid Vicious.

"Ladies? Am I interrupting?" Although he looked smooth, he was still Elliot, still her little brother.

"No. We had to get out of there."

"Kind of gruesome, isn't it?"

Penelope gave him a light punch on the shoulder. "Don't say that."

But Lotus smiled at him gratefully and laughed. "No, he's right. It is."

Penelope, Lotus and Elliot chatted in the corner, almost achieving a defensive huddle. But as guests filtered in and out and offered condolences, the trio smiled and shook hands, never forgetting their Southern manners. Hattie would have been proud. *I wish I could be anywhere else but here.* As soon as Penelope thought it, guilt washed over her. Saying goodbye to Grandma Hattie mattered, but this event—with people she'd known in her youth, those who felt obligated to attend, and family members she'd rather not see—felt uncomfortable.

And then Mom ended up in the same room as Penelope. She pressed her thin lips together tightly in her perpetual look of disdain for the whole world. Or maybe it was just for her daughter. "Penelope, how are you?"

"Fine."

She gave Penelope a shoulder squeeze, almost like she was attempting an effort at hugging but couldn't quite bring herself to do it. "Rose needs someone to go back to the house and start the casseroles and dinner prep. She's planning to feed the extended family. I told her I'd ask you."

Mom carefully avoided asking for herself by pretending to be the messenger. And she avoided saying *she* had suggested Penelope for the job. But Penelope had played this game too many times to be fooled.

"Sure." Penelope wouldn't give her the satisfaction of knowing she was flustered.

One of Mom's eyebrows rose. "Thank you." Her words sounded forced.

"No problem. By the way, I wanted to ask you if I can have the knit dolls. The ones Gram made me. I left all that when I moved out."

"I know," her mom said, only acknowledging the last of what Penelope said.

Penelope waited for the answer, refusing to ask again. She mirrored her mother's eyebrow of skepticism.

Mom pressed her already flat lips together. "That's fine. Come by and get them."

Even though they would see each other at the funeral and would be together at Aunt Rose's the next day—even though the dolls belonged to Penelope, and she hadn't asked for anything of Mom's or Hattie's—somehow, Penelope had agreed to go by her mother's place in Athens to get the dolls. Gram was dead, and Penelope didn't care about her jewelry or her money or anything else she owned. Every year, on Penelope's birthday, her grandmother had given her a special handmade knit animal. Gram was the one who had taught Penelope to knit. No matter how old she got, she'd always looked forward to her annual handmade gift. The mouse. The lion. The octopus.

Lotus, Elliot, and Penelope were the first of the family to leave. Once Penelope told them she was leaving early for dinner prep, the other two jumped at the opportunity to join her and get away from smiling at guests. Anything to avoid the room where Grandma Hattie lay still and frozen.

Chapter 43

Lotus faced away from the middle of the bed and concentrated on making her breathing even and believably sleeplike as Rob fumbled in the dark room, his belt buckle clanking as he stripped off his jeans, oblivious to how much noise he made. She peeked at the clock on her side table. It was 4:05 a.m.

She didn't trust herself to deal with him at the late hour. Enough was enough. A loud thud startled her. A soft, deep giggle emanated from the floor on his side of the bed. Lotus imagined him twisted in his jeans, down on his ass on the floor, unable to figure out how to extricate himself.

His weight on the mattress shifted her, and she forced herself to remain still, her body pillow clutched between her knees, the weight of her belly pulling her into the bed. She was going to have to tell Rob the truth. This was not the life she wanted. *When did I stray so far away from my plans? When did he?* If she was honest with herself, her change of heart was triggered by more than the suspicion that he was using. She wasn't in love with him anymore.

The change had been subtle, an evolution that occurred gradually and accidentally. His attention had turned away from her, and hers had done the same, until they were living together, circling each other with their own lives and own plans but not coming into each other's orbit often enough. She began to resent him. He pulled away from her and found girlfriend after boyfriend to keep him occupied. She felt annoyance at his boyish, carefree attitude, which she'd used to admire. She'd made excuses for his daily pot smoking and ignored all the nights out and late returns. And finally, she was here, cringing as he stumbled in from a club, high and drunk, having difficulty finding his place in their king-sized bed. If she was honest with herself, she'd become emotionally closer to Jagannath in the past months than her own husband.

The dim light from Rob's phone cast an eerie glow from his side of the bed. Lotus closed her eyes and pretended it wasn't there. But she could feel a tightness in her chest that would not let up. Rob's hands found her and caressed her tight, turned-away shoulder. At first, she was repulsed. *Why didn't he go home with someone else?*

"I know you're awake," he said quietly.

"So?"

"So, what's the deal? You've been really cold to me."

"You think four in the morning is the time for this conversation?" She flopped over without a shred of grace and faced him.

"I think you're holding back, and it's starting to turn into resentment."

"Starting to?" She couldn't keep the disgust out of her voice.

"If you have a problem, you're supposed to talk to me about it. That's what you do in a marriage."

Lotus threw the covers aside and sat up. "Oh, *that's* what you do in a marriage? By your example, I thought you were supposed to ignore your son, get high, fuck anything that walks, and leave all the responsibilities for someone else." The tightness in her chest lifted. It was out, and there was no putting it back.

"How long have you been feeling this way?" he asked so quietly she barely heard him through the pounding in her ears.

"How long?" she said, her voice rising. "Well, let's see. How long have you been doing that shit? Oh, since Blaze was born. Grow the fuck up. I'm done having a man-child as a partner. I don't need another mouth to feed and ass to wipe."

She stood. The thought of staying in bed with him or sleeping at all was completely out of reach. It was over. She'd finally stopped holding it all in and told the truth. She didn't love him anymore.

Lotus knew she had to say more. He didn't get it. But the danger of crossing into the territory of the drugs and her real suspicions was choked off in her throat. She stomped out of the room and down the stairs, her feet slapping on the hardwood floor.

This wasn't the Appalachian Trail anymore. This was her real life. *How did things get this bad?* She thought of their first time together, on the zero day in Tennessee, and the trail time that followed. She thought of getting her trail name and how she'd embodied that name for too long.

The morning after the zero day they'd spent in Erwin with Jason, she and Rob had hiked together as usual. The other hikers must have known what had passed between them, but she held her tongue from confessing. She didn't need to ask for permission or approval. They were adults—sort of.

Rob stopped pitching his own tent at night and instead slept in hers. She worried the rest of the bubble might want to break off from them as they fucked their way through the Appalachian Trail. But they stayed, taking zero days together and ignoring their perma-grins.

The new relationship was more than sex, though. There was an intimacy and passion to it—a connection without a label coupled with the intensity of the AT. They went unwashed for a week at a time, having dirty sex and no actual dates—not exactly the way most couples started off. In the six-by-four tent, they had their first argument when a knee connected with a temple. It was hard to believe they'd been able to keep up the sex pace of a fresh couple. But by that point, after more than three hundred miles of trail, they'd grown hiking legs and somehow still had energy at night.

On a rainy evening in the shelter, HotMama shucked off her rain pants and called Lotus over to look at her calf. The left one was red and swollen.

Lotus put two fingers on the tender spot. Warm. "This does not look good. How much pain are you in? Guys, come look at this."

She waved over Rob and Banana Split to look at HotMama's calf. When they'd gathered, a look of sadness eclipsed Rob's face.

Banana Split's eyes widened. "That's messed up."

"No shit. I think we need to get her off the trail," Lotus said.

"Take a couple zero days?" HotMama asked.

Rob shook his head. "No. This looks like a blood clot. My uncle had one. This needs to be looked at."

"I can take her," Lotus said. "Can you walk?"

"I stumbled the last bit," HotMama said. "But I think it's gotten worse. I wish I could ice it and see."

Rob shook his head again. "We'll carry you if we have to. But you need to get off the trail tonight. Blood clots can be serious."

Banana Split was already two glasses into the moonshine, and his words blurred together as he offered to help. "I can carry her too."

"You stay here," Rob said. "We can take her. I've got her if you can get her gear."

Lotus turned her phone on to find a bit of battery life. "I'll get a shuttle service."

After three phone calls and a shuttle ride, they arrived in the emergency room. The ER confirmed the clot. They gave their tearful goodbyes. The bubble was down to three.

That night in the shelter, Lotus curled against the wall in the space where she'd left her pack.

"You've gone a long time on this trail without a trail name," Rob said.

"I know." She rolled toward him. "Banana Split still alternates between calling me Patchouli, Lasso, and TripAdvisor."

"I think I finally figured you out."

"Oh?"

"I don't think you have a trail name because you're holding back. It's like we don't really know you yet. I mean, you hang your own bear bag and won't let anyone help you. But you sleep by the wall in the path of the mouse track. You came up here because your brother died, so you're in mourning. But instead of crying and being depressed, you feel like you have something to prove—maybe just to yourself. You're independent. And somehow, you still wanted a bubble. Am I getting it right?"

She considered how Rob had just put a finger inside her wound. "Maybe. But I don't see how it translates into a trail name."

"You're a cool chick, you know that? And now that we're close, I'm just wondering why you haven't opened up more."

Stone had died, and she'd shared about that. But Rob dug into the wound, like a child plucking at a scab, forcing it away from the healed edges, prying at it until the bleeding began again.

"What do you want me to say?" she pleaded. Then she picked up speed. "That I'm here because my brother overdosed?" Heat rose in her chest. "That I found him dead in a hotel room with a needle still in his veins? Does that make you feel better? You feel closer to me now?" The words spilled out and, with them, tears. She sat up, throwing her bedroll aside. "You want to hear about how I left my brother alone in New Orleans to get laid and how he would still be alive today if I hadn't?"

She had to get out of the shelter. Rain pounded on the roof as she opened the door and went out. The water assaulted her body, pelting her dry pajamas and slicking her disheveled hair. Lotus opened her arms, and the rain soaked her through. She had tried to escape, but she couldn't run far enough to get her away from the truth.

When her shirt was suctioned to her body, clutching like a second skin, and she was numb to the rain, a light emerged from the shelter. He was a silhouette framed in the doorway before he stepped into the rain.

"I was not trying to trigger you," Rob said. "I just want to know you. I wanted you to know I see you and I can be here for you."

"What about what I want? I just want to get away from it. I want to stop seeing Stone lying dead every time I close my eyes. I want my brother back."

"I know." Rob looked into her, his deep-brown eyes holding her in place. He was soaked through. "But he's not coming back." The finality of his words felt like a kick in the throat. "When this is over, you'll go back and have to live it without him."

How? She still thought of funny things to tell Stone. She wanted to pick up the phone and call him or sit down together for a beer. She would give everything to hear his voice and laughter for just five minutes. She never forgot that he was dead, but the knowledge always arrived late.

Rob folded around Lotus, pressing against her rain-soaked body, arms snug. If she collapsed, he would hold her in place forever. The rain became syncopated as if it couldn't decide if it wanted to keep on or let up.

He leaned down, his breath on her ear and neck. "I know this is crazy, and we were just having fun. But there's something here, Lotus. When we get off this trail, I want to know you. In real life."

She wanted that, too, so she nodded, her face rubbing against his wet shirt.

He pulled back and squeezed her on the upper arms. "A fresh start?"

She looked at him through a blur of tears. "I'll try."

The rain slackened. Maybe they were between clouds, or maybe it had cleared.

"So, trail name? Too soon?" The disarming smile reappeared.

"Okay, what've you got?" Lotus was relieved to change the subject and gave her best effort at a good-sport smile.

"This is what I say fits you: Atlas. You take on the weight of the world and bear it as if it's your own. I want to help you carry it. But I accept that it is yours to move. What do you say?"

"Atlas. I like it," she'd said.

Lotus sat on the porch swing, wrapped in her favorite thick sweater, taking slow, deep breaths. The early morning was cool before dawn but not cold. She didn't feel like Atlas anymore. The door behind her clicked, and she looked up to see Jagannath coming outside, Morgana on his heels to join them in the backyard.

"You okay?" he asked.

"You heard?"

He shrugged. "You were kind of yelling."

"It's over," she said. "I'm going to ask him to move out. And I know you were his friend when you got here, and that might put you in an awkward place. But you're welcome to stay. This has nothing to do with you."

"May I?" Jagannath asked, pointing at the empty seat on the porch swing.

Lotus nodded, and he sat down beside her.

"I'm sorry your marriage is over," he said.

"I'm sorry I handled it that way. I didn't want to explode like that. I just can't keep tucking it away and tucking it away and thinking it's not going to happen, though. I kept wanting to wait for some definitive evidence. But you know what? My own unhappiness is evidence enough. The drugs—well, *suspected* drugs—were enough to send me over the edge."

"And if he's not using, does that change things?"

Lotus didn't answer right away, pulling the sleeve of her sweater over her hand and then peeling it back. "I don't know. I don't think so."

"I'll stay if you'll have me." Jagannath looked at her in the way that made her feel like he was looking *into* her.

She nodded, the emotions of the night still welling inside her.

"But I have to tell you something that might change things for you. And I'll understand if you want me to leave."

She shook her head. *No. Not now. Not today. Can't he see it's not the time for this?* If her instincts were right, he'd been developing feelings for her, just as she had for him. If they were wrong... well, she didn't know what he might say.

"I think I already know. But can we not have this conversation today? Not now. I just can't."

He put a hand on hers and looked her in the eyes again. He might as well have said it. She could feel it all around him, like an aura. "Okay. Not today."

She wanted to hug him and tell him she had feelings for him. But things were so fucked-up. She couldn't complicate it more. Rob was going to have to leave. It was definitely over. Jagannath was going to stay. Something might be beginning.

And the baby. She was still going to have Rob's baby, no matter what happened to their marriage.

Chapter 44

Penelope trudged out of the hospital in the dawning light of the winter morning, spent. She couldn't imagine anything better than soaking her feet then putting them up, stretching on her couch to watch trashy TV while the swelling in her ankles went down. She used to love the night shift, but the pregnancy had worn on her, and the fatigue of a twelve-hour shift left her swollen and exhausted.

As she stepped off the curb in the direction of her car, she heard her name. Penelope turned to see Jasper striding toward her. She bit the inside of her cheek. *Not now.* Things hadn't exactly gone well the last time she'd seen him.

"What do you want, Jasper? I just finished a twelve-hour shift, and I'm not in the mood for you." No point in holding back.

"I want to talk to you. Can I have five minutes? Buy you a coffee?"

She narrowed her eyes at him. "I don't want coffee. I want sleep and to get off these sausages." She gestured to her swollen feet.

"Tea? And ten minutes?"

Tea. Typical Jasper, he offered her coffee first and then remembered she preferred tea. She craved the warmth of the Epsom-salt soak on her poor feet. And then falling asleep in front of *Real Housewives* or maybe *The Bachelor*.

"Please give me a few minutes. I just want to talk." His earnest eyes pleaded with her in a way she'd never seen from him. He didn't mention their last interaction, though, or use it to guilt her into a concession.

If it wasn't so cold in the early morning, she would cross her arms and let him talk right there in the parking lot. But the thought of standing there beside her car, outside the hospital, did not feel inviting. Neither did the idea of going back inside. And considering she'd ruined his marriage during their last interaction, she could probably spare ten minutes. They were having this baby for real, and she'd have to figure out a way to deal with him eventually.

"Okay, ten minutes."

At Tea Leaves and Thyme, she ordered an herbal black tea and sat stiffly in her chair, waiting for it. Though he'd caught her off guard coming from her work shift, she still had to deal with him, probably better than she had in the past. Now that she was sitting, the baby rumbled across her belly. She tended to do that whenever Penelope was still.

"Okay, talk," she urged him. The fatigue that settled in as she left her shift had lifted somewhat.

"I want to be there when the baby is born." The words rushed out of him.

That was not what she'd expected to hear. "Why did you tell my wife like that?" or "Fuck you for ruining my marriage" or maybe even "Please reconsider the adoption"—those were all phrases she could imagine coming from Jasper.

"What?" she asked.

Jasper clutched his coffee cup with both hands, looking into it. "I know I didn't want this baby." He looked up, his shaggy blond hair hanging beside his face. "Frankly, neither did you. But here we are, and I want to be there—at the birth and after. And it's not because my marriage is fucked. Or because I want to get back together with you. I can't change that I cheated on my wife. And I can't change that you fell in love with me." He paused for a second like he might regret that. Then he pressed on. "Neither of us can change the fact that you got pregnant. I'm not here to change your mind about the adoption. So if you're keeping this baby, then *we* are keeping this baby. And I want to be there." He took a sip of his coffee, maybe just to stop himself from talking more.

Penelope narrowed her eyes. She'd been involved with Jasper far too long to think he'd take responsibility and ask for it. *What the hell happened between him and Jessica?* The baby rumbled across her belly again, trying to tuck a foot or something beneath her rib.

"So, you want me to, like, call you when I'm in labor? And you want to be in the room when I deliver?" She couldn't keep the skepticism from her voice.

"Like it or not, I'm going to be a dad. As I see it, I can be a shitty dad, or I can try. I don't have much to go on. But I'm willing to give it a go. I'm sure there are dozens of other men you'd probably rather deal with. But you've got me. And this is our baby." He looked nervously toward her protruding middle. Even in her scrubs, the lateness of her pregnancy was apparent.

In the room? She swallowed. "I'm going to have to think about it. I mean, this was not what I expected." She'd seen a lot of deliveries and a lot of family dynamics at work, including boyfriends and baby daddies. And it wasn't as if Jasper hadn't seen her naked many, many times.

"Don't get me wrong, Penelope. I'm not happy with the way things went down at my house. I wish I'd had time to consider the news that you were keeping the baby before we told Jessica. Still, I probably deserved that." He took another sip of coffee.

Penelope thought of the look on Jessica's face—how she'd turned the whole thing on Jasper and how irrationally calm she'd been toward Penelope. *A sex addict? Can that really be true?* Penelope doubted it. More Jasper excuses to get away with his typical Jasper behavior. A twinge in her belly told her she'd been stupid enough to buy it all at one time.

"Did she leave you?" Penelope asked.

"Yes." He didn't elaborate.

"You really a sex addict?" Now that the power had shifted to her, and he was asking for favors, she figured she could get away with it.

He shrugged. "I don't know. But you weren't the first, if you want the truth."

The pain of getting over Jasper hadn't completely subsided, and there he was, pouring salt in the wound. She'd just been a fling for him. Another in a line of other women, probably before and after his short-lived marriage. But there were moments of vulnerability, after his aunt died and after he'd saved that kid in the fire, when he'd come to her and shared. That was when she'd fallen in love with him.

She pushed the thoughts aside. No sense in ruminating over what was lost. She knew better than to want a partnership with him. Coparenting was going to be the best they could do.

"Well, this has been awkward," she said. The baby pushed forward, elbowing near her belly button.

"You okay?"

He must have seen the look on her face. She couldn't get used to the person taking up space inside her, pushing around, hiccupping, jabbing her in the ribs, and compressing her bladder.

"Uh, yeah. The baby is moving. I just—can't get used to it."

He raised an eyebrow and looked down at her distended belly. "May I?" There was a hopeful lilt in his voice. "You can say no if you don't want me to." The words rushed out.

She swallowed. There was a strangeness at being asked and considered in a way she never had been when they were together. She considered saying no, keeping a wall between them, forcing Jasper out. She might have to let him into her child's life, but she didn't have to let him into hers. But no. She would rather have an interested father in her child's life than the absent one she had.

"Okay. Right here." She reached across the table, grabbed his calloused hand, and placed it next to her belly button where the last kick had come. "You might have to wait a—"

"Whoa."

The kick of the baby startled them both. Penelope could not get used to it, maybe because she'd spent so much of the pregnancy ignoring the alien changes happening in her body. She had a heightened sense of the being inside her growing, moving, and getting ready to meet her. She held her hand over his for another minute, neither of them talking but both sharing the movements of their baby.

After no kicks came for a bit, he pulled his hand away. "Thank you."

She nodded. "You're welcome."

"And thank you for thinking about it."

Do I really want Jasper in the room, watching me give birth? As they parted, she watched Jasper get into his car. He sat slumped with two hands grasping the steering wheel. He looked less and less like the hottest guy she'd ever been with and more and more like a broken individual.

Maybe there was a chance they could figure out the coparenting thing. Maybe there was a chance that her daughter wouldn't grow up as messed up as Penelope had.

Chapter 45

The complications of Lotus's life had mounted in the past weeks. The store. The growing distance and then the break from Rob. And the stirring that occurred within her when she thought of Jagannath. Even though he hadn't said it aloud, it seemed clear that he'd developed feelings too.

But what am I feeling? That was a puzzle she hadn't quite worked out yet.

Alone at the store on closing shift, Lotus shut down the register, counted the deposit, and did her final check. Rain pounded on the roof. The storm had kept the street and her shop clear for most of the evening.

As she snuffed the last stick of incense, she heard the door bells chime. She looked up to tell the patron they were closed and saw Jagannath standing in the doorway, soaking wet.

Her breath caught. So much for avoiding the situation.

The door shut behind him, muffling the sound of the downpour. He slicked a hand across his bare head, sloughing off fat drops of rain onto the welcome mat. "Hi." His voice was deep and melodious.

"Hi," she repeated quietly.

Her stomach did a flip. Maybe on another day in another place at another time in her life, a man she had all these weird, unsorted feelings for showing up unannounced would have been okay. That day, round with pregnancy, in the midst of a folding marriage and confused about her feelings, she felt ambivalent.

"I want to talk to you." He walked toward her.

"I know."

Jagannath nodded slowly. "So you don't need me to say it?"

"It might be harder if you did."

Maybe she needed to hear it, but she wasn't sure what the point would be. Even if something was stirring, she was about to give birth.

She and Rob were ending, but they still had a family together. It was more than the fact that she was feeling *something* for Jagannath. The timing of all these months of feeling less and less for Rob scared her.

"So that's it? Tell me you don't feel anything for me, and I can pack up and go. But I need to hear it from you. I don't know what happened, but I'm not afraid to say it. I think I love you, Lotus. I don't know how you feel, but if you think there's any chance that what's happening is mutual, then tell me to stay."

Tears sprang up. She was right—it was harder to hear him say it than to leave it unsaid. She wanted to hug him. To tell him she felt something for him too.

"I think you should go." She could barely say the words.

Jagannath looked at her with confusion. He didn't believe her. Maybe he knew she wasn't being entirely honest.

"Tell me, Lotus. Say it. Say you don't love me. Say you don't have any feelings for me at all." He stood his ground, meeting her eyes.

"I... I don't..." She couldn't do it. She didn't mean it.

Jagannath stepped forward and wrapped his arms around her. He touched her cheek gently and then kissed her deeply. Everything inside her stirred and woke. She kissed him back until a sob choked up. She hadn't wanted it to be like this.

She pulled back, feeling salty tears on her lips. "I'm sorry. I can't. My marriage is ending. And I'm not sure if what I feel about you is—"

"Real?" Jagannath ran his hands along her shoulders as he let go. A chill ran through her at his touch. "I know. I'm afraid of that too. I don't want to be your rebound. But I know what I feel is real."

"And this?" She pointed to her pregnant belly. "What about this?"

He shrugged. "I get it. It's complicated. It doesn't change how I feel. I've been over it in my head dozens of times. And if you feel the same—"

"I do." Lotus reached out and grabbed both his hands in hers. "But I need some space for my marriage right now. I've felt it too. I wanted to call it friendship. I wanted to see you as *his* friend, but over time, you became mine. You've really been here for me during these chaotic months with Rob. I appreciate that. I don't want my appreciation for you to cloud my judgment. I have to know these feelings are real and not just here to replace my hurt over Rob."

"I'll wait. I'll be your friend. Do what you have to with your marriage. But as long as you let me, I'm not going anywhere."

She squeezed his hands. "Deal."

Chapter 46

Deciding on a name for her baby had proven to be easier than Penelope expected. Grandma Hattie was Penelope's closest relative before she'd died. Gram would have insisted that she not call the baby Hattie, so Penelope decided to use Gram's middle name, Dolores, instead. She hadn't decided on a first name yet.

After Grandma Hattie's wake, Penelope had pulled the macaroni and cheese out of the oven. Mac and cheese casserole was served like a vegetable in the South. Aunt Rose had everything prepared and labeled in the large second refrigerator in her garage. Penelope set down the deep nine-by-thirteen dish and wiped her forehead with the back of her hand.

"This one's done," Penelope reported to the other helpers.

Elliot was dressing a salad, his silvery jacket discarded over the back of a barstool. He hardly seemed like the same person who'd eaten four bowls of boxed mac and cheese when Penelope used to scrounge up a dinner for him back when they were kids.

"Oh goody. Now if we can just pour some gravy on everything, it'll be like Thanksgiving," Elliot said.

"As if you'd know what Thanksgiving is like anymore. How long has it been since you've come back?"

"Bitch, please," he said with a flourish and a smile. "You know you don't go either. I saw your last Friendsgiving post. You do that just to fuck with her, don't you?"

"And what about you?"

"I avoid the social media she's on. Besides, I really had to work last year."

"Mm-hmm," Penelope said, pressing her lips together. As soon as she realized she was making that tight-mouthed look of perpetual disappointment, she relaxed her face. "I'm not saying I care. I'm saying thanks. You were the one who got me started on skipping out every year."

His face dropped. "Except now you can't go to Palm Coast anymore."

The reason they'd all come together slammed her back into the present. She'd been trying to avoid processing Gram's death while surrounded by her old life. Elliot and Lotus didn't understand what it was like. Penelope had called Gram every week. She'd gone down there when no one else had. She'd played bridge with Gram's best friends. In her mind, she could still see Gram's face shining with pride as Penelope took her first trick. She could still feel the papery velvet of Gram's wrinkled hand as she traced the puffy green veins that had sprouted there. She had run her thumb around the glistening ruby Gram wore in place of wedding and engagement rings. Gram had kept a strong face for so long, only showing her vulnerability at the end of her life. Penelope was still haunted by the memory of Gram's mask cracking as death came for her.

Dinner included a great-aunt Penelope had only met twice in her life. Gertie told stories of Hattie as a young woman and promised to bring pictures the next day, the ones of Hattie at the lake, Hattie as a scrawny gazelle-like teen, and Hattie with Thomas, the man she'd almost married. Penelope couldn't help entertaining the idea that things might have been different if Thomas had been her grandfather and not Frank.

Though Penelope was sitting almost as far as she could from her mother, she watched her at the other end of the table, tipping back a glass of white wine like an amateur marathoner, taking gulps instead of sips. It never ended well. Penelope needed to leave. It felt like the layer of fascia beneath her skin was rippling and had a mind of its own, as if a feeling from deep within was trying to get out but the rest of her was stopping it. Penelope tried to shove it away. That same feeling had moved through her the time she told her mother she hated her. It had crawled over her when she decided she was moving out and never wanted to speak to her mother again. And she'd had it the night Mom had that party in the house and Penelope had snuck out, not in defiance but as a way to protect herself from the strangers who might try to crawl into any bed. When the feeling persisted, she knew something was going to burst forth, something she wouldn't be able to put back.

Penelope stood. "I'm not feeling so well. I'm sorry to excuse myself."

Aunt Rose didn't protest but instead nodded in support. Uncle Roger didn't look up from his plate.

Penelope escaped the ornate dining room, pushing the swinging farm door, and stepped into the kitchen, searching for a moment to breathe. *What would happen if I just got in the car and drove away, off to Palm Coast—forgot this funeral and celebrated with Gram's real friends?*

The door swung, and she turned to find Lotus. "Can I make you some tea?" her cousin offered.

Penelope shrugged. "I think I just want to lie down."

But it was a lie. She wanted to run until her legs collapsed beneath her, plummeting to the dirt in the woods behind Aunt Rose's house, lying on roots and leaves and twigs on the forest floor and pressing her face into the cool earth.

Lotus nodded. "I saw her drinking."

Lotus and Penelope had never talked about Mom's drinking. No one in the family admitted she was an alcoholic because then they would have to deal with it. The silence stretched. Lotus looked Penelope in the face in a refusal to observe how uncomfortable the whole thing had become.

"She can do whatever she wants. But I don't want to sit around for it when she starts dishing it out."

Lotus nodded.

"I just can't ignore it like everyone else. I lived with it. I know how this ends."

"So do I," Lotus said quietly. She crossed the kitchen and took Penelope's hand.

After a walk through the back of the property, they sat on a tree log lying sideways near the water's edge. An hour turned into two, and Penelope remembered why she liked her cousin so much. After repeated attempts to send Lotus back inside, Penelope settled on the fact that Lotus was not going to leave her alone in the woods. They slid from the log onto the ground in front of it, using the tree as back support.

"So, she wants me to go over there and pick up the knit dolls," Penelope said.

"And you don't want to?"

"I mean, she's just making me work for it. What's wrong with throwing them in the car tomorrow when she comes back down for the funeral? She's just trying to make it difficult for me."

"Maybe not. In her mind, she may not see anything wrong with asking you to come and get it if you want it. I know that doesn't seem like the nicest way to handle it, but it's possible that it's not malicious."

Penelope thought her mother might be jealous of her relationship with Gram, but it sounded too petty to say it out loud.

"Do you want me to go with you?" Lotus asked. "We could go up tomorrow afternoon or Sunday."

Penelope stopped swirling the stick in the dirt and looked up. "Would you?"

"Of course I will."

"Poor Rob. We just ditched him in there with all the crazies."

"He's fine. He and Elliot started bonding over their trips to Asia, and now he's got a buddy. Besides, we need someone on the inside to tell us when the coast is clear." Lotus pulled out her phone, and the screen lit her face. "Not yet, but it's winding down, he says."

They sat until the sun had dropped from the sky and the darkness filled the world with shadow. "We should probably head back," Penelope said with a sigh.

Lotus rose and led the way, lighting their path with the flashlight on her phone. Penelope trudged toward the gravel driveway, and when they reached it, she saw that Elliot's car was gone. A sense of foreboding washed over Penelope at seeing her mother's rusty Dodge in the gravel drive.

She stopped, standing in the open, no longer surrounded by trees. Lotus kept walking for a few paces before realizing Penelope was not behind her anymore. She turned back.

"She's not here. Elliot had to drive her home."

Of course he did. Penelope's unease melted into anger. "Now someone is going to have to go pick her up for the funeral tomorrow." Sometimes, the only way to deal was to fixate on concrete details and problem solve. "This is about Gram, not about her. Not about her problems."

Lotus gave her a sympathetic look. "I know. But her problems still exist. Even on the days we have to bury Gram."

"Probably even more so."

***

Sunday arrived with a grief hangover. They'd buried Gram after the service at Aunt Rose's rural Southern Baptist church, where a five-person church choir sang "Amazing Grace" from a raised choir stall. They'd caravanned a mile to the gravesite to lower Gram's casket into the ground. All of Gram's children and grandchildren had been given a single flower to place on the casket before it was lowered. Mom was crying as she placed her white rose on the casket. Aunt Rose began to sob into her husband's chest, and coincidentally, Mom's cries became more pronounced.

Penelope's eyes were puffy and achy. She barely noticed Elliot having a fight with his boyfriend over the phone in the empty kitchen as she poured her first cup of coffee. He hung up and rolled his eyes, leaving the room with his cup and a heavy thud to his steps.

Penelope met Lotus in the living room once she'd dressed and was feeling more human on her second cup of coffee. The only way to get the knit dolls Gram had made was to go to her mom's turf and pick them up. She would never forget sitting next to Gram, two knitting needles in hand, clumsily bringing her yarn up and around as Gram taught her with the rhyme, "Through the door, grab the sheep, over the fence, off we leap." The memory, the immeasurable value of the knit dolls, and Lotus's offer to traverse the gates of hell alongside her, was exactly what she needed to face it.

"Ready?" Lotus asked.

"As ready as I'll ever be."

The drive to Mom's house was familiar and at the same time strange. Although Penelope had made the drive north to Athens on 441 a number of times to see a '90s grunge band or to shop at the Junkman's Daughter's Brother, she'd never done it to visit her mother or see her new place. In a way, she was proud of Mom for selling the old concrete block house in Watkinsville and relieved that she didn't have to revisit her childhood home. But at the same time, it was odd that Mom lived up in Athens now. It was as if she'd tried to leave her home and barely got out of the neighborhood before deciding she'd rather stay nearby. Filling herself with a sense of pity for her mother prevented Penelope from filling with anger.

They pulled onto her street to find that the "townhouse" she supposedly lived in was actually a duplex. Three young men sat outside the adjoining unit, smoking cigarettes. The parking was not so much a driveway as it was an unmarked slab of concrete that served as a lot to hold four cars. One of them was up on blocks, beside it a Cadillac that looked to be from the seventies, and then next to that, her mother's car. Penelope slid the Honda in next to them and smiled cordially at the gentlemen sitting outside.

"This is it," she said.

There was a doorbell by the front door, but the casing was broken, and Penelope was not too sure about touching the exposed mechanism. Penelope's mother answered the door after three loud knocks. She wore a bathrobe and a scowl and held a chipped coffee mug, which might or might not have contained coffee.

"Hey," she said, turning to go back inside after opening the door.

Penelope reluctantly followed at Lotus's nudging. There were dishes in the sink and a ratty blanket thrown over the back of the couch. The house smelled like stale cigarettes. There was a time when Mom had tried to quit, but it had ended with a screaming match, nicotine patches spilled all over the linoleum floor, and her red-faced mother leaning against the wall, inhaling deeply, chain smoking a whole pack. Their house had always smelled like smoke after that.

"I thought you might want to check the attic because I didn't find that box you were talking about," she said, pointing at the ladder extending down from the ceiling in the narrow hallway.

Penelope glanced at Lotus, who nodded encouragingly. Anger boiled beneath the surface, but Penelope refused to let her mother see that she was getting to her. "Sure." She handed her purse to Lotus and started up the ladder.

A wave of heat greeted her as her head cleared the opening. It smelled better up there than on the ground floor, like sawdust and old books instead of stale smoke. The attic wasn't navigable, and once she was waist-high, she could pretty much reach every box stuffed up there.

Penelope pushed aside the plastic crate with a masking tape label marked *Christmas* and slid the six-foot prelit-artificial-tree box along the attic floor to see what hid behind it. She popped the tops of two gray plastic bins that didn't have labels and found old blankets and a box of pictures. Asking for anything that might require generosity on her mother's part was out of the question. Instead, she sorted through the pictures until she found one of Gram at what looked to be Easter. She had one hand on the back of her head, holding her hat in place while her flowered spring dress swirled around her in the wind. Penelope slid the picture into her top, careful to tuck it into her bra.

Moving the remaining bins, she came to a brown box. For a moment, she was sure it was her belongings. But then she opened it to find Elliot's old band uniform hat and letters from old boyfriends—and girlfriends back then. A sense of defeat settled over her. *If Mom didn't find it, and it isn't here, where is it?*

Advice from Gram came to mind: "The problem, my dear, is expectation. You expect more of her than she is capable of giving."

Empty-handed except for the photo she'd secreted away, Penelope descended the ladder. "It's not there. Is there somewhere else I can check?"

Mom shook her head. "Anything that wasn't mine got shoved up there during the move. If it's not there..." She trailed off, but she might as well have said it.

Penelope couldn't resist. "Those were important to me." Her voice was quiet. She strained to tame it.

"Well, I know. But maybe you should've taken them with you. Or gotten them before I moved."

Penelope's fault, as always.

"Those can't be replaced," Penelope said.

"Well, it's not like I lost them on purpose."

"That was all I wanted." Instinct told her to hide her hurt, but she couldn't see the point of that anymore.

"Well, if that's the case, I'll take the ruby," Mom said.

Penelope looked up at her, searching her face for meaning or validity.

Mom nodded. "Oh yeah, she left you the ruby ring. You know, the one she bought herself after she divorced Daddy." She said it with a sneer, but both women knew what she meant without the description.

Lotus had stayed silent beside Penelope. Her neutrality was fading more and more the longer they stood in Penelope's mother's house. "Aunt Ruthie, are you sure there's nowhere else we can look?" Lotus asked.

Mom gave a shrug. "Don't think so."

Lotus and Penelope drove away from her mother's house, leaving behind the need for the knit dolls Penelope wanted and her sad, stale life. They went back to their aunt's house, where Penelope kissed her and Lotus and hugged Elliot goodbye. She drove by the funeral home and picked up the box marked with her name.

Sitting in her car, Penelope opened the box and pulled the ruby ring from its nestled home on the silk pillow. It was huge, not something Penelope would typically wear, especially going to and from the hospital, sliding surgical gloves off and on repeatedly. The sunlight caught it, and it shone like the early-morning sheen on Lake Oconee in the summer, glinting in a surreal way. She could see it on Gram's withered hand, shining bright against her green-and-purple veins, flopping sideways when she became too thin for it to fit properly anymore.

Penelope slid it onto her left ring finger, just where Gram used to wear it, and gripped the steering wheel. She drove back home, wearing the ring the whole way. But the weight of Gram's death was unleashed on her, and she couldn't bear to look at the ring anymore.

Penelope slipped it off her finger, slid it back onto its silk pillow, and shut the box. Maybe one day she would take it out and put it on. But not that day.

Chapter 47

Lotus rolled slowly away from Blaze, removing herself from the sleeping toddler. She never tried to leave until she knew he was completely asleep. Waking him would start the lengthy bedtime process all over again.

She crept from the room, shutting the door, and stepped around the creaky floorboard in the hall. In the living room, she found Rob lounging on the couch, his face lit by the glow of his phone.

"Can we talk?" she asked.

"Sure," he said, tucking his phone away.

"I thought we might go outside." She couldn't risk a heated discussion waking Blaze. They'd never get through this if she had to go up and comfort him back to sleep.

Their backyard had a large weeping willow. It had been her favorite thing about the house back when it belonged to her grandfather. She would walk through the long, slender leaves of the wispy branches hanging near the ground and imagine she'd entered another world.

Now the backyard was home to a wooden swing set and a firepit. Lotus sat in front of the pit. It was too late to start a fire and dark enough that she could avoid looking at Rob directly.

"I'm glad you wanted to talk. I wasn't sure after the other night. I'm sorry I've been disappointing you lately. I guess I'm having a hard time with all these changes."

Typical Rob. She wanted to talk, to try to be rational with him at a time when he wasn't already mad. But it was never about her. It was always about him and how he was struggling. She swallowed hard and didn't answer right away.

"I know you're using again."

He looked up from across the dark, empty firepit. "What makes you say that?"

"Your drug dealer came by. Said he left a message for you and didn't hear back."

Rob kept his face smooth and unreadable, but he started to rub his thumb along the side of his index finger, a tic she'd discovered years ago and never revealed to him.

"You going to deny it? You think that's how we go from here?" she asked.

He met her eyes then nodded. "Okay. I guess there's no reason to deny. I have a problem."

The moment of triumph melted instantly. She'd come outside anticipating another fight. Instead, she was met with a transparency she hadn't been expecting.

"You also have a son. And a baby on the way. Now what? If you really wanted to get help for this problem, why didn't you come clean on your own? Why didn't you tell me you needed help?"

He shrugged. "Stone. I know this is a trigger for you. I didn't want to hurt you."

"You didn't want to hurt me? You think this hurts less?"

"You think it doesn't hurt me? You think I don't know that I've ruined our marriage? You've been so wrapped up in the store and this baby. And I haven't been here for you. And I know Jagannath has."

The baby? She'd barely given any thought to the baby. It was nothing like the first pregnancy, when she had counted every week and knew the milestone for growing eyelashes. She could barely remember how far along she was this time. She sat with the silence, stunned that he'd realized the situation with Jagannath.

"Our agreement in this marriage is to be open. When were you going to tell me something was developing between you two?" His words were cold.

"Nothing has happened." *Unless you count that little kiss.* But no—she'd stopped the kiss. Even though she hadn't talked to Rob before her feelings had grown, it was because she could hardly understand them herself. "And don't turn this on me. You're the one who's been using. You're the one who hasn't been there for his son. Or wife."

"How do you think this is going to work? He's my ex."

"That didn't stop you from inviting him to live here," Lotus said.

"I want to get help. I think we can get past this. But I think Jagannath has to go. I'm not sure we can get through it like this."

"You just don't get it, Rob. I'm sick of being unhappy. I'm sick of doing everything for everyone. I'm sick of asking every time I need you to help with *your* son. I'm sick of getting no gratitude from you while you goof off at the comic book store and act like I'm putting you out when I ask for help. I can't do everything and be expected to be happy with an immature partner who gives so little." Outside had been the right choice. She didn't care what the neighbors might overhear. "And the bottom line is, you knew drugs were a deal breaker. I trusted you. I told you everything out there on the trail. You made promises to me. So the rest of it hardly matters, but I'm tired of being Atlas. I can't hold the weight of the world by myself anymore."

"That's what you think? I give so little?"

"Come on, Rob. When's the last time you had a real job? If it wasn't for the store, what would you be doing? And every time you do help, it's because you're asked. Or told. I don't want a child for a partner. Grow up."

Maybe she'd gone too far. She'd been trying to convince herself that the muted feelings she was having for Rob had only been because they stood in stark contrast to the stirring she felt for Jagannath. But the truth had escaped her lips. She didn't want him. She resented him. It wasn't like the other night when she was mad as hell at four in the morning. It was over.

"What are you saying?" His voice had dropped to a near whisper. "What are you saying about us?"

"I'm saying I'm done. I'm saying I meant it the other night. And I wanted to talk again and be rational about it. But I really am done."

"But you're about to have our baby. You don't get to be done." His voice took on a menacing tone.

She hadn't planned for the conversation to go like this, but she'd had enough. Lotus looked down at her belly, where her round, full uterus sat like a globe in her lap. Their baby. It wasn't like she and Jagannath had discussed the birth plan or what would come after. And Rob was the father, no matter what they decided. *Am I just going to rashly dismiss him because I'm overwhelmed and overworked and in love with someone else?*

In love... am I?

"I know this baby is yours. And if you're clean, we will find a way to coparent. But the marriage is over."

He reached out for her hands again. She let him take them, her skin starkly pale against his in the moonlight.

"You can feel how you want to feel and explore this thing with Jagannath if you want. I can't deny his allure. It drew me in too. But this baby is ours. This life is ours." He rubbed the back of her palms with his thumbs as if that would soothe her.

Maybe she had fallen out of love with him. She had been aggravated with him so often, but it was more than that. The drugs were a dealbreaker. She couldn't come home to find him dead like she had with Stone. She couldn't let her children be raised by an addict.

Chapter 48

Nia was sitting at her Mamá's kitchen table when the call came. "We have a baby for you."

She stood up with her cell phone clutched to her ear and walked to the back door, her steps slow and deliberate. "A baby?"

"That's right. The teen parents you and Edward met a few weeks ago. They chose you."

Nia could feel her pulse beating against the phone. "We're going to have a baby?" Sucking in a deep breath, she repeated, "A baby? We're going to have a baby! When?" Her mind flitted to the Drakes, the couple Penelope had chosen before deciding to keep the baby.

"She's already in the window for delivery, so it'll be soon. They waited a long time to make their choice. But they chose you. Now, I want you to keep in mind that nothing is guaranteed. Sometimes adoptive parents get all the way to the birth and bonding with the baby, and the birth mother changes her mind. There's a seventy-two-hour window before it can be finalized."

"I know. I remember." But the warning could not cause her excitement to ebb.

"They said they're happy to notify you when she goes into labor, and you can go to the hospital."

"Wow. Okay, that's wonderful. Day or night. Anytime. I want to be called."

"You will be."

"Thank you, Marianne. Thank you so much. Lotus was right about you, and I am so happy we hired you to help match us to our baby."

"My pleasure."

Nia hung the phone up and turned to find her mother standing behind her. "Mamá. How long have you been standing there?"

"Long enough."

Nia stiffened, bracing herself for an argument.

"Long enough to know how much this baby means to you. Sweet Jesenita... I'm sorry." She reached over and took Nia's hands in her own stubby, calloused ones.

She hadn't called her that name since Papi's funeral. She reserved the endearment for moments like this, when she'd softened completely. It was a version of her stern mother that Nia rarely saw.

Nia squeezed her mother's hands and then pulled her into a hug. She tucked the short woman beneath her chin and breathed in the smell of her. Honey and hibiscus. Her mother had smelled the same ever since Nia could remember. "It's okay, Mamá."

"This baby will be my *nieto*. And I'm sorry it took me so long to realize that."

Nia nodded, her chin bobbing against her mother's head. She pulled back and wiped a finger beneath her eye. "I have to call Edward!"

"I have to call your brother and sister. Oh, or maybe you do?"

"Call them, Mamá."

Nia didn't want to celebrate prematurely, but on the way home from Mamá's, she called Penelope and Lotus. They both shared her excitement. She was right. Their babies were going to grow up best friends, born within weeks of each other.

It was going to be difficult to wait a few weeks for the baby, but she'd waited a lot longer than that. *What difference will a few weeks make?*

Chapter 49

The aftermath of Penelope's baby shower blanketed Nia's posh Buckhead apartment. It was everything cheesy Penelope had dreaded about a baby shower. It was perfect. Nia had gone shabby chic with the theme but still included all the silly games.

Penelope took a tray stacked with leftover bacon-wrapped dates from the table into the kitchen.

"Do not clean up. You're going to be asked to leave if you don't relax," Nia said.

"Oh, please. You know I'm doing way heavier lifting than this at work. And by the way, Lotus is helping, and she's still pregnant." Penelope pointed at Lotus's round belly.

"But you're the guest of honor this time." Lotus wore a skirt that looked like it was borrowed from a Bollywood actress with a top that hugged her round belly. She carried her pregnancy like a badge of honor and smiled like she had three months to go even though she was overdue. She didn't like to tell people her exact due date, but for Penelope and Nia, she'd revealed it.

Nia was dressed in a black-and-white chevron dress with a shiny narrow belt. She looked effortlessly gorgeous, as usual. Her optimism over the adoption was convincing. But Penelope knew her friend was not going to feel quite right until she had her baby in her arms.

Penelope fingered the banner hanging above the gift table. *Welcome Baby Ruby*. Ruby Dolores. Gram would have liked that. Of course, if Gram were still alive, Penelope probably wouldn't have thought of the name Ruby at all.

She looked down at her hands. The swelling had been just slight enough that she'd had to squeeze Gram's ruby ring onto her finger for the baby shower. Before leaving the house, she'd pulled out the old picture of Gram wearing a flowered spring dress. She considered how much she looked like her grandmother and wondered if Ruby would favor her too.

A peace had settled over Penelope. Once she'd decided the baby was hers, she'd started to think of Ruby as a person—a real, actual human growing inside her. A child she would raise and teach and love. The *love* part scared her. Her lack of parental role models scared her. Nevertheless, she pictured their lives together.

"Now that the guests are gone, we have one more thing for you," Lotus said. She and Nia exchanged looks, and then Nia pulled a brown shipping box from the closet. "Sit."

It didn't look like the rest of the gifts, which had all been wrapped in thick decorative paper and accented with ribbon, twine, or flowers. Except the gifts from the Labor and Delivery nurses. They'd all topped their boxes with surgical-glove balloons.

"What's this?"

"Open and see," Nia said.

The girlish excitement that usually danced in Nia's eyes was gone. *Is she tired?*

Penelope pried off the tape and unwrapped the unremarkable brown package. She pulled the white tissue back to find a collection of more than a dozen hand-knit stuffed animals amassed in the box, cradled by a brown basket beneath crinkly white paper. She picked up the stuffed knit octopus Gram had given her when she was eight. She twirled the mouse's whiskers in her fingers and flipped the lion's yarn mane as she had when she was a child.

Her voice caught in her throat. "Gram," she whispered. "How did you get these?"

Lotus lifted her eyebrows apologetically. "I know we have a pact never to talk about certain people, so I'm not sure you want to hear it."

Penelope nodded solemnly. "You talked to my mom?"

Lotus nodded. "Aunt Ruth reached out to me. She didn't try to invite herself. She didn't even send a message for you. But she asked me to give you your collection because she thought you might want to pass it to Ruby."

"How did she know I was pregnant?"

Lotus looked down. "I think my dad told her."

Penelope wiped away a tear. She didn't want to consider what it meant that her mother might be in AA and trying to make amends, because she wasn't ready for that. But this was a step of sorts, and that had to be enough for the moment.

She put the box aside and hugged Lotus. "Thank you."

"Are you going to give them to Ruby?" Nia asked.

Penelope fingered the brown-and-white owl and the gray dolphin. "No. It's all I have left from Gram. But I think I'll knit Ruby her own. Just like Gram taught me."

Lotus wiped her eyes.

"Don't you start, too, or we'll all be in a puddle soon," Nia said. "Your hormones are no joke."

Penelope gathered up the knit animals and placed each one lovingly in the basket. Lotus helped her load the baby-shower gifts in her car. Nia talked about how their children were going to be best friends. No one said anything when she talked about her soon-to-be-adopted baby as if it were certain. Nia had a way of joining the club, no matter what she had to do to be part of it.

Things were changing. And Penelope was going to be okay. Nia was right. Their kids would grow up together. Soon they would all be holding tiny newborns in their arms, changing diapers, feeding babies, and pushing strollers. Gone would be the bars and the club and the girls' days out. Here would be the mommy-and-me classes, playdates, and sleepless nights. Penelope couldn't think of anyone she'd rather be on that journey with than Nia and Lotus. Things were finally looking up.

Chapter 50

Oscar wasn't a small baby. Nia held his warm, pudgy body against hers, trying again to get him to take his bottle. He kept dozing off, ignoring her efforts. Their first night, he'd slept more than she'd expected. His nurse finally made her wake him up to feed him. Nia wouldn't let him go to the nursery.

He was her baby. She and Edward had their baby. It was surreal. Logically, she'd known it was coming. But after the miscarriage and the repeated warnings from Marianne about the seventy-two-hour waiting period, she hadn't let herself completely believe that it was going to work out. But the feelings of love and joy at having him there, in her arms, overwhelmed her. There was no way she would send him down the hall.

Then forty-eight hours later, they'd brought him home. Marianne offered interim care for him if they didn't want to bring him home before the birth mother signed everything. But she, Edward, and the birth mom had wanted the baby to go home with them. One day later, papers were signed, and Oscar was officially theirs.

A soft knock on the bedroom door brought her back to the present. "Come in," she called quietly.

Pixie ran over to see who was visiting, but she didn't bark. Oscar didn't stir. Maybe he was going to be a really good sleeper. Penelope came in, holding balloons, followed by Lotus carrying a plate of something and a small gift bag.

"You're here!" Nia said. She'd spent two days in the hospital in a rooming-in space and had been home for barely a day. She hadn't let anyone visit the first day back.

The women hugged. Circles under Lotus's eyes contrasted with the smile on her face. It was the most worn Nia had seen her. Penelope smiled radiantly, looking the way she had at the baby shower, truly happy and content in a way that Nia had never expected from her. Penelope tended to be cynical, and this new version of her, excited about her pregnancy and impending baby, was refreshing.

Lotus handed over the plate. "Normally, I bring new moms lactation cookies. I just made you oatmeal chocolate chip."

Nia laughed at "lactation cookies." She was a little sad about not breastfeeding her baby, but her gratefulness overshadowed her moments of wanting.

The women oohed and aahed over Oscar, and Nia passed him to Lotus. He slept the whole time, not stirring when he changed arms. Penelope checked in with her about wet diapers and feedings and all the same things her nurse had been asking about. She wouldn't take her nurse hat off, and Nia appreciated that.

"Where's Edward?" Penelope asked.

"He went out to get me some pho. I was craving it. He's spoiling me rotten and keeps calling me Mommy and feeding me since I can't seem to do anything but stare at Oscar all day."

Penelope laughed. "Yum. Tell him to keep it up. You're going to be new-mom tired, getting up for feeds every two to three hours, until he gets a little bigger."

Lotus stood silently, looking down at Oscar.

"How are you feeling?" Nia asked. "Ready to have that baby yet?"

Lotus shook her head.

"How long is the midwife going to let you go?" Penelope asked.

Nia commended Penelope for being diplomatic. Her careful tone told Nia she was concerned about Lotus's late-term pregnancy.

"She said the risk of stillbirth increases in the forty-third week, but I think we have my due date wrong. I'm comfortable waiting."

Nia and Penelope exchanged looks. Lotus kept her face down, looking at Oscar. Nia knew what Penelope thought about waiting. She was a nurse. She'd seen too much. Just like Edward had.

"You okay, Lotus?" Penelope asked. She clearly didn't want to discuss their differing philosophies.

Lotus looked up from Oscar, her eyes shining with tears. "I'm fine."

"You don't look fine," Nia said. "What's the matter?"

"He's so beautiful. You guys, we're so lucky."

Is it hormones? No, Lotus would be the first to blame the hormones if she thought that was the cause. She looked genuinely upset.

Nia reached a hand out to Lotus. "Thank you for the cookies. And for all the texts of encouragement. I'm sorry I kept you guys away for a few days. But I just couldn't bear to introduce him to everyone if she changed her mind."

Lotus smiled at her, but it didn't reach her eyes. "You're welcome."

"Now, tell me the truth. What's going on?" Nia's tone was firmer than she had intended.

Lotus bit her lower lip. "You just got your new baby. You need to focus on that. You don't want to hear about my drama."

Nia rolled her eyes. "Well, that's where you're wrong. I always want to hear about drama." She leaned forward.

Lotus passed the baby to Penelope and sat at the foot of the bed. "Everything is crumbling. With Rob. I just feel so resentful all the time. He's doing nothing. I finally told him it's over. But this is his baby, and it's complicated. And I think—" She looked down, not making eye contact with either of them. "I think I love Jagannath," Lotus continued miserably. "I've been feeling like this for a while."

"Why didn't you tell us?" Penelope asked.

"I don't know. You just decided to keep your baby, Pen. And, Nia, I know it's been hard with the modeling job and the adoption and stuff."

Nia crossed her arms. She didn't want to be harsh with Lotus, but enough was enough. "What do *you* want, Lotus? Tell us that. You don't have to try to make everyone happy."

Lotus shrugged, tossed a section of her long hair over her shoulder, and wiped her nose. She looked positively miserable. "I mean, I think I'm going to try to make it work. Rob and I had a big fight, and then he was so sweet, and he wants me to see where it goes with Jagannath but not walk away from what we have. I'm about to have his baby, again. That makes sense. I told him the marriage was over. But I'm not so sure. He wants to get help."

What a mess. "You didn't answer the question," Nia said.

Lotus shrugged.

Penelope looked at Nia over Lotus's head and shrugged. Nia continued, "I think you do. Stop trying to please everyone. Do what you want. Do you want to be with Rob or not? Even if he 'lets' you explore things with Jagannath, is staying with Rob what you really want? I get it—you don't have to leave him. You can do both. But is that what *you* want? And is he really going to rehab?"

Lotus shrugged again. The bags under her eyes made sense. She'd probably been up half the night, crying.

"I'm doing everything. I can't keep doing it on my own. Rob and I have children. It's not like I'm breaking up with a boyfriend. We'll have to coparent no matter what we choose for our relationship." Her shoulders slumped. "Sometimes I wish I'd never gotten pregnant. I know—that's an awful thing to think."

Penelope raised her hand. "Well, it's something I can definitely identify with. But the men in your life don't determine what kind of person and what kind of mother you are. You're successful all on your own. Sure, Rob helps run the store and sometimes even effectively. But *you* built that. And we're here for you no matter what you choose. I'm going to be raising Ruby on my own, and I'll have to figure out Jasper's involvement, whatever that might be. I know it's different because you guys are married, and you have Blaze already, but your happiness matters, too, Lotus. You've got to put yourself first sometimes. I was so afraid of being like my mother. I was afraid to do that for myself. But now I finally am."

Penelope handed Oscar back to Nia and went to Lotus. She pulled her into a hug. The two women stood over Nia's bed, their bellies beside one another.

Lotus drew back and looked up, the sorrow on her face melting into surprise. "I think my water just broke."

Chapter 51

"She's on her way. About an hour." Penelope hoped it wouldn't take the midwife an hour.

This wasn't Lotus's first labor, and her body knew it. "I'm not going to do anything medical. I can't," Lotus had said.

Penelope was determined to just be her cousin and friend and not to be the most medically experienced person in the room. She'd chuckled to herself as they left Nia's place, right next to the hospital, and headed to Lotus's peace-and-love hippie home birth. But once they reached Lotus's house, labor had started fast and furious. It wasn't funny anymore. Lotus sat, naked, her legs folded beneath her, steam rising off the water of the freshly filled corner bathtub.

"Can I get you anything?" Penelope needed an excuse to leave the stuffy, humid room. The bathroom had been updated in Lotus's Victorian home, and an enormous soaking tub took up a whole corner. Jagannath sat on the corner of the tub, massaging Lotus's shoulders.

"If there's coconut water, I would love some," Lotus said.

Maybe the hippie thing was what permitted Lotus to sit naked in front of a guy she'd just realized she was in love with while she labored to give birth to another man's baby. Rob hadn't come home yet. Penelope could imagine how it might feel to Rob, seeing his ex-boyfriend sitting on the edge of the tub, massaging his naked wife.

At least my situation isn't the most fucked-up. Immediately, she regretted that thought. She didn't want any of it to be fucked-up. *How is it that Nia has the most normal life at this point? When did she become the stable one?*

Penelope returned from the kitchen with coconut water to find Lotus midcontraction. Her faced tensed, and she exhaled loudly, making a hissing noise, her head thrown back into Jagannath's lap. He stroked her face.

"Two and a half minutes," he said when it ended. "That's the fifth in a row."

"The water isn't doing much to slow them," Penelope muttered.

"The water is making them manageable." Jagannath squeezed a washcloth over a bowl of ice water and ran it across Lotus's sweaty forehead and lips.

Penelope sat down on a low wooden stool. A turquoise dribble of toothpaste along the side reminded her that Lotus had a little person using her bathroom. The next contraction started, coming too close on the heels of the previous one. It wouldn't be long. If she had to, Penelope would deliver the baby. *Nothing will go wrong. When it happens quick and easy like this, it's because everything is going right.* She thought of Alicia, the young, healthy mom with the prolapsed cord. No one had anticipated that problem with a low-risk mother. But there she had been, riding along on the mom's hospital bed, her hand inside the patient's cervix, trying to hold the cord back before the loss of oxygen killed her baby.

Penelope exhaled. It wouldn't be like that for Lotus. She had to believe that.

The door slammed, followed by "Lotus? Lotus!"

Penelope stood and went to the bedroom door, calling down, "We're up here."

Rob. *Time to get this party started.* After Lotus's confession at Nia's bedside, Penelope had wondered how tense it would be between them.

He stomped into the bathroom, went to his knees beside the bathtub, and took Lotus's hands. "I'm here. How are you?"

"Fine," Lotus said. "Who's at the store?"

His eyebrows drew in. "Chelsea has the store covered. Can't you trust me to handle it?"

She gave him a wry look. Jagannath sat behind Lotus, his hands on her shoulders protectively, his face passive.

Poor Lotus. What has she gotten herself into?

Jagannath checked his phone, which he'd been using to time the contractions, and watched Lotus.

"Can I get you anything?" Rob asked. "What can I do?"

"I'm pretty good. Um, actually, I need someone to go get Blaze. Is it one o'clock?" Her eyebrows arched, and she looked at Penelope with pleading eyes.

"I can go. Where is he?" Penelope said.

"No. You can't leave, Penelope, please. You're the one I need if the midwife doesn't get here."

Rob looked at Jagannath kneading Lotus's shoulders. Then he turned to Penelope, who was sitting down again on the low stool. She shrugged at him, not sure what she was supposed to do. She'd offered to get Blaze. Lotus didn't want her to leave. She *couldn't* leave her.

Rob's face fell. "It's not quite one yet. But I don't want to go. I want to stay with you. Can't you send Penelope?"

"No," Lotus said, shutting her eyes again. Penelope watched her, waiting for the next contraction to start. But it didn't come.

They waited. Penelope checked her watch. Maybe it was the anticipation of the contraction that was due any second. Maybe it was the push and pull between Rob and Lotus.

Does she really not love her husband anymore? Is Jagannath her new boyfriend? The whole thing was fucked, all the way back to the history between Jagannath and Rob. Their situation hung in the room, stretching between them, heavy like the humid air.

"I don't want to leave you, Lotus," Rob said.

She opened her eyes, fixing them on Rob. "You want to be helpful? You want to be involved? Then go pick up your son. That's your responsibility. Be a grown-up. That'll impress me." She shut her eyes again.

Penelope wanted to leave the tense space. But Lotus needed her. Rob looked at Lotus, lips slightly parted, eyes wide, stunned. Lotus didn't talk to people like that—not that Penelope had ever heard.

Rob turned and left, his lips pressed together. Penelope thought she saw a glimpse of tears shining in his dark eyes. He knew he'd gone too far and it might really be over between them.

Lotus kept her eyes shut until the front door slammed. "Sorry, you guys," she said.

"Don't apologize to us," Penelope said just as Jagannath said, "You have nothing to apologize for."

Jagannath started back at rubbing her shoulders, trying to ease the tension. She shrugged him off. "I'm good."

Jagannath and Penelope exchanged a look. Clearly, she wasn't good. *But what are we going to do about it?*

Jagannath started Lotus's yoga music, and Penelope offered sips of water. Within ten minutes, Lotus seemed back to herself, except she hadn't had a single contraction. Not when Rob was there and not in the ten minutes following his departure.

And then one hit her, and she closed her eyes. Her face was screwed up in a mask of pain. She let a noise out with this one, groaning and then moaning through it. Jagannath coached her to relax. Penelope checked her watch and then stood, looking outside the bay window into the street, watching for the approaching midwife's car.

When it ended, Lotus slumped limply against Jagannath, worn from the effort. *Will the contractions resume their pace at two and a half minutes? Is this gap the space between laboring and pushing?* Penelope wished again that she could check Lotus. But no. It wasn't her job. Not this time. The midwife was on her way.

To her relief, the steady, evenly spaced pushing contractions didn't follow. But the contractions didn't go back to being two minutes apart either. She studied Lotus closely—the bedside watch Penelope had done so often—but there was no sign of the strong,

fast-paced contractions that once plagued her. Instead, they were erratic, as if to tell Penelope her expectations didn't matter.

Seven minutes.

Three minutes.

Twelve minutes.

"Mommyyy!" A loud, long call from the hallway revealed that
Rob and Blaze had returned. Blaze ran to the edge of the tub, putting
his hand gently on Lotus's protruding belly. "Where'sa baby?"

Lotus opened her eyes, looking up at Blaze standing beside the
tub, and ruffled his russet hair with her wet hand. "You'll get to see
your baby soon. Is it going to be a boy or a girl today?"

Penelope had seen that game before. Lotus asked Blaze about the
baby, and he thought about it and answered questions, guessing the
baby's sex and other features.

"Girl. Wif hair yike me, not you." He grabbed the messy bun
atop her head, squeezing the roll like it was one of Gram's yarn balls.
She smiled up at him, letting him grab at her hair and trail a finger in
the warm bath water.

"Okay, buddy, that's enough. Mommy's working hard to have the
baby now. You want to go get a snack?" Rob looked calm and composed, but there was a rim of redness around his eyes like he'd been
crying.

Blaze looked up at him, still patting the ball of hair like he was
playing the drums. "No, I stay wif Mommy."

Lotus smiled at her son, but the tightness around her eyes
showed the wear on her. She wouldn't tell the boy no. She wouldn't
ask him to leave, even if he played her hair like a drum solo through
the rest of the labor. That was how she was with him.

Rob stepped into the bathroom, trying to gently take Blaze's
hands. "I think there's some dippy down there. Do you want some
hummus dippy?"

Jagannath sat at the foot of the tub. It was a good thing the bathroom was huge. There was still room for the midwife and doula and whatever other circus Lotus had invited over.

"Aren't you hungry?" Jagannath asked Blaze.

Blaze pursed his lips, looking from Lotus to Rob to Jagannath.

"I go wif you," he said to Jagannath, letting go of Lotus's hair and holding out a hand for Jagannath.

"Okay, buddy, I'll take you." He shrugged at Lotus, but she waved back at him, shooing them both out.

Eight minutes.

Four minutes.

Two minutes.

Nine minutes.

It looked like an early, nonprogressing labor pattern. Lotus tensed. She yelled. She turned red. She clenched. At the rate they were going, Penelope would not be delivering any babies that day. *How did she transition from the steady every-two-minute pattern to this?*

"Lotus? How're you feeling?" Penelope asked in between the erratic contractions.

Lotus looked up, her eyes drooping with the familiar fatigue of a laboring mother. "I'm fine. I don't know why they stopped coming close together. I thought I was in transition for a minute."

"So did I," Penelope said.

Lotus closed her eyes again, shutting them out.

Rob and Lotus weren't talking to each other. They weren't looking at each other. Rob wasn't rubbing her back or feet or saying anything to her as she contracted, but he stayed, keeping vigil at her side. *Does she want Jagannath?* He hadn't come back yet after getting snacks for Blaze.

As Penelope looked out the window again, the midwife, Elaine, arrived, pulling a rusted gray Oldsmobile into the street outside of

Lotus's Victorian home and unloading a few bags from her trunk. She was large with a gray braid down her back. Her eyes reminded Penelope of a bloodhound. They were clear and alert, but the bags beneath them told of the many nights she'd spent at the bedsides of women.

She entered the room and approached Lotus with the unbounded confidence of a doctor and the gentle, reassuring presence of a nurse. Penelope liked her immediately. Or maybe it was the breath of air Penelope could finally take now that she wasn't the most experienced person in the room.

Having a medical professional who had done all this without all the hospital equipment both relieved Penelope and seemed alien. She thought of herself, in her apartment, laboring away and waiting for a midwife to come over. No. That was way outside her comfort zone, and she certainly wouldn't choose home birth, but she supported Lotus's decision.

Penelope sent a text to Nia: *Midwife is here. Labor was kicking and now it's slow. I'll update you when I know more. How's Oscar? Does he miss me?* She smiled, sliding the phone back into her pocket. She hoped Ruby would be chubby like Oscar.

Eventually, the midwife reported that Lotus was eight centimeters dilated. *So, she* was *in transition.*

An hour passed. Then another. Nothing changed. Jagannath eventually returned, and Blaze played happily with the midwife's assistant until his naptime.

Lotus had long since given up on the bathtub and moved to the bedroom. She paced the room like a caged lioness, stalking from one corner to another. When she contracted, she stopped, falling into a supported embrace with Jagannath, dangling from his arms as she attempted to relax.

The midwife offered suggestions on occasion. The doula pressed some kind of pressure point on Lotus's back as she contracted. Rob sat in the overstuffed chair in the corner, looking on. He wasn't involved in the labor, but once Blaze had gone down for his nap, he stayed on, watching but not interacting.

"Her labor has stalled," the midwife announced. Her voice was calm and direct. Lotus had gone into the bathroom and shut the door.

The crowd in the bedroom turned to the midwife. "What does that mean?" Jagannath asked.

"It means something is stopping her labor from progressing. Is it the baby's position?" Penelope asked the midwife.

Elaine shook her head, "I'm afraid not. The baby is lined up. Physiologically, everything looks right."

How long will the midwife let her hold in this nonprogressing pattern? Lotus's broken bag of waters meant the time clock to keep her at home was ticking. Penelope had seen the transfers. Not all of the home birth midwives stuck to a conservative protocol and shifted to the hospital at the first sign of trouble.

Physiologically. There was something else going on, then, maybe psychologically. *Is it Rob?* The whole love-triangle thing between them felt stressful to Penelope, and it wasn't even her life or relationships at stake.

She wanted to help Lotus. She didn't know how, but she knew Lotus needed to sort out her labor if she was going to have her baby at home.

Chapter 52

Alone at last. Stay present. Birth is not inherently dangerous.
So, what is wrong? Why am I still eight centimeters?

Lotus should have birthed her baby by now. She couldn't stop the negative thoughts. Only the old wooden door separated her from everyone else. Rob. Penelope. Jagannath. Blaze. All of them. Even the midwife was out there, watching. Waiting. Their muffled voices told her she was probably the topic of conversation.

She looked down at her naked belly and rubbed it. *Come on, sweet baby. Why aren't you coming out?*

The spaced contractions confused her. A low, dull ache that never receded plagued her back. The anticipated rhythmic feeling of labor eluded her. There was something comfortable and predictable about the continually expected contractions coming in waves as they had with Blaze. These were sporadic and unpredictable. Like her life.

She swallowed hard and resisted the urge to push out the *ha* sound and expel it. The negative thoughts had a place. She couldn't banish them with an exhalation as she once had.

Did that ever really work?

No. She'd used it to avoid facing her own harsh judgments about others and about herself.

When did life become so complicated?

Maybe she shouldn't have let Jagannath in. If she'd been able to draw a boundary with Rob in the first place, she wouldn't be in this situation. Jagannath never would have moved in. The thought came with a twinge of pain in her chest. That wasn't what she wanted either.

What exactly do I want? Why did I wait so long to confront Rob's drug problem?

No matter the state of her marriage, Rob was the father of her children. There was no avoiding or denying Rob's place in her children's lives if he was truly clean. *But what about his place in* my *life? Have I really fallen out of love with him, or is this a hardship we'll be able to overcome? Do I want to overcome it?*

A gentle knock on the door preceded Elaine's soft voice. "Lotus? May I come in?"

Lotus squinted at the bags beneath her eyes in the bathroom mirror. She looked as bad as she felt. "Yes," she called to the closed door.

Elaine slipped into the bathroom and shut the door behind her, blocking the rest of the room out. She carried a handheld doppler. "I just need a quick listen."

Lotus turned her belly away from the mirror and toward the midwife. Elaine was short and stout, coming only to Lotus's shoulder. But she had an air of authority that commanded a room.

Elaine squeezed gel onto the T-shaped wand head and pressed it against Lotus's lower abdomen, searching for the baby's heartbeat. It came immediately, pulsing rhythmically.

"Good, strong heart tones. The baby is tolerating labor well. For now." She paused. "I have to tell you, I am bound to certain protocols based on the rupture of your membranes. I'd like to see a more consistent pattern of labor so that we can stay here and have your baby at home, as you wanted. I know this may be hard to hear, but I need you to understand that plans might change if we can't establish that. Do you understand?"

She met Lotus's eyes with a direct stare, not afraid to look away. Not holding back. Her light-gray eyes were alert, and she held Lotus's gaze firmly.

Transfer? She might have to transfer. The thought terrified her. Everything that she had wanted for her home birth had dissolved. This was supposed to be her place of comfort. Instead, it had become a place of chaos. She thought of Ina May Gaskin, the famous farm midwife who had signed the ratty copy of her book from the seventies. The one her mother had passed down when Lotus was pregnant with Blaze. *The energy that gets the baby in is the energy that gets the baby out.*

Did she mean sex? Love? Is that it? The energy that had been present at the making of her child was certainly absent from her labor now. Disintegrated.

"I understand," Lotus said. Her only choice was to tell the truth. She had no other recourse. "I don't know how to fix it. I don't think I love Rob anymore. But this is his baby. This is *our* baby, no matter what else I choose."

Maybe that was why her baby wasn't coming. She didn't want to bring a child into this mess—that was true. She was starting to accept that she might love Jagannath. But she was afraid of what he would think of her postpartum, holding and nursing Rob's child. Her family of four would be together but apart, with Jagannath as the fifth wheel.

But he wasn't that. *He* was her choice. Not an obligation to Rob. She wanted to refuse the pressure to "make it work" with Rob. *And why does that have to all be decided now?*

Her midwife nodded knowingly. "I see. I think your labor has stalled because you are emotionally stuck. That can cause you to be physically stuck. You've produced catecholamines, which interfere with your process. Like an animal hiding from a predator. Your body doesn't know the difference between a real and a perceived threat. The hormone response is the same and signals threat."

She stated it matter-of-factly but, at the same time, stroked Lotus's arms, a soothing gesture Lotus knew was meant to calm her.

"What do I do?" She felt helpless. "I'm sorry."

"No, child. Don't be sorry. This is normal. But you will have to deal with things. Clearly, you cannot shove them down and ignore them. This is the result."

As if in defiance, her body seized, the sensation of a contraction coming on. It was low in her abdomen and circled around to her back like a belt worn too tightly. She leaned into the counter, rocking her hips through it. The midwife reached out with the doppler, getting a read on the baby during the contraction.

Rob. Jagannath. This baby. Blaze. Her family. Drugs. Her dead brother. She wanted to push it all back down, but it bubbled inside her, spilling out with the tears that flowed freely with the contraction.

Nia's voice rang in her thoughts. *What do* you *want, Lotus?* That was the million-dollar question.

She didn't want to hurt anyone. She didn't want to push Rob out, but she didn't want to come home and find him overdosed. They had a history, and this was his baby too. She didn't want Jagannath to change his mind about her. She didn't want a bigger mess once the baby was born.

But that didn't answer the question. *What do* you *want, Lotus?*

Everything she'd wanted, she'd gone after. The Appalachian Trail thru-hike. She'd started that journey alone, determined.

Am I the same woman who struck out, fearless, for a six-month hiking journey?

Rob. She had wanted him. She had loved his free spirit, his openness, and his ability to make her feel like she was the only thing that mattered in the world. And at some point, that had changed.

She didn't want to be Atlas anymore. Her store, the Lotus Garden. She'd built that from nothing, out of a dream. Her home birth with Blaze. Despite the naysayers, she'd accomplished that on her terms, the way she wanted it. And it seemed she was about to give that possibility up this time just because she couldn't get her head in the right space.

What do you *want, Lotus?*

She opened her eyes after the contraction ended. Her tearstained face felt sore and swollen. But the determination had sunk deep into her bones.

She nodded at the midwife. "I want Jagannath. Ask him to come in here. I want everyone else to leave. Everyone."

The midwife squeezed her shoulder and left the room.

Chapter 53

Penelope found herself back in the bathroom once the midwife declared that Lotus was complete. She'd sat in silence in the living room, checking her phone, texting Nia, rubbing her swollen feet until the midwife said Lotus wanted her back in.

"Mommyyy. I heard brave noises. Can I do it?" Blaze walked into the bathroom, removing his clothing as he went. "I wanna get in."

Lotus smiled at the boy. "Okay, let's hear your brave noise."

He mimicked her labor noises, pretending that he was having a contraction, with his shirt off and his round, toddler belly sticking out as far as he could push it. Penelope found herself wishing someone was taking a video.

Lotus pursed her lips and looked seriously at Blaze, nodding in approval. "That's a very brave noise."

"Okay. Now I get in," he stated.

Lotus didn't protest. He stripped down to his rocket-ship underwear and climbed belly down over the side of the massive tub then plopped into the water in front of Lotus.

"Remember, there will be blood, Blaze. If you decide to get out, Daddy will help you." She spoke calmly and rationally, not like a woman fully dilated, about to push a baby out. She was not talking down to her three-year-old but instead was giving him the autonomy to choose how he wanted to be involved in his sibling's birth.

Penelope didn't think she would ever be like that with Ruby. She would be involved, that was for sure. She would be present not just at dance recitals or softball games but at the practices too. She imagined reading books to Ruby, teaching her how to read, taking her on playdates with Lotus's little one and Oscar. *Will I be the mom pushing my baby around in a stroller, or will I let Lotus talk me into those wraps or carriers she used with Blaze?*

Penelope hadn't been with Lotus for the labor with Blaze. She and Lotus hadn't been as close back then—although they'd bonded after the funeral, they hadn't gotten close enough to share an experience as intimate as childbirth. Penelope had still been deciding if she wanted those family ties. Lotus had no boundaries. She let Rob, Blaze, her brother, and everyone walk all over her.

The ache in her low back drew her attention. She was used to being on her feet for long periods of time, but then again, she'd never been pregnant. The tension of Lotus's labor turned her inward to her own labor and to Jasper. *Will there be tension with Jasper if I let him be here for the labor? Will fear of motherhood stop my own progress?*

She shoved the thoughts aside. Her labor wasn't going to look like Lotus's. She'd been through enough labors as a nurse to know that. Every woman's labor looked different.

Lotus finished a push and looked up, taking in the people surrounding the tub for her waterbirth. "Where's Rob? I want him here. Tell him I'm sorry for earlier. Penelope, tell him I want him here. This is his baby."

Penelope nodded, taking Lotus's hand. "I'm sure he'll be right back. He sends his love. Want me to call him?" As soon as the words were out, she wanted to pull them back in. *He sends his love. How lame is that?*

Lotus's face was ashen, and her cheeks were flushed. In a moment, her child would come into the world, but Rob wasn't going to be there to see it.

Is this how I want it to be for Jasper? No. Jasper deserved to be there. If he wanted to be an involved father, she would encourage that from the beginning, starting with the birth of his child.

"Where the hell is he?" Lotus asked, her face growing red.

Jagannath sat behind her, searching Penelope's face for an answer. Rob had been downstairs with Penelope when he'd gotten a phone call. He'd told Penelope to tell Lotus he loved her. She hadn't realized he was leaving.

Another contraction took over, and Penelope didn't have to answer. The midwife was there, kneeling beside the tub on a thick gardening mat, encouraging Lotus to push with each exhalation.

Chapter 54

It all happened faster than it had with Blaze once the pushing contractions came. After three pushes, Lotus was holding her baby.

I don't care where he went. I don't need him. Lotus heard the thoughts in her head but didn't really believe them. Maybe he was hurt and didn't want to be there. Maybe he couldn't stand it that Jagannath was there, by her choice, sharing in this experience.

During Lotus's final push, the midwife said, "Reach down and get your baby."

Lotus had pulled the slippery newborn up from beneath the water. The relief of the baby leaving her body released something within her. She cried, stroking the vernix on the baby's back. Rob was supposed to announce the sex. They'd waited to find out, just like they had with Blaze. But he'd chosen not to be there.

Anger boiled up behind her tears. *How could he choose that?*

She looked up at Penelope. "Where's Rob? Did he really decide to leave?"

Penelope shook her head. The seriousness in her eyes betrayed her.

Something is wrong.

"I didn't know he was going to leave. He just said, 'Tell Lotus I love her,' and then he was gone."

"Tell me *what*?" She could hear the alarm rising in her voice.

Penelope put a hand on her naked shoulder. "I don't know. He said he needed help. Maybe this is a good thing."

Tears began anew. He'd missed the birth of his child. She'd shut him out and chosen Jagannath. In the moment things were stalled and she was afraid, she hadn't wanted her husband. She hadn't even wanted her best friend.

She held her tiny newborn, not yet knowing the sex. It should have been an exhilarating moment, rubbing the soft vernix in, rolling the tiny baby over to check if they had a boy or a girl. Instead, her husband had chosen to leave, and her thrill in that moment was dampened by that.

"Lotus? You hear me? You don't need to worry about this right now. Look at your beautiful baby. Rob will be back."

Lotus nodded, meeting Penelope's eyes. "Thank you."

She rolled the baby over, which incited a loud cry from the child. She scooped the baby up, checking for the sex. "It's a girl. Rob wanted a little girl. We already picked out the name." She looked down at the baby. "Her name is Shanti. It means peace."

Chapter 55

Three days past her due date, Penelope woke to use the bathroom in the night, just like always. The tiny subway tiles glittered in the glow of the night-light. The harsh overhead light remained off, which helped her pretend she wasn't waking up.

Her heavy-lidded eyes hovered half-open as she trudged to the toilet. Sweet relief. She imagined Ruby pinching her bladder. Ruby had dropped a week before, settling deep into her pelvis, preparing to be born. Penelope's newfound ability to take a deep breath was a gift, but the price was a bladder flattened like a pancake. During the day, she couldn't make it more than an hour or two. At night, she was up two or three times, like clockwork.

Bloody show. Penelope's heavy eyes lightened and opened at the first sign of labor.

She grabbed her phone and sent off a text to Nia: *It might be baby day. Tell Edward I have show! I'm going back to bed... promise. Hope I didn't wake you.*

Nia replied immediately: *Sleep now. You know that. Text me in the morning unless something else happens. I was up—feeding peanut again. So excited to meet Ruby! Soon!*

Nia's enthusiasm fed Penelope's confidence. She could do this. She should tell Jasper that she might be in labor. Or maybe she needed to wait for another sign. Jasper might have been a terrible boyfriend and husband, but she didn't want him to be a terrible father. But he wasn't going to be the one helping her through the labor—thank goodness, she had Nia, Lotus, and Edward for that.

She waddled out to the refrigerator and squinted at a copy of Jasper's schedule hanging there. He was at work. He could be up, and he might want to give his boss some notice.

She typed up the message: *Might be baby day. Only one sign. Just wanted to give you a heads-up. I'll let you know if anything more happens.*

Penelope opened the refrigerator. She was awake now. She'd meant it when she said she was going back to bed. She would do that—after she had some watermelon.

The cold melon juice dripped down her chin. She wiped it off and stood in the glow of the refrigerator, the bottom of her abdomen peeking out from beneath her sleep tank. The tiny pink lines on her belly weren't something she thought she'd appreciate, but she found that she didn't mind the feathery marks where her baby had grown and stretched the skin.

Ruby kicked. She loved the watermelon too. Penelope nudged the door shut and waddled back to the bedroom. Her bed was a nest of pillows that had grown with each month of pregnancy. She couldn't imagine how other pregnant women slept comfortably with another person in bed.

Penelope's phone rang. Her first thought was of Jasper, but when she picked up the phone, she saw that it was Nia.

"You didn't have to call," she said.

"But I wanted to check on you," Edward replied.

"Oh, hey there. I thought you were Nia. And I thought patients usually called the doctor, not the other way around."

"You get special treatment."

"Are you calling to check up on me? I told Nia I was fine."

"I just wanted to hear it from you. Nia said you had show."

"Yes. It's all normal, not too much, not bright red. Give me some credit. I know what I'm doing, remember?"

"You don't get to be a nurse today, Pen. You get to be the mom."

Her nickname again. But she couldn't bring herself to tell him not to say it. "Okay. Well, I'll work on trying to forget years of training and the thousands of labors I've been to."

His laughter rang in the phone in a deep bass. "Get some sleep."

"I will. I'll update you in the morning."

They hung up. *Why is Edward being so overprotective?* Maybe Nia was worried and had made him call.

Penelope stared down at her cell phone. Nothing from Jasper. Oh well. She would reach him in the morning. She climbed into her nest of pillows and drifted back to sleep.

Waves rolled over Penelope as she lay in the sand. The sand didn't itch—it was soft, like the kinetic sand Lotus's son played with. She was on her back, sprawled on the sand, clumping it in her fists and then letting it go. It ran like water. The sun warmed her, but there was no glare from the globe above her. The lump of her belly blocked her feet from view. Waves started at her feet and climbed up her body, rolling up to her neck and then back down again. She never worried that they might come up over her face. Always it crept up to her chin and then retreated, back down her body and out to sea. She was warm and dry as soon as the water rolled off her skin. Then it came again, warmer than the sun, heating her from her toes to her neck and then back again.

A gush of fluid yanked Penelope out of the dream. The water. The water had betrayed her. But no. That wasn't it. She was in bed. She'd been dreaming. The gush of fluid had come from her.

She sat up, realizing her amniotic sac had ruptured. A contraction seized her then, wrapping from her low back around to her abdomen. She breathed slowly, trying to focus on relaxing. Her abdomen hardened like a rock.

She'd expected the contractions. She'd witnessed enough of them. But then they'd happened, and they were nothing like she'd anticipated. It seared like fire, scorching her low back and abdomen. When she was sure the contraction would rip her in half, the muscles began to release. She rubbed her belly as the intensity faded and took a deep breath as it ended. She didn't know how much time she had until the next one, so she got up, trailing fluid to the bathroom, intent on cleaning up her mess. The fluid had gotten everywhere.

She was halfway through changing when the next contraction seized her. *Not again.* This time, it was better as she stood at the bathroom sink, rocking her hips and breathing. Labor had definitely started. There was no denying that. As soon as she could move, she went for her phone.

There was a text from Jasper: *Just saw this. No fires tonight. I can leave and come if you need me.*

She closed his message and texted Lotus first: *Labor has started. Water broke. Ctx close.*

She sent the same to Nia, who rang back almost immediately. "Do you want me to come and get you? Is Lotus there?"

"No one is here." That last word came out strained as another contraction seized her. "Hang on." She labored through it, breathing heavily. At first, she clutched the phone, then dropped it onto the vanity and bent her knees, gripping the edge of the sink. The searing through her back and abdomen caught her off guard every time. When it subsided, she brushed the hair out of her face and picked the phone back up. "Sorry about that." She licked her dry lips.

"You're in serious labor. Get Lotus over there now, or I'm going to come pick you up."

Lotus had offered to attend as Penelope's doula. Since she wasn't expecting Jasper to support her, she'd taken Lotus up on the offer. Penelope hadn't thought she needed a doula, but she wanted Lotus there, and it would be good to have someone to drive her to the hospital.

"I don't know. I'm feeling weird about calling her. You know she won't want to leave Shanti," Penelope said. Shanti, born a little later than expected, was only two weeks old.

"So? Let her bring her. I'm leaving Oscar with the au pair. You can give her the option to say no, but you know she'll be hurt if you take the choice away from her."

"You're right. I'll call her." Another contraction started as Penelope hung up, seizing her into a frozen position, leaning over the sink. When it ended, she dialed quickly. Lotus answered on the first ring.

"Do you never sleep?" Penelope asked.

"It's baby time?"

"You got it. Can you come over now? Or listen, I know Shanti is so little, and you weren't expecting that. If you can't, I understand."

There was a long pause.

"It's not that I don't want you here—I do. But you always say yes, and you always do things for everyone, and I just want to give you the out to stay with your baby if you need to."

"Penelope, I appreciate that. But I had already considered this. Mom is here, so it's fine."

"I—" The next contraction cut her off, gripping her body. It came out of nowhere earlier than she'd expected. If she could just take a deep breath before a contraction began, she could get on top of it.

She had to drop the phone on the countertop again. She could hear an animal growling, a low-pitched, teeth-gritting moaning. It was coming from her. She tried to stop it, to hold her breath, to keep it in, but the pain spiked in response. So she let the growl go on.

When it was over, she picked the phone back up. "Sorry about that," she said in a breathy voice.

The sound of a car ignition turning over roared at her through the phone. "I'm coming," Lotus said. "Hang on."

Chapter 56

Shanti will be okay with Mom. Lotus repeated it to herself as she drove, whipping around the slow-moving car in front of her on the dark street. Penelope needed her. Lotus had to drive her to the hospital because she'd offered to be her support partner.

Penelope was right—Lotus always said yes. But this was different. Her instinct was to say yes to her baby, not to leave Shanti, only two weeks old, in someone else's care. Shanti needed Lotus. But no, Penelope needed her too. Lotus fought the need to be in control. She fought the idea that the only person her baby needed was her.

Penelope hadn't sounded good on the phone. She was already struggling through the early part of labor. Maybe it wasn't early labor. Lotus had only been there for a handful of births and her own. She didn't have the experience her doula or Penelope had. But Penelope needed her. Nia would be there too. And Jasper's position at Penelope's side was bound to be as difficult as Rob.

Rob. His absence from Shanti's birth had initially been a shock. As much as Rob had betrayed her during the months leading up to their split, she'd never imagined he would leave during their child's birth.

She'd gotten the full story later when he called her from the rehab center. "My dealer called me. Everyone was outside of the room, waiting for you to call us in when you were ready. It was use or leave. I chose to leave. I knew if I didn't check myself in right then, I'd be high. Would that have been better for our daughter's birth? No. I had to prove to myself that I can kick this. Because I need a chance to be there for my children—regardless of what happens to us."

The dark streets were slick with an evening rain. Lotus guided the Prius carefully through the wet streets. A chill hung in the air, clinging to her as she parked at Penelope's apartment building.

Lotus's heart pounded. She had to calm herself down to be calm for Penelope. She took three deep breaths while crossing the parking lot. Lotus's mom and Jagannath had been there at every turn since Shanti's birth, taking care of her and taking care of Blaze. Penelope had none of that. She just had Lotus and Nia. *Who's going to make her a sandwich while she nurses her newborn? Who's going to hold the baby while she showers? Who's going to keep the baby when Penelope goes back to work?* Lotus had decided that she'd just have to bring Shanti over and help Penelope in the postpartum period. She and Nia could do it. Or maybe Lotus could convince Penelope to come and stay with her for a little while.

She knocked on Penelope's door then tried the handle. It was unlocked. Inside, she found Penelope crouched on the floor on her hands and knees, breathing deeply, moaning as she had on the phone.

"I'm here, Pen. I'm right here."

Penelope's head moved in a nod. A throaty moan greeted Lotus. It wasn't going to be long. Lotus could see that, and her only knowledge of labor was her own childbirth classes and the few friends' home births she'd been to.

The contraction ended, and Penelope looked up. "What the hell? It's going too fast."

Lotus nodded, helping Penelope stand. "It's going to be okay. Time to go to the hospital. Do I need to call Edward and Nia?"

"Yes." It was all Penelope could get out before she dropped back to the floor, another contraction seizing her.

Lotus's stomach flipped. She had no idea how to handle someone else's labor by herself. She opened her phone and texted Nia. There was a comfort knowing Nia and Edward lived closest to the hospital and were meeting them there. Everything would be ready.

Now she just had to get Penelope there. One step at a time. One contraction at a time.

Chapter 57

It had taken four stop-and-go tries to get down to Lotus's car. Each time a contraction came, they had to drop everything. Lotus would hold Penelope up as she leaned into the pressure tearing through her.

"Why is this kid trying to rip roar out of me at this pace? I've been doing this long enough to know how much longer it takes than most people think," she said between contractions. "What the hell is this kid doing?"

"Every labor is different. You know that." Such a typical Lotus response.

"Okay, well, let's just tell Ruby to chill out a little. I need a moment to breathe between them."

They reached the car, and Lotus finished loading the hospital bags into the trunk.

"You know, I'm not leaking that bad," Penelope said, sitting down on a black garbage bag covering the front seat.

"I did that days ago. Just in case."

The drive to the hospital didn't take long, but Penelope wanted to stand up or get on her hands and knees. The contractions crushed her in her folded position in the car. The labor pains rushed together, and Penelope couldn't talk to Lotus anymore. Lotus was far away, on the other side of a misty veil. Every time she spoke to Penelope, it was like her voice came down through a tunnel. Penelope was alone.

They arrived at the hospital. Nia and Edward met them just outside the locked double doors to triage. Penelope was A-list, and they skipped right past triage as Edward led her to a room. Somehow, she had made it up the hallway to the Labor and Delivery floor. Voices told her to sit and use the wheelchair, but she couldn't bear the thought of being crushed through each contraction again. The car ride had been unbearable.

In the labor-and-delivery room, hands had eased her into the hospital bed. She heard screaming and then realized it was her. *Why is the baby trying to kill me?* "No, no, no, no, no."

"Look at me. Penelope. Look at me." Hands touched her on the cheeks, and she opened her squeezed eyes. Edward's face filled her field of vision. He really was a handsome man and incredibly gentle. She could see why Nia had agreed on that first date.

"Why? Edward? What's happening? I can't."

"That's it, Penelope. Look in my eyes. It's going to be okay. I think you are pretty close to having this baby, but I need to check you, and the nurses need you to be still for a moment to get you on the monitor. Can you do that?"

Another contraction seized her. "Why?" She could hear the long cry. *Am I crying?*

She ground her teeth together. She tried to imagine relaxing her bottom like the childbirth educator, Beth, had taught her. That woman was crazy. She wasn't opening like a flower—she was on fire. She didn't melt and relax—she grabbed the cold plastic on the side of the hospital bed and squeezed it. She squeezed her eyes closed, shutting out Edward, Nia, Lotus, and the nurses who tried to talk to her. She could feel the monitor groping at her abdomen. Her belly was tight and hard, like the bone in her forehead, just like that stupid Beth had said. She felt a gush through the contraction. It had been happening through most of them, but this one was bigger and warm and on her thighs.

Am I naked? When did I get naked? It didn't matter. She'd been hot, and anything touching her skin made it crawl.

She couldn't do it. *Fuck it. I want the epidural.* She heard herself say, "Epi-epi-epi-dural."

Did they hear me? Where is my epidural?

A mask came down over her nose and mouth, forcing oxygen into her. It smelled stale. She batted it, but a soft hand enveloped hers and guided it gently away. She opened her eyes and looked into Lotus's face. Her big blue eyes shone with tears. Lotus was so in touch with her emotions. *Geez.*

Penelope turned to the other side of the bed. Nia and Jasper were there. *When did he get here?* Jasper looked as handsome as ever, but there was a crease in his forehead and a deep, concerned look in his eyes. Men. He couldn't stand looking at a labor. And he was supposed to be the tough guy. *Who's the tough one now?*

Beside him, Nia held her other hand. But that look on her face. It matched Jasper's. Penelope turned back to Lotus. The look was there, too, beneath the tears. Penelope sat up. Between her knees, Edward looked grim.

What the hell is going on?

She hadn't said it aloud, but everyone started answering her all at once. "Sit back, Penelope. Edward's going to check now."

The cold ultrasound liquid squirted out again. The monitor searched across her abdomen. The nurse—it was Karen—kept moving and tracing her belly with the monitor, like a child trying to dig tracks into the sand. Karen. *Why do I have the charge nurse? Is the floor busy? Why don't I hear the heartbeat on my monitor?* She knew she was being uncooperative. But damn, it hurt.

"Did you hear me, Penelope? We are going to help you. I need you to bear down on Karen's count," Edward said.

"Is it time? Where's my epidural?"

"The baby needs to come now," Edward said.

Penelope did as he said, pushing on the nurse's count. She hated the count. She secretly called those the drill-sergeant nurses, wondering why they counted in that demanding, condescending tone. As if the patients were idiots. As if she couldn't push without the counting.

"Six. Seven. Eight."

She let the push go.

"Deep breath. Come back into the push. Hold it for ten."

Pressure was building in her face. Around her eyes. She'd seen moms burst blood vessels in their eyes from pushing so hard. And so wrong. *Am I pushing wrong? Is the baby coming?*

More gushes came as she pushed. Poor Edward. He was probably covered in her amniotic fluid. The noise in the room increased with her gushing push. *Don't these people know when to shut up? What happened to everyone collectively holding their breath?*

How she wished she was the nurse, calling out those numbers and pressing the cold monitor lead into the abdomen. Not the patient, red-faced and frog-legged in the hospital bed, trying to get that watermelon out of her.

She pushed again, holding it longer this time until the push devolved into a scream. She hadn't wanted to be so out of control. She'd imagined how well she would handle her labor, unafraid, knowing what was happening and easy about it. But as the contractions ripped through her, she didn't care about composure or control, and through the screaming she could feel the baby pressing down farther and farther. It burned. Fire. The fire had moved down.

"Puffs. Short puffs," Karen said. Penelope opened her eyes and saw Karen puffing, mimicking the breaths she wanted Penelope to take. She had big bushy eyebrows, and with her lips pursed, blowing short puffs, Penelope was suddenly reminded of the big bad wolf.

She tried to copy the breaths, but Edward stopped her. "No, bear down again."

"I can't. I think the contraction is gone." Suddenly, she felt better. Her bottom was stretching. The fire had subsided. But the contraction was gone.

"No, there isn't time. Listen to me, and push as hard as you can." His tone was so serious.

"As hard as I can?" She wasn't sure if she'd said it aloud. *But why is Edward trying to tear me open? He knows slower is better.*

"Now, Penelope." The demand in his voice scared her.

So she pushed.

As hard as she could.

The baby ripped through her. She could feel it between her thighs. She bore down and held her breath and pushed as hard and long as her breath allowed her.

Ruby slipped free. Penelope could breathe. Her head fell back. Free. The baby was out.

She exhaled and looked down between her knees. Edward palmed the baby with one hand, his other on the baby's back. The newborn hung from Edward's hands as if asleep, limbs drooping.

The silence roared in her ears. But there was no noise except a soft swishing as Edward's glove pumped up and down her baby's back. Ruby. Ruby was supposed to be red and screaming. But she hung from his palm, blue.

Blue. Why is Ruby blue? Why isn't she crying?

Then Karen said, "I need peds in three, stat. Code blue."

Her baby wasn't breathing. Code blue.

Chapter 58

Sometimes, mothers went home with only their grief. The hallway passed in a blur as Penelope's wheelchair glided to the exit. Karen pushed her as Jasper walked alongside, carrying her hospital bag. She'd been the nurse to deliver the postpartum patient to the sidewalk before. Always, the mother sat in her yoga pants and baggy T-shirt holding a newborn baby to her chest.

Penelope's arms were empty.

When she got home, the bassinet was empty. The drawers were full. Onesies and sleepers, socks that fit in the palm of her hand, and dresses with matching headbands for every occasion.

"What are we going to do with all the clothes? And the diapers and the bassinet?" she asked Jasper.

He looked down at her, green eyes rimmed in red. "I can donate them," he said gently.

The despair came over her in unsuspected swells. She'd cried all the tears and exhausted herself into sleep on the first night. The nightmares started right away.

Jasper stayed. It was over between them. She no longer held desire for it to work out. But he stayed because he was the only one in the world who understood her. She wasn't the first woman to ever lose a baby, and maybe he didn't feel the ache in his breast like she did or the heaviness of an empty uterus. But he'd lost a child in the same moment. Odd how there wasn't a word for a parent who lost a child.

So, what does this make me? A childless mother? Am I a mother if I have no child?

"Can I get you some tea?" Jasper asked.

She shrugged. "I don't care." The numbness felt better than the despair.

Lotus and Nia visited in the days that followed. They never brought their babies with them.

The nights were the worst. Penelope didn't want to close her eyes. If she could sleep a dreamless sleep, night would have been a welcome respite from her circling thoughts. But no. It came with dreams. Nightmares. Ruby's body dangling from Edward's hands. Limp. Blue.

Her body had betrayed her. Penelope went over the timeline again and again. *How could I have prevented it?* She knew the failure was hers somehow. Ruby had kicked during labor. She'd been alive. And then the placenta abrupted, severing the connection between Penelope and Ruby. The gushing fluid in the hospital bed had been her own blood.

Why did my body detach the placenta too early? Why did my body eject the life support for my baby, cutting off the oxygen, abandoning Ruby in my uterus with no way to breathe? She'd asked Edward the questions, sobbing into his lab coat.

"Sometimes this happens," he'd said. "It's rare, but it happens."

Tea appeared at the side table. Jasper sat beside her on the couch, and she hunched into the crook of his arm, soaking his crisp baby-blue shirt in her grief.

Chapter 59

The coffee shop just inside the Hartsfield-Jackson airport was not the easiest to get to, but it made the most sense as the place to see Penelope off. Lotus sat with Nia in the corner, looking at the scroll of latest pictures of Oscar on her phone. She and Nia had made weekly playdates a priority, but the last few weeks had gotten away from them. In baby time, big milestones could happen within a few weeks' time.

"Think she's going to be okay?" Nia asked, putting her phone away.

Lotus shrugged. "Her brother is in Denver. Maybe it'll be good to have some family nearby."

"You're family. And I am too."

"I know. But she couldn't go back to work. She couldn't function here."

"I just worry about her. She's not the same," Nia said.

"She never will be again."

Penelope rounded the corner, wheeling a carry-on suitcase and carrying a large purse over her shoulder. "Hey," she said, a smile spreading on her face. It was a rarity to see that these days.

Lotus and Nia both stood and hugged Penelope in turn.

"Want to get some tea and coffee? How much time do you have?" Lotus asked.

"You guys, thanks for coming to see me off." Penelope checked her watch. "I have about forty minutes before I need to get through security and to my concourse. I have time to grab a coffee."

Lotus felt a heaviness whenever she was around Penelope. The energy in the room was like a pelican in an oil spill, black and weighted. She and Nia had visited every week since Ruby's death but never brought Shanti or Oscar along. It was like an energetic space had opened around Penelope, and that space was void of life.

Penelope came back with her coffee. "Elliot said he found a place a few blocks from him with a one bedroom for rent. We're going to look at it tomorrow."

"That's great," Nia said, reaching across the table to take Penelope's hand. "I just can't believe you're leaving."

Penelope winced. "I love you guys. But I just can't. I expected it to get easier, and it hasn't. It's been six months. When am I going to stop driving by the hospital? When am I going to quit going to the cemetery all the time? I don't want to work in L and D anymore, and this job is a good opportunity. Maybe instead of trying to live in the fantasy of the family I don't have, it'll do me some good to rekindle a bit with the family I *do* have."

Nia looked down, but it didn't hide the tears that leaked down her face.

Penelope squeezed her hand. "I'll be back. I already decided to visit regularly. I just can't live here anymore."

Lotus nodded. She understood. She'd left California after Stone died and hiked the Appalachian Trail. She didn't have the heart to tell Penelope that she hadn't been able to escape the ghost of her brother. Just like she still sometimes saw Stone lying on that hotel bed, Penelope would never stop seeing her limp blue baby dangling from Edward's hands.

Nia pulled a stone statue from the large bag beside the table. Lotus knew she'd intended to give it to Penelope because Nia had run the idea by her already.

"I want you to have this," Nia said, shoving the six-inch carved stone across the table.

Lotus recognized the Jizo statue Nia's mother-in-law had given her during the miscarriage.

Penelope took the carved monk into her hand. She traced the stretched ears with her finger and ran a hand along its bald head. The monk wore the red knitted bib Penelope had made for it in the Jizo tradition, just after Nia's miscarriage.

"Are you sure?" she asked Nia. "This seems like it belongs in your family."

"Okasan passed it to me when she didn't need it anymore. Now I think it needs to go to you. I didn't tell anyone, but I'm out of the first trimester now, so I'm far enough along to tell you. Edward and I are pregnant."

"Holy shit, Nia, I can't believe you kept that secret." Penelope's eyes teared, but this time, it wasn't the desperate cry of loss Lotus had seen on her so many times.

"I know. I'm sorry. I wanted to tell, but I just couldn't get excited about it until we were out of that window."

That window. There was no such window for Penelope, Lotus thought. She'd been outside of the common window for loss when Ruby died. No one had expected that.

Penelope took the monk from Nia and brought it to her heart. "I'll keep him. For now."

It wasn't a promise to give him back. But it was a promise that there could be more for her someday.

Chapter 60

EIGHT YEARS LATER

The level of noise never ceased to amaze Nia. Penelope's flight would be landing soon, and Nia had to find a way to rein in the chaos before she left for the airport.

"If you want to walk to the playground, you have to help your brother put on his shoes, Oscar." She handed him the size 13 Nikes and turned to her four-year-old. "Let Oz help you, please?"

She walked to the foot of the stairs, picking up a discarded pair of socks and soccer cleats on her way. "Emi! You're going to miss out if you don't come down!"

She shoved the cleats into the shoe bin in the mudroom. While the space was perfect for their big family, the challenge to the new house was that they were so spread out. She was tired of shouting up the stairs or down to the basement to get their attention. Yes, she was going to call the electrician to put in the intercom system. *Before* the baby was born.

Emi trotted down the stairs, wearing a sparkly pink-and-purple dress and tennis shoes. She spun, her dress flaring out. Her hair was pulled into uneven pigtails, parted delicately by a six-year-old hand, which bobbed and bounced with the movement. "Do you like my hair? And my outfit?"

"I love them! Did you do it yourself?"

Emi smiled proudly, showing the gap where she'd just lost a tooth. "Sí!"

"You remembered to put shorts on?"

In response, Emi lifted her dress to show her mom that she'd put her play shorts under the sparkly dress. "Are the boys ready? Can we take Nico with us?"

Emi, her only daughter, loved to mother her baby brothers. She loved to mother *all* her brothers, but especially those two.

Nia smiled down into the wide brown eyes of her child. "No." She leaned down, pitching her voice to a whisper. "It's time for his N-A-P, so he's going to stay here with Katy while I go pick up Aunt Penelope. You take Frankie and Oscar and have fun."

Oscar had finally wrestled the shoes onto Frankie. "Ready!" He snatched the walkie-talkies off the stand and handed one to Nia.

"It's not your turn," Emi shouted. "Mami, tell him it's not his turn. He had the walkie last time!"

Nia turned her mom look on Oscar. "Is that true? Whose turn is it?"

Oscar pursed his lips and put a hand on his hip. "But she thinks she's the boss when she has the walkie. *I'm* the oldest. *I'm* the boss."

"No one is the boss. You are a team, and you all work together. Or we can stay here. I think I have some chores for you to do..."

Oscar shoved the walkie-talkie into Emi's hand. "She can have it. It's her turn."

Emi smiled triumphantly. Oscar shot her a glare when he thought Nia wasn't looking.

Katy, the nanny, came down the stairs. "Nico's asleep." She took the other walkie-talkie from Nia. "You'd better go so you aren't late."

"Thank you, Katy. I don't know what we'd do without you." Nia hugged her and kissed each of the kids by the front door. "No tree climbing until I get back. Promise?" She directed the question at Emi.

"I promise," Emi said with reluctance. "No trees." She stuck a pinkie out, offering a solemn vow. Nia wrapped her pinkie finger in her daughter's tiny one, comforted to know she wouldn't climb the tree.

Nia grabbed her keys. *Big kids across the street to the playground. Nico to nap. It's time.* It had been a year since she'd last seen Penelope.

Chapter 61

Penelope had considered not going on her annual pilgrimage to Atlanta this year. Her flight touched down in the Hartsfield-Jackson airport, and she once again thought about skipping it altogether. But this year, it felt more important than ever to go. The first couple of years had been the hardest even though those were the shortest trips. Now that she was settled in Denver permanently, her life had almost gotten in the way of her annual Atlanta visit.

She exited the plane at her gate and made her way down past security. The tiny baby cuddled into her chest, and she pressed him in with her free hand. He'd slept through the landing and woken happy, nuzzling against her in a blissful half-sleep.

A loud "Squee!" caught Penelope's attention, and she looked up from the half-parted pink baby lips and droopy hazel eyes to find Nia practically sprinting toward her. Nia skidded to a stop in front of her like a twelve-year-old running the bases in her backyard and threw her arms around Penelope. "You made it! Yes! I am so happy to see you!" Nia bumped Penelope with her round belly.

Pregnant again. Penelope had never pegged her as the one who would want a gaggle of children. No one had become what Penelope had expected.

Nia peeked into the pouch Penelope wore strapped to her chest. "Oh my God, Harrison is precious! Even better than the pictures! Look at those lips. His eyes." Nia cooed over the baby for several minutes. "Oh, look at me going on. I'm sorry." Nia waved a hand at Penelope. "Let's go. Lots to do."

Pregnancy suited Nia. She was tiny everywhere except in the middle and carried her belly around like it wasn't even there. Penelope followed her onto the light-rail transport, around to the baggage claim, and out of the crowded airport.

"You've been really quiet. You okay?" Nia asked.

"The usual. I'm always like this the day I land."

"I know. I just thought it might be easier this time." Nia conspicuously made an effort not to look at the baby when she said it.

"It's not."

"Oakland first? Or you want to go to the house first?"

"Oakland, please." Penelope strapped Harrison into the car seat Nia had brought for him and climbed into the front seat.

"I can come or stay, same as always."

"I know. Thank you."

Nia reached over and squeezed Penelope on the knee. She didn't offer condolences, and for that Penelope was grateful. Nia could sit with the discomfort and not try to fix it. She'd learned that from Lotus.

"Jonathan comes in tomorrow?" Nia asked.

"Yes. He had an overlap with the conference, so he's coming after it ends tomorrow. Lands at nine, I think."

"Edward adores him, you know. And we haven't seen him since the wedding, with his crazy schedule."

"I know. He's excited to see you guys too." The change of subject should have relieved Penelope, but it felt tedious. She could hear her own voice, flat and lifeless.

Nia turned up the radio and didn't push Penelope for more conversation. Penelope drifted into the past as she always did on that drive, back to eight years before, staring down between her knees at her blue baby girl, until they arrived at Oakland Cemetery.

Chapter 62

"Tabouli salad," Rob said, setting a large wooden bowl on the table in front of her. "Do you want the edamame hummus or the traditional?"

"Edamame," Lotus said. "They'll be converted once they taste it. Besides, it's *me*. They know what to expect by now."

"So true."

Lotus shut the laptop and stood up. "I'm done now if you want some help."

"I'm the chef in this house. And didn't you get up at five today? Go rest. I'm sure you ladies are going to be up late together tonight."

"Think so? Sometimes I wonder what there is to talk about after all these years."

"You haven't seen Penelope in a year," Rob said, looking up from the colander of edamame beans.

"But I see Nia every week."

"So let Penelope talk."

"It's hard her first day back. We should've scheduled for another night."

"There isn't another night. Oscar's birthday party is tomorrow." Rob put the washed edamame into the food processor.

"Did you pick up the gift?" she asked.

"No, Jagannath did. Shanti wanted to pick it out, but of course, Blaze had an opinion, too, so he took both of them."

Jagannath was so great with the kids. Even Blaze didn't remember a time when he wasn't part of their lives.

"Where's Derek? At work?"

"He'll be home by dinnertime. I told him we had kid duty tonight, so he planned some games and a movie for the kids."

"Oh, that reminds me—I found something for you." Lotus flopped her yoga bag up onto the table and dug around. "Flowers," she said, handing over a business card.

Rob turned off the food processor and took the business card. "I'm so relieved. I thought you would never get it."

"I told you I had the flowers figured out. She's the only one you want doing the flowers. Now, when are the two of you picking out the wedding cake? You're going to run out of time if you don't get a move on it."

"As soon as I can talk Derek into tasting the pink champagne cake," he said, raising an eyebrow and flicking the spatula.

Lotus laughed. He'd always had eclectic tastes. "I know I've said it before, but I'm happy for you guys."

"Thank you. Who knew we'd end up like this?"

"Not me, that's for sure."

Chapter 63

Oakland Cemetery was one of the oldest and largest in Atlanta. The classic Victorian cemetery was just north of Grant Park. Penelope used to take afternoon walks there in the early spring through late fall. When it had come time to find a place for Ruby to be buried, she knew Oakland was where she wanted her to be.

The plots were not easy to come by, but one of Penelope's patients had known someone selling one, so she was able to get a tiny space for Ruby. She didn't imagine she would be able to bury her whole family there, but it felt like the right place for her baby. She wanted Ruby to stay in Atlanta, where she'd been born, though at the time, Penelope had wanted to get out. Leaving Atlanta had felt like the only way to remove herself from the grief and start to heal.

She reached over and squeezed Nia's hand. "Thank you. Thank you for bringing me and for understanding that I have to go alone."

Nia nodded and brushed the back of her hand across a cheek. "We'll be fine. You go."

Penelope looked into the back seat at her sleeping baby and got out of the car, leaving Nia to tend to him. The trek up to Ruby's spot sloped, and she climbed the sidewalk in a trancelike state. The days and weeks following her birth had blurred together into a heap of pain that collected in her body and ached. There were moments of clarity when she looked up into Nia's eyes and asked, through the pain and tears, "Am I being punished?"

Memories from those days were etched in her mind. The baby-blue shirt Jasper had been wearing when she laid her head on his shoulder and cried for their lost child—she could smell his cologne when she thought of that moment. Her baby, blue and limp in Edward's hands. That image was as sharp as if she were looking at it right then. The rest of it blurred from sleepless nights into her losing twenty pounds and falling into depression. The tiny box they'd had to choose for their baby still haunted her some nights.

Large oak trees, for which the cemetery had been named, shaded her path as she approached her child's plot. A small and modest headstone stood watch over the site, adorned with a single date marking the day Ruby had both come and gone from the world. Ruby Dolores Banks-Martinelli. She hadn't planned to give Ruby Jasper's name. But after she died, it felt right to use both surnames. And her grandmother's name—that had felt right all along.

The cool grass in front of her baby's grave blanketed beneath her as she clutched the knit octopus in her palm. Tattered loose yarn threads splayed off her old octopus in every direction. Penelope had giggled that day in her ruffled pink dress about the eight arms being perfect for her eighth birthday. In her other hand, she held the soft one, knitted from newly spun yarn into somewhat of a twin to her tattered old one.

"This one is for you," she whispered, placing the new octopus on the grave. The years had washed away the others.

"Eight years already?" The deep voice startled her even though she'd been expecting him.

She turned to find Jasper looming above her, holding a bouquet of roses. Even with the extra weight, he managed to look big instead of flabby. His five-o'clock shadow deepened his naturally rugged look. Despite the creases at the corners, there was a light in his eyes that softened the sadness.

"Feels like it was yesterday, huh?" she said.

Jasper leaned over and placed his flowers on the headstone. "You need a few more minutes alone?"

"Sit."

Her hate for Jasper seemed a lifetime ago. It had been eclipsed by their loss. Now it felt like he'd given her a precious thing that she never knew how to love. Until she did. And as soon as she had accepted and loved her baby, she'd had to tell her goodbye.

"Penelope." His tone was gentle and serious.

"Yeah?"

"I know it might not mean much now, but I have to tell you something."

Oh boy. She braced herself, never knowing what to expect from Jasper.

"I'm sorry." His eyes pleaded with her not to look away and shut him down. "Not just sorry for being a shitty, unfaithful person. Not just sorry about Ruby. But I need you to know that I am sorry to *you* for everything I put you through—before, during, and after."

"You weren't so bad after." She pictured his baby-blue shirt and pressing her face into the soft fabric as he held her. He'd understood. His baby had died too.

"I'm serious, Penelope. I never took responsibility. I was such a dick, and I blamed a lot of it on you—because then I didn't have to face myself. I've done a lot of thinking, and I need you to know that I am truly, deeply sorry for all the pain I caused."

"It's not your fault she died, Jasper."

He reached over and put his hand on hers. "It's not yours either."

She let his words resonate. For once, she didn't argue or quip back but just told herself, *It's not yours either.* She'd spent a lot of sleepless nights trying to figure out what she'd done wrong to cost her baby's life. She blamed herself for not loving Ruby deeper and sooner, right after she blamed herself for being with Jasper in the first place. The guilt of wishing she had never been pregnant at all hung like a cloud over the rest of her emotions. She blamed herself for wanting an abortion. *It's not yours either.* And then she'd blamed herself for Ruby's death. She should have known something was going wrong. Eventually, the search for blame had turned into a dull acceptance. But it wasn't until after she'd reached that point that she'd met and married Jonathan and then given birth to Harrison.

The silence enveloped them both, cradling them in that moment together in front of their baby's grave. She and Jasper would never be friends. They would never be more than that either. But they would always be Ruby's parents.

The life she had included Jonathan and now Harrison and her dream job in Denver, plus a new closeness to her brother. She didn't have a life with Jasper in the suburbs of Atlanta, but she didn't want any of that anymore.

She didn't want to be the mother of a dead baby either. But she was. And she accepted it all as part of who she'd become. On the cool grass, with Jasper's hand over hers, she knew that she had always lived the life she was meant to—during the good moments and the bad.

Acknowledgments

This book would not be possible without the people who supported me through my process as a writer. I have so many people to thank, so here they are, in no particular order.

I'd like to thank my beta and sensitivity readers, Brandee Anderson, Michael Harper, Courtney LeBlanc, Jennifer Knight, and Chris Lee. Your thoughtful consideration and devotion to my pages helped me make critical changes to the book, even when it was almost ready. Brandee, thank you for hosting my namestorm, asking me a million questions, and always treating my characters like real people. But most of all, thank you for your friendship. Harper, thank you for the dude perspective. Courtney, thank you for being the fastest reader I know and for always volunteering your insight. Jenn, I know it took me forever to give you the book, but it's only because I care so much about your opinion. Thank you for seeing pieces of me in the book and understanding it in a way that only a friend of seventeen years could possibly do. And Chris, thank you for being the most woke cisgender white man I've ever known. I appreciate you helping me remove all the cringey bits and offering me lessons in your areas of expertise.

Thank you, Carina Bisset, who talked thoroughly through this plot with me at AWP in 2017 and helped me realize the surprising yet inevitable ending.

The MFA program at Queens University of Charlotte was where the first draft of this novel was born, and every person who laid eyes on this work added a value to it—especially those peers who shared a small or large group pod with me. Your support and encouragement helped me shape the book. This includes my stellar mentors at Queens program—Fred Leebron, Susan Perabo, David Payne, and especially Ashley Warlick, my thesis mentor, who worked with me through the first complete major edit of the project. To my faculty readers, Jonathan Dee and Myla Goldberg: your insightful feedback enabled me to revise this novel to what it needed to be. Also, I'd like to thank my MFA wives, Whitney Roberts Hill and Courtney Leblanc, the women who held me through the hard moments of the book and the crippling self-doubt. Thank you for long drives, coffee dates, scene-by-scene analysis, walks, and talks and for always believing in me. Whitney, thank you for always reminding me that these stories need to be told and for supporting me through hard writing and hard parenting moments.

To the Long Haulers, my longest-lasting real writing group and the readers of the earliest draft of this novel: you helped shape the initial direction the book needed to take. To Eleanor, a midwife and a gift to birthing families in her community, thank you for talking me through some very technical aspects of labor-and-delivery emergencies and helping to inspire Penelope's profession. To Heather, thank you for teaching me what real grief looks like, which only exists so starkly next to real, unconditional love.

Many thanks to the TGIF Rogue Writers, a group of talented women who helped me through the pandemic, my writing, and personal-growth moments with nothing but encouragement and support. I'm grateful to the Women's Fiction Writers Association for connecting me to my beloved community of writers who insist that women's voices are powerful and that their stories must be told.

Thanks also to my editors, Angie Gallion Lovell and Sarah Carleton, without whom I never would have seen this book rise to a publishable condition. I'm grateful to my publishing mentor, Erica, for her guidance and support through the publishing journey, and to Lynn, for believing in this book and taking a chance on it.

Thanks to my street team, the inside group that has been watching the publishing of this book unfold behind the scenes. And to Kiana, my assistant, for your encouragement and hand-holding through all the tasks that make me freeze.

A big thank-you to my husband, Marcos, whose unwavering love and support has bolstered me on this journey as a writer, and to my children, who made me the person I am and without whom I wouldn't be able to tell this story.

And finally, many thanks to every mother, father, and baby I have ever had the joy of working with. You all taught me about the thin veil present during the moments a new life passes into this plane, and for that, I will forever be changed.

About the Author

Before finding her way to writing full time, Sita Romero spent fifteen years in women's health, teaching childbirth classes and attending hundreds of births. Her writing has been published both online and in print literary journals and anthologies.

Now, Sita teaches academic writing at a local community college, where she serves as the faculty advisor for the student creative arts journal. She is a graduate of Queens University of Charlotte's MFA program and a member of Women's Fiction Writers Association and Science Fiction Writers of America.

Sita lives in Virginia with her husband, three children, two dogs, and over two hundred fifty board games. When she's not writing or editing, she's playing boardgames, drinking tea, and working yarn into shawls and blankets.

Read more at sitaromero.com.

About the Publisher

Dear Reader,

We hope you enjoyed this book. Please consider leaving a review on your favorite book site.

Visit https://RedAdeptPublishing.com to see our entire catalogue.

Don't forget to subscribe to our monthly newsletter to be notified of future releases and special sales.

CPSIA information can be obtained
at www.ICGtesting.com
Printed in the USA
BVHW030237120422
633959BV00021B/241

9 781948 051866